CRIME MOVIES 2

with contributions from

Brian Clemens
George Harmon Coxe
Dick Francis
Antonia Fraser
Erle Stanley Gardner
Tony Hoare
Elwyn Jones
Richard Levinson
William Link
Edgar Lustgarten
William F. Nolan
Ruth Rendell
Georges Simenon

CW01496444

Further titles in this series from Severn House

CRIME MOVIES 2

Famous Television Crime Series

Collected & Introduced by
Peter Haining

with contributions from

Brian Clemens
George Harmon Coxe
Dick Francis
Antonia Fraser
Erle Stanley Gardner
Tony Hoare
Elwyn Jones
Richard Levinson
William Link
Edgar Lustgarten
William F. Nolan
Ruth Rendell
Georges Simenon

This first world edition published in Great Britain 1997 by
SEVERN HOUSE PUBLISHERS LTD of
9–15 High Street, Sutton, Surrey SM1 1DF.
First published in the USA 1997 by
SEVERN HOUSE PUBLISHERS INC. of
595 Madison Avenue, New York, NY 10022.

British Library Cataloguing in Publication Data

Crime movies 2
    1. Detective and mystery stories
    I. H   r, 1940–

are fictitious and
ns is purely coincidental.

oduction Limited,

in by

PROGRAMME

Note: This is a list of television titles. The original works on which these television series were based may have had different titles from those listed above.

CREDITS

The Editor and publishers are grateful to the following authors, their agents and publishers for permission to include copyright stories in this collection: Hutchinson and Kingsmarkham Enterprises for 'A Case of Coincidence' by Ruth Rendell; Magazine Enterprises Inc for 'Reward for Survivors' by George Harmon Coxe; Davis Publications Inc for 'Forbidden Fruit' by Edgar Lustgarten, 'The Case of the Howling Dog' by Erle Stanley Gardner and 'Inspector Maigret Hesitates' by Georges Simenon; William F. Nolan for his story 'Down The Long Night'; London Weekend Television Enterprises for 'The Embassy Incident' by Brian Clemens; Weidenfeld & Nicolson Ltd for 'Your Appointment is Cancelled' by Antonia Fraser; Michael Joseph Ltd for 'Odds Against' by Dick Francis; *TV Times* Ltd for 'Saint Nick Alas' by Tony Hoare; H.S.D. Publications Inc for 'The End of an Era' by Richard Levinson and William Link. While every care has been taken in seeking permission for the use of stories in this anthology, in the case of any accidental infringement interested parties are asked to write to the Editor in care of the publishers.

PROLOGUE

'The Cops on the Box'

In March 1992 in Paris, the American actor Peter Falk was awarded one of France's highest arts honours. The prestigious *Knight of the Order of Arts and Letters* was given to Falk not for his lifetime career in films and on television, but specifically for one role: that of the disheveeled Los Angeles homicide detective, Columbo, familiar all over the world for his grubby raincoat, cheap cigars and line of shrewd but gentle questioning with suspects. The honour climaxed 25 years in the role for Falk, during which time his character has become a cult figure with millions of television viewers and even entered the French language. For as the actor himself learned after the award ceremony, *un Lieutenant Columbo* is now a common expression in the country to mean a particularly dogged investigator.

The award notwithstanding, it still poses the question as to *why* a fictitional and far from typical homicide detective from a television series should so capture the public imagination? The simple answer, perhaps, is that we all need heroes whatever their appearance or methods

Prologue

– and most of all in the world of law and order or otherwise we fear that the very basis of our organised society is under threat. Certainly on the evidence of all the crime serials that have been put out over the years on television, few other genres are more popular with viewers.

Currently, 'cops on the box' are among the top rated TV shows – and have often been so in the time since television became a fully nationwide broadcasting medium in the years after the Second World War. Today, even the most cursory glance at the TV schedules reveals how widespread these men – and women – have become. *Inspector Morse*, Wexford in the *Ruth Rendell Mysteries, Frost*, DCI Jane Tennison of *Prime Suspect, Hill Street Blues, Taggart, The Bill, NYPD Blue, Cracker* – the list is almost endless: and they are just the police characters. Cheek by jowl with the officers in blue can be found Sherlock Holmes, Hercule Poirot, Jane Marple and the other amateur sleuths, not forgetting the newspaper reporters, television investigators, lawyers and private detectives who also regularly turn up as the central characters in crime series.

In a recent article in *The Mail on Sunday* about the popularity of these crime serials, journalist David Hughes wrote, 'In the days of Stratford Johns a cop show like *Z Cars* made stars but not money. Now the police series is so central to culture, or rather so popular, that the stars line up. Cop shows are nowadays key shows.'

Hughes also makes the point that well-shot locations have also given these shows an air of reality that is missing from anything made in the studios, and this provides viewers with a fresh perspective on where and how we are living. Crime shows can also, of course, tackle the kind of significant issues that affect everyone. They can focus on the perpetrators of crime and their victims. They can look at issues of liberty and the threat to lives.

And they can particularly discuss the use and abuse of the law.

Although it is true to say that the earliest productions treated crime in very black and white terms (and I do not mean those fuzzy grey pictures on the screen), the increasing sophistication of recent shows and the boldness of their producers has enabled them to address the fallibility of policemen, the weaknesses of the legal system, and in some cases the corruption of those entrusted with enforcing the law.

At its most basic, the cop show offers escapism in the form of crime, pursuit and capture, and in the best of them the viewer's loyalty is alternately switched from one side of the law to the other. Over the years they have also reflected the changing moral and political climates of the day ranging from the culture shocks of the Sixties to the violence of the Seventies and so on. As David Hughes concluded in his article:

'It's good and evil made good and funny – that's what draws the millions. Instead of going to church or into politics or charity or enlisting as a social worker, we let these programmes be our conscience. Thanks to their efforts we fight society's battles from the fortress of our armchair. Without a flicker of contradiction we become all at once burglars, liars, WPCs, juries, cheats, murderers, the man on the beat.'

In truth, though, ultimately we all enjoy seeing the villain getting his just deserts and the cop on the box provides a sense of certainty that is not available in life. And this, I believe, has been the secret of the success of the crime series. Many of them, of course, have drawn their raw material from the well-stocked library of mystery fiction, while others have been especially created by scriptwriters from life – or at least from recognisable models with whom we can identify. In this collection, however, I have concentrated on short stories – those which have inspired or are based upon crime series – and through them attempted to offer a representative cross-section of some of the most important shows of the past fifty years. Together I believe they provide an interesting and revealing guide to the development of the genre through some turbulent but nevertheless fascinating times.

If there is not an actual crime series awaiting your attention on the small screen in the corner of your sitting room at this moment, then may I invite you instead to be an armchair detective in the equally dramatic and exciting medium of the printed page . . .

PETER HAINING

THE RUTH RENDELL MYSTERIES

(ITV, 1987–)
Starring: Keith Barron, Ronald Pickup &
Don Henderson
Directed by John Davies
Story 'A Case of Coincidence' by Ruth Rendell

Amidst the plethora of highly rated crime series on television in the Nineties – *Cracker* with Robbie Coltrane, David Jason in *Frost* and John Thaw as *Inspector Morse* are just three that spring quickly to mind – one mystery writer has retained her status as 'a Queen among the Queens of Crime', as she was described by the *Observer* in 1991: Ruth Rendell. The first adaptation of one of her stories, 'Wolf to the Slaughter', which launched *The Ruth Rendell Mysteries* in August 1987, also introduced George Baker as Detective Chief Inspector Wexford, and such was its appeal and that of its successors that the authoress shows every sign of continuing to dominate the genre throughout the Nineties. What has made Ruth Rendell's work so popular is her ability to write murder mysteries that constantly extend boundaries as well as display an insight into the minds of psychopaths, murderers and rapists that is quite unmatched by her contemporaries. In this context, she has developed a second identity as 'Barbara Vine' (from her middle name and her grandmother's maiden name, Vine) and her first pseudonymous novel, *A Dark Adapted Eye* (1986)

– the dramatic story of a war of attrition between two sisters and their niece over some dark family secrets – was recently adapted for television by BBC 1 starring the excellent acting trio of Celia Imrie, Sophie Ward and Helena Bonham-Carter. The Barbara Vine tales, if they are all adapted, promise to earn the BBC the same kind of audiences that her real name has been gaining for ITV.

The success of *The Ruth Rendell Mysteries* is just one of many milestones in the career of Ruth Rendell (1930 –) during the past 30 years since she switched roles from that of a rather unsuccessful local journalist in Essex to become a novelist of international renown. The saga began with her first Wexford novel, *From Doon With Death* (1964), for which she was paid the princely sum of £75! The appeal of the rather dour Chief Inspector – who Ruth admits is partly based on her father – has turned her into a cult figure, and Wexford is now unique among the 'cops on the box' as he is the only English policeman to have a big following in Japan! Apart from the cases of Wexford and the 'Barbara Vine' novels, several of Ruth's short stories have also been adapted for *The Ruth Rendell Mysteries*, notably 'A Case of Coincidence' which was broadcast as a two-parter in March 1996. The account of a serial killer in the Cambridgeshire fens, it starred Keith Barron as the policeman Masters who has serious doubts that his colleague, Ronald Pickup, has actually arrested the right man when he brings in a suspect. It was an unforgettable adaptation that reads just as chillingly on the printed page . . .

Of the several obituaries which appeared on the death of Michael Lestrange not one mentioned his connection with the Wrexlade murders. Memories are short, even journalists' memories, and it may be that the newspapermen who wrote so glowingly and so mournfully about him were mere babes in arms, or not even born, at the time. For the murders, of course, took place in the early fifties, before the abolition of capital punishment.

Murder is the last thing one would associate with the late Sir Michael, eminent cardiac specialist, physician to Her Royal Highness the Duchess of Albany, and author of that classic work, the last word on its subject, so succinctly entitled *The Heart*. Sir Michael did not destroy life, he saved it. He was as far removed from Kenneth Edward Brannel, the Wrexlade Strangler, as he was from the carnivorous spider which crept across his consulting room window. Those who knew him well would say that he had an almost neurotic horror of the idea of taking life. Euthanasia he had refused to discuss, and he had opposed with all his vigour the legalizing of abortion.

Until last March when an air crash over the North Atlantic claimed him among its two hundred fatalities, he had been a man one automatically thought of as life-enhancing, as having on countless occasions defied death on behalf of others. Yet he seemed to have had no private life, no family, no circle to move in, no especially beautiful home. He lived for his work. He was not married and few knew he ever had been, still fewer that his wife had been the last of the Wrexlade victims.

There were four others and all five of them died as a result of being strangled by the outsized, bony hands of Kenneth Edward Brannel. Michael Lestrange, by the way, had exceptionally narrow, well-shaped hands, dextrous and precise. Brannel's have been described as resembling bunches of bananas. In her study of the Wrexlade case, the criminologist Miss Georgina Hallam Saul, relates how

Brannel, in the condemned cell, talked about committing these crimes to a prison officer. He had never understood why he killed those women, he didn't dislike women or fear them.

"It's like when I was a kid and in a shop and there was no one about," he is alleged to have said. "I had to take something, I couldn't help myself. I didn't even do it sort of of my own will. One minute it'd be on the shelf and the next in my pocket. It was the same with those girls. I had to get my hands on their throats. Everything'd go dark and when it cleared my hands'd be round their throats and the life all squeezed out . . ."

He was twenty-eight, an agricultural labourer, illiterate, classified as educationally subnormal. He lived with his widowed father, also a farm worker, in a cottage on the outskirts of Wrexlade in Essex. During 1953 he strangled Wendy Cutforth, Maureen Hunter, Ann Daly and Mary Trenthyde without the police having the least suspicion of his guilt. Approximately a month elapsed between each of these murders, though there was no question of Brannel killing at the full moon or anything of that sort. Four weeks after Mary Trenthyde's death he was arrested and charged with murder, for the strangled body of Norah Lestrange had been discovered in a ditch less than a hundred yards from his cottage. They found him guilty of murder in November of that same year, twenty-five days later he was executed.

"A terrible example of injustice," Michael Lestrange used to say. "If the M'Naughten Rules apply to anybody they surely applied to poor Brannel. With him it wasn't only a matter of not knowing that what he was doing was wrong but of not knowing he was doing it at all till it was over. We have hanged a poor idiot who had no more idea of evil than a stampeding animal has when it tramples on a child."

People thought it amazingly magnanimous of Michael

that he could talk like this when it was his own wife who had been murdered. She was only twenty-five and they had been married less than three years.

It is probably best to draw on Miss Hallam Saul for the most accurate and comprehensive account of the Wrexlade stranglings. She attended the trial, every day of it, which Michael Lestrange did not. When prosecuting counsel, in his opening speech, came to describe Norah Lestrange's reasons for being in the neighbourhood of Wrexlade that night, and to talk of the Dutchman and the hotel at Chelmsford, Michael got up quietly and left the court. Miss Hallam Saul's eyes, and a good many other pairs of eyes, followed him with compassion. Nevertheless, she didn't spare his feelings in her book. Why should she? Like everyone else who wrote about Brannel and Wrexlade, she was appalled by the character of Norah Lestrange. This was the fifties, remember, and the public were not used to hearing of young wives who admitted shamelessly to their husbands that one man was not enough for them. Michael had been obliged to state the facts to the police and the facts were that he had known for months that his wife spent nights in this Chelmsford hotel with Jan Vandepeer, a businessman on his way from The Hook and Harwich to London. She had told him so quite openly.

"Darling . . ." Taking his arm and leading him to sit close beside her while she fondled his hand. "Darling, I absolutely have to have Jan, I'm crazy about him. I do have to have other men, I'm made that way. It's nothing to do with the way I feel about you, though, you do see that, don't you?"

These words he didn't, of course, render verbatim. The gist was enough.

"It won't be all that often, Mike darling, once a month at most. Jan can't fix a trip more than once a month. Chelmsford's so convenient for both of us and you'll hardly notice I'm gone, will you, you're so busy at that old hospital."

But all this came much later, in the trial and in the Hallam Saul book. The first days (and the first chapters) were occupied with the killing of those four other women.

Wendy Cutforth was young, married, a teacher at a school in Ladeley. She went to work by bus from her home in Wrexlade, four miles away. In February, at four o'clock dusk, she got off the bus at Wrexlade Cross to walk to her bungalow a quarter of a mile away. She was never seen alive again, except presumably by Brannel, and her strangled body was found at ten that night in a ditch near the bus stop.

Fear of being out alone which had seized Wrexlade women after Wendy's death died down within three or four weeks. Maureen Hunter, who was only sixteen, quarrelled with her boyfriend after a dance at Wrexlade village hall and set off to walk home to Ingleford on her own. She never reached it. Her body was found in the small hours only a few yards from where Wendy's had been. Mrs Ann Daly, a middle-aged widow, also of Ingleford, had a hairdressing business in Chelmsford and drove herself to work each day via Wrexlade. Her car was found abandoned, all four doors wide open, her body in a small wood between the villages. An unsuccessful attempt had been made to bury it in the leaf mould.

Every man between sixteen and seventy in the whole of that area of Essex was closely examined by the police. Brannel was questioned, as was his father, and was released after ten minutes, having aroused no interest. In May, twenty-seven days after the death of Ann Daly, Mary Trenthyde, thirty-year-old mother of two small daughters and herself the daughter of Brannel's employer, Mark Stokes of Cross Farm, disappeared from her home during the course of a morning. One of her children was with its grandmother, the other in its pram just inside the garden gate. Mary vanished without trace, without announcing to anyone that she was going out or where she was going. A massive hunt was mounted and her strangled body finally found at midnight in a disused well half a mile away.

All these deaths took place in the spring of 1953.

The Lestranges had a flat in London not far from the Royal Free Hospital. They were not well off but Norah had a rich father who was in the habit of giving her handsome presents. One of these, for her twenty-fifth birthday, was a Triumph Alpine sports car. Michael had a car too, the kind of thing that is called an 'old banger'.

As frontispiece to Miss Hallam Saul's book is a portrait photograph of Norah Lestrange as she appeared a few months before her death. The face is oval, the features almost too perfectly symmetrical, the skin flawless and opaque. Her thick dark hair is dressed in the high fashion of the time, in short smooth curls. Her make-up is heavy and the dark, greasy lipstick coats the parted lips in a way that is somehow lascivious. The eyes stare with a humourless complacency.

Michael was furiously, painfully jealous of her. When, after they had been married six months, she began a flirtation with his best friend, a flirtation which soon developed into a love affair, he threatened to leave her, to divorce her, to lock her up, to kill Tony. She was supremely confident he would do none of these things. She talked to him. Reasonably and gently and lovingly she put it to him that it was he whom she loved and Tony with whom she was amusing herself.

"I *love* you, darling, don't you understand? This thing with Tony is just – fun. We have fun and then we say goodbye till next time and I come home to you, where my real happiness is."

"You promised to be faithful to me," he said, "to forsake all others and keep only to me."

"But I do keep only to you, darling. You have all my trust and my thoughts – Tony just has this tiny share in a very unimportant aspect of me."

After Tony there was Philip. And after Philip, for a while, there was no one. Michael believed Norah might have tired of the 'fun' and be settling for the real happiness. He was working hard at the time for his Fellowship of the Royal College of Surgeons.

That Fellowship he got, of course, in 1952. He was surgical registrar at a big London hospital, famous for successes in the field of cardiac surgery, when the first of the Wrexlade murders took place. Wendy Cutforth. Round about the time the account of that murder and of the hunt for the Wrexlade strangler appeared in the papers, Norah met Jan Vandepeer.

Michael wasn't a reader of the popular press and the Lestranges had no television. Television wasn't, in those days, the indispensable adjunct to domestic life it has since become. Michael listened sometimes to the radio, he read *The Times*. He knew of the first of the Wrexlade murders but he wasn't much interested in it. He was busy in his job and he had Jan Vandepeer to worry about too.

The nature of the Dutchman's business in London was never clear to Michael, perhaps because it was never clear to Norah. It seemed to have something to do with commodity markets and Michael was convinced it was shady, not quite above board. Norah used to say that he was a smuggler, and she found the possibility he might be a diamond smuggler exciting. She met him on the boat coming from The Hook to Harwich after spending a week in The Hague with her parents, her father having a diplomatic post there.

"Darling, I absolutely have to have Jan, I'm crazy about

him. It's nothing to do with us, though, you do see that, don't you? No one could ever take me away from you."

He used to come over about once a month with his car and drive down to London through Colchester and Chelmsford, spend the night somewhere, carry out his business the following day and get the evening boat back. Whether he stayed in Chelmsford rather than London because it was cheaper or because Chelmsford, in those days, still kept its pleasant rural aspect, does not seem to be known. It hardly matters. Norah Lestrange was more than willing to drive the forty or so miles to Chelmsford in her Alpine and await the arrival of her dashing, blond smuggler at the Murrey Gryphon Hotel.

Chelmsford is the county town of Essex, standing on the banks of the river Chelmer and in the midst of a pleasant, though featureless, arable countryside. The land is rather flat, the fields wide, and there are many trees and numerous small woods. Wrexlade lies some four miles to the north of the town, Ingleford a little way further west. It was some time before the English reader of newspapers began to think of Wrexlade as anywhere near Chelmsford. It was simply Wrexlade, a place no one had heard of till Wendy Cutforth and then Maureen Hunter died there, a name on a map or maybe a signpost till the stranglings began – and then, gradually, a word synonymous with fascinating horror.

Bismarck Road, Hilldrop Crescent, Rillington Place – who can say now, except the amateur of crime, which of London's murderers lived in those streets? Yet in their day they were names on everyone's lips. Such is the English sense of humour that there were even jokes about them. There were jokes, says Miss Hallam Saul, about Wrexlade, sick jokes for the utterance of one of which a famous comedian was banned by the BBC. Something on the lines of what a good idea it would be to take one's mother-in-law to Wrexlade . . .

Chelmsford, being so close to Wrexlade, became public knowledge when Mrs Daly died. She was last seen locking up her shop in the town centre and getting into her car. It was after this that Norah said to Michael: "When I'm in Chelmsford, darling, I promise you I won't go out alone after dark."

It was presumably to be a consolation to him that if she went out after dark it would be in the company of Jan Vandepeer.

Did he passively acquiesce, then, in this infidelity of hers? In not leaving her, in being at the flat when she returned home, in continuing to be seen with her socially, he did acquiesce. In continuing to love her in spite of himself, he acquiesced. But his misery was terrible. He was ill with jealousy. All his time, when he was not at the hospital, when he was not snatching a few hours of sleep, was spent in thrashing out in his mind what he should do. It was impossible to go on like this. If he remained in her company he was afraid he would do her some violence, but the thought of being permanently parted from her was horrible. When he contemplated it he seemed to feel the solid ground sliding away from under his feet, he felt like Othello felt – "If I love thee not, chaos is come again."

In June, on Friday, 19 June, Norah went down to Chelmsford, to the Murrey Gryphon Hotel, to spend the night with Jan Vandepeer.

Michael, who had worked every day without a break at the hospital for two weeks, had two days off, the Friday and the Saturday. He was tired almost to the point of sickness, but those two days he was to have off loomed large and glowing and inviting before him at the end of the week. He got them out of proportion. He told himself that if he could have those two days off to spend alone with Norah, to take Norah somewhere into the country and laze those two days away with her, to walk with her hand in hand down country lanes (that he thought with such maudlin romanticism is evidence of his extreme exhaustion), if he could do that, all would miraculously become well. He would explain and she would explain and they would listen to each other and, in the words of the cliché, make a fresh start. Michael was convinced of all this. He was a little mad with tiredness.

After she was dead, and they came in the morning to tell him of her death, he took time off work. Miss Hallam Saul gives the period as three weeks and she is probably correct. Without those weeks of rest Michael Lestrange would very likely have had a mental breakdown or – even worse to his way of thinking – have killed a patient on the operating table. So when it is said that Norah's death, though so terrible to him, saved his sanity and his career, this is not too far from the truth. And then, when he eventually returned to his work, he threw himself into it with total dedication. He had nothing else, you see, nothing at all but his work for the rest of his life that ended in the North Atlantic last March.

Brannel had nothing either. It is very difficult for the educated middle-class person, the kind of person we really mean when we talk about 'the man in the street', to understand the lives of people like Kenneth Edward Brannel and his father. They had no hobbies, no interests, no skill, no knowledge in their heads, virtually no friends. Old Brannel could read. Tracing along the lines with his finger, he could just about make out the words in a newspaper. Kenneth Brannel could not read at all. These days they would have television, not then. Romantic town-dwellers imagine such as the Brannels tending their cottage gardens, growing vegetables, occupying themselves with a little carpentry or shoemaking in the evenings, cooking country stews and baking bread. The Brannels, who worked all day in another man's fields, would not have dreamt of further tilling the soil in the evenings. Neither of them had ever so much as put up a shelf or stuck a sole on a boot. They lived on tinned food and fish and chips, and when the darkness came down they went to bed. There was no electricity in their cottage, anyway, and no running water or indoor sanitation. It would never have occurred to Mr Stokes of Cross Farm to provide these amenities or to the Brannels to demand them.

Downstairs in the cottage was a living room with a fireplace and a kitchen with a range. Upstairs was old Brannel's room into which the stairs went, and through the door from this room was the bedroom and only private place of Kenneth Edward Brannel. There, in a drawer in the old, wooden-knobbed tallboy, unpolished since Ellen Brannel's death, he kept his souvenirs: Wendy Cutforth's bracelet, a lock of Maureen Hunter's red hair, Ann Daly's green silk scarf, Mary Trenthyde's handkerchief with the lipstick stain and the embroidered M. The small, square handbag mirror was always assumed to have been the property of Norah Lestrange, to be a memento of her, but this was never proved. Certainly, there was no mirror in her handbag when her body was found.

In Miss Hallam Saul's *The Wrexlade Monster* there were several pictures of Brannel, a snapshot taken by his aunt when he was ten, a class group at Ingleford Middle School (which he should properly have never, with his limitations, been allowed to attend), a portrait by a Chelmsford photographer that his mother had had taken the year before her death. He was very tall, a gangling, bony man with a bumpy, tortured-looking forehead and thick, pale, curly hair. The eyes seem to say to you: The trouble is that I am puzzled, I am bewildered, I don't understand the world or you or myself and I live always in a dark mist. But when, for a little, that mist clears, look what I do . . .

His hands, hanging limply at his sides, are turned slightly, the palms half-showing, as if in helplessness and despair.

Miss Hallam Saul includes no picture of Sir Michael Lestrange, MD, FRCS, eminent cardiac specialist, author of *The Heart*, Physician to Her Royal Highness the Duchess of Albany, professor of cardiology at St Joachim's Hospital. He was a thin, dark young man in those days, slight of figure and always rather shabbily dressed. One would not have given him a second glance. Very different he was then from the Sir Michael who was mourned by the medical elite of two continents and whose austere yet tranquil face with its sleek silver hair, calm light eyes and aquiline features appeared on the front pages of the world's newspapers. He had changed more than most men in twenty-seven years. It was a total metamorphosis, not merely an ageing.

At the time of the murder of his wife Norah he was twenty-six. He was ambitious but not inordinately so. The ambition, the vocation one might well call it, came later, after she was dead. He was worn out with work on 19 June 1953, and he was longing to get away to the country with his wife and to rest.

"But, darling, I'm sure I told you. I'm going to meet Jan at the Murrey Gryphon. I did tell you, I never have any secrets from you, you know that. *You* didn't tell me you were going to have two days off. How was I to know? You never seem to take time off these days and I do like to have *some* fun *some*times."

"Don't go," he said.

"But, darling, I want to see Jan."

"It's more than I can bear, the way we live," he said. "If you won't stop seeing this man I shall stop you."

He buried his face in his hands and presently she came

and laid a hand on his shoulder. He jumped up and struck her a blow across the face. When she left for Chelmsford to meet Jan Vandepeer she had a bruise on her cheek which she did her best to disguise with make-up.

They had a message for her at the hotel when she got there, from her 'husband' in Holland to say he had been delayed at The Hook. Hotels, in those days, were inclined to be particular that couples who shared bedrooms should at least pretend to be husband and wife. It was insinuated at Brannel's trial that Jan Vandepeer failed to arrive on this occasion because he was growing tired of Norah, but there was no evidence to support this. He was genuinely delayed and unable to leave.

Why didn't she go back to London? Perhaps she was afraid to face Michael. Perhaps she hoped Vandepeer would still come, since the phone message had been received at four-thirty. She dined alone and went out for a walk. To pick up a man, insisted prosecuting counsel, though he was not prosecuting *her* and the Old Bailey is not a court of morals. Nobody saw her go and no one seems to have been sure where she went. Eventually, of course, to Wrexlade.

Brannel also went out for a walk. The long light evenings disquieted him because he could not go to bed and he had nothing to do but sit with his father while the old man puzzled out the words in the evening paper. He went first to his bedroom to look at and handle the secret things he kept there, the scarf and the lock of hair and the bracelet and the handkerchief with M on it for Mary Trenthyde, and then he went out for his walk. Along the narrow lanes, to stop sometimes and stand, to lean over a gate, or to kick a pebble aimlessly ahead of him, dribbling it slowly from side to side of the long, straight, lonely road.

Did Norah Lestrange walk all the way to Wrexlade or did someone give her a lift and for reasons unknown abandon her there? She could have walked, it is no more than two miles from the Murrey Gryphon to the spot where her body was found half an hour before midnight. Miss Hallam Saul suggests that she was friendly with a second man in the Chelmsford neighbourhood and, in the absence of Vandepeer, set off to meet him that evening. Unlikely though that seems, similar suggestions were put forward in court. It was as if they all said, a woman like that, a woman so immoral, so promiscuous, so lacking in all proper feeling, a woman like that will do anything.

Her body was found by two young Wrexlade men going home after an evening spent at the White Swan on the Ladeley–Wrexlade road. They phoned the police from the call box on the opposite side of the lane, and the first place the police went to, because it was the nearest habitation, was the Brannels' cottage. Norah Lestrange's body lay half-hidden in long grass on the verge by the bridge over the river Lade, and the Brannels' home, Lade Cottage, was a hundred yards the other side of the bridge. They went there initially only to ask the occupants if they had seen or heard anything untoward that evening.

Old Brannel came down in his nightshirt with a coat over it. He hadn't been asleep when the police came, he said, he had been awakened a few minutes before by his son coming in. The detective superintendent looked at Kenneth Edward Brannel, at his huge dangling hands, as he stood leaning against the wall, his eyes bewildered, his mouth a little open. No, he couldn't say where he had been, round and about, up and down, he couldn't say more.

They searched the house, although they had no warrant. Much was made of this by the defence at the trial. In Kenneth Brannel's bedroom, in the drawer of the tallboy, they found Wendy Cutforth's bracelet, Maureen Hunter's lock of red hair, Ann Daly's green silk scarf, and the handkerchief with

M on it for Mary Trenthyde. The Wrexlade Monster had been caught at last. They cautioned Brannel and charged him and he looked at them in a puzzled way and said: "I don't think I killed the lady. I don't remember. But maybe I did, I forget things and it's like a mist comes up . . ."

Michael Lestrange was told of the death of his wife in the early hours of the morning. Their purpose in coming to him was to tell him the news and ask him if he would later go with them to Chelmsford formally to identify his wife's body. They asked him no questions and would have expressed their sympathy and left him in peace, had he not declared that it was he who had killed Norah and that he wanted to make a full confession.

They had no choice after that but to drive him at once to Chelmsford and take a statement from him. No one believed it. The detective chief superintendent in charge of the case was very kind to him, very gentle but firm.

"But if I tell you I killed her you must believe me. I can prove it."

"Can you, Dr Lestrange?"

"My wife was constantly unfaithful to me . . ."

"Yes, so you have told me. And you bore with her treatment of you because of your great affection for her. The truth seems to be, doctor, that you were a devoted husband and your wife – well, a less than ideal wife."

Michael Lestrange insisted that he had driven to Chelmsford in pursuit of Norah, intending to appeal to Jan Vandepeer to leave her alone. He had not gone into the hotel. By chance he had encountered her walking aimlessly along a Chelmsford street as he was on his way to the Murrey Gryphon.

"Mrs Lestrange was still having her dinner at the time you mention," said Chief Superintendent Masters.

"What does that matter? It was earlier or later, I can't

be precise about times. She got into the car beside me. I drove off, I don't know where, I didn't want a scene in the hotel. She told me she had to get back, she was expecting Vandepeer at any moment."

"Vandepeer had sent her a message he wasn't coming. She didn't tell you that?"

"Is it important?" He was impatient to get his confession over. "It doesn't matter what she told me. I can't remember what we said."

"Can you remember where you went?"

"Of course I can't. I don't know the place. I just drove and parked somewhere, I don't know where, and we got out and walked and she drove me mad, the things she said, and I got hold of her throat and . . ." He put his head in his hands. "I can't remember what happened next. I don't know where it was or when. I was so tired and I was mad, I think." He looked up. "But I killed her. If you'd like to charge me now, I'm quite ready."

The chief superintendent said very calmly and stolidly, "That won't be necessary, Dr Lestrange."

Michael Lestrange shut his eyes momentarily and clenched his fists and said, "You don't believe me."

"I quite believe you believe it yourself, doctor."

"Why would I confess it if it wasn't true?"

"People do, sir, it's not uncommon. Especially people like yourself who have been overworking and worrying and not getting enough sleep. You're a doctor, you know what the psychiatrists would say, that you had a reason for doing violence to your wife so that now she's dead your mind has convinced itself you killed her, and you're feeling guilt for something you had nothing to do with.

"You see, doctor, look at it from our point of view. Is it likely that you, an educated man, a surgeon, would murder anyone? Not very. And if you did, would you do it in Wrexlade? Would you do it a hundred yards from the home of a man who has murdered four other women? Would you do it by strangling with the bare hands which is the method that man always used? Would you do it four weeks after the last strangling which itself was four weeks after the previous one? Coincidences like that don't happen, do they, Dr Lestrange? But people do get overtired and suffer from stress so that they confess to crimes they never committed."

"I bow to your superior judgement," said Michael Lestrange.

He went to the mortuary and identified Norah's body and then he made a statement to the effect that Norah had gone to Chelmsford to meet her lover. He had last seen her at four on the previous afternoon.

Brannel was found guilty of Norah's murder, for he was specifically charged only with that, after the jury had been out half an hour. And in spite of the medical evidence as to his mental state he was condemned to death and executed a week before Christmas.

For the short time after that execution that capital punishment remained law, Michael Lestrange was bitterly opposed to it. He used to say that Brannel was a prime example of someone who had been unjustly hanged and that this must never be allowed to happen in England again. Of course there was never any doubt that Brannel had strangled Wendy Cutforth, Maureen Hunter, Ann Daly and Mary Trenthyde. The evidence was there and he repeatedly confessed to these murders. But that was not what Michael Lestrange meant. People took him to mean that a man must not be punished for committing a crime whose seriousness he is too feeble-minded to understand. This is the law, and there can be no exceptions to it merely because society wants its revenge. People took Michael Lestrange to mean that when he spoke of injustice being done to this multiple killer.

And perhaps he did.

CRIME PHOTOGRAPHER

(CBS, 1951–1952)
Starring: Darren McGavin, Cliff Hall & Jan Miller
Directed by Sidney Lumet
Story 'Reward for Survivors' by
George Harmon Coxe

Curious as it may seem, the first heroes of crime series on television were not detectives or policemen, but reporters, who launched the genre in America in the late Forties and early Fifties. In 1948, what its producers, NBC, claimed was the very first regularly scheduled mystery series, *Barney Blake: Police Reporter*, appeared: a live show starring Gene O'Donnell as a formidable newspaperman who, with his secretary, Jennifer Allen (Judy Parrish), specialised in solving murder cases – all in less than 30 minutes! Although the series only lasted 13 weeks before being cancelled, this did not deter rival network, ABC, from screening *Photocrime*, a year later with Chuck Webster as an investigator with the unlikely name of Hannibal Cobb. In 1951, however, CBS hit the jackpot with *Crime Photographer* based on a popular series of novels and short stories about Jack 'Flashgun' Casey, the tough cameraman of the *Boston Express*. Written by George Harmon Coxe, the tales of Casey had first appeared in *Black Mask* magazine in 1934, and later been transferred to the cinema in 1936 (starring Stuart Erwin) and then formed the basis for a long-running radio series, *Casey, Crime Photographer* (from 1946 with Stats Cotsworth) before making the transition to the tiny, black and white TV screen of American viewers in April 1951. Like its predecessors, *Crime Photographer* was broadcast live, and most episodes were set in the Blue Note Cafe where Casey recounted his triumphs to his girlfriend, Ann Williams (Jan Miller), also a reporter, and a barman with the extraordinary name of Ethelbert (Cliff Hall). In the early episodes of the series, Casey was played by Richard Carlyle, but he was soon replaced by Darren McGavin who would later become famous as Mike Hammer in the TV version of the Mickey Spillane novels. The series ran successfully for two years and undoubtedly helped to establish crime stories as popular viewing with audiences. The quality of acting and general stylishness of the series owed a lot to the rapidly developing talent of its director, Sidney Lumet, who later became one of the most famous directors in Hollywood.

George Harmon Coxe (1901–1989), the creator of Flashgun Casey, had himself been a newspaper reporter in Santa Monica, Los Angeles and New York, before starting to write crime stories for the pulp magazines in the Thirties. It was Coxe's own interest in photography that led to his creation of Casey to fill a gap in the fictional detective field – previously there had been plenty of reporter-sleuths, but never a cameraman who took pictures and solved crimes. Later, Coxe created another newspaperman, Kent Murdock, who also enjoyed great popularity with readers. The success of these two characters resulted in Coxe becoming a contract scriptwriter for MGM in Hollywood – although he did find time to help in adapting the first Casey story for the screen, *Women Are Trouble* (1936), and then a decade later when

the radio series was launched on CBS. His contributions to the crime story genre earned him a Grand Master Award from the Mystery Writers of America in 1964. 'Reward for Survivors' is a typical Flashgun story in which he has to solve the double mystery of a missing judge and the murder of a reporter – it was adapted for the TV series by producer Charles Russell and screened in May 1952.

Casey, number one camera, for the *Express*, filled the exposed film holder from his camera and shoved it into the bulky plate-case at his feet. He took out a fresh holder, slipped it into the camera, fastened the case and swung the strap over his shoulder; then he leaned his stomach against the fire rope and watched the blaze.

There was not much to it; the very nature of the source limited the spectacle. A three-storey, wooden tenement; old, crumbling, dilapidated even for Kaley Street. A kindling wood structure which seemed to glory in the display and nourish the broad spearheads of fire belching from the windows along the front and one side, and rapidly making the ground floor a continuous spread of flame.

The hot, yellow glow made a glistening bronze mask of Casey's rugged face, and after a minute or so he became aware of what felt like an acute attack of sunburn.

He said, "What the hell," irritably, as though disgusted at his rapt attention, and ran his hand over the soft fabric of his ulster.

It was hot to the touch and he grunted, turned away and began to look for Wade, his fellow cameraman, in the crowd behind the fire lines.

A white helmet caught his eye. He bucked through to a battalion chief whose name escaped him, but whose face was familiar. He saw then that the chief was talking to Jim Trask.

Trask said: "Hi, Flashgun."

Casey grunted an answer, let the plate-case slide from his shoulder, spoke to the chief.

"I hear there was a guy caught in there."

"If he was," the chief growled, "he's still there."

"Well," Casey said, "it won't be long, anyway. In an hour you can wet down the foundation and go home."

"If it don't spread and wipe out the block." The chief's tone was annoyed and he cursed as his eyes swept the adjoining buildings.

Casey fell silent and followed the chief's gaze. A half dozen fat hose lines criss-crossed on the street, continued to drench the side walls of the adjacent brick tenements which, fortunately, were set back from the flaming structure. A derricklike water tower had waddled into position in the middle of the pavement and was alternately wetting down every nearby roof.

Casey glanced at Trask. "You eat it up, huh?"

Trask shrugged. One of the city's leading criminal lawyers, he was a nut on fires. Given an honorary appointment to the fire department, he had promptly ordered a gold replica of the official badge. A flash of that got him into the front row at every blaze.

Trask shrugged thick, overcoated shoulders. He was a heavy-set man with an imposing mien, a course, brutal face and a contradictory, booming voice that was nurtured for courtroom use.

"I get a kick out of it, yes," he admitted defiantly. "Liked fires as a kid and never got over it."

Casey said: "Must be a complex," and then turned around in response to a tug on his arm.

Tom Wade was doing a dance, the routine of which

27

consisted mainly of hopping from one foot to the other so that his chunky body bounced his plate-case in and out from his hip. His round, good-natured face looked strangely aggravated and he said: "We got enough. Let's go."

"Why?" Casey said. "It's warm here, ain't it?"

"Warm hell! It's hot – all but my feet. They're froze."

Casey hesitated, glanced down the street again. The side opposite the blaze was, with one exception, made up of third-rate apartment houses and tenements. The exception was a four-storied, brick loft building with a plumbing supply house on the ground floor. His glance slid up the dingy facade, focused on the roof and he said:

"Okey. One more shot. There's an alley back of that loft building. If there's a fire-escape I can get to the roof. It oughta make a good shot from there – and I might catch her when the walls go."

He started through the crowd. Wade stopped hopping and grinned. "I'll go with you."

"You stay here," Casey grunted. "You'd never make it with those cold feet of yours."

Once one of the crowd, Casey broke into a trot. He swung right at the corner, jogged into thick shadows. The mouth of the alley was an opaque black curtain, and to eyes accustomed to the glare of the fire, the alley, itself, was an inky crevasse with no end, no floor.

He jogged on, keeping to what he thought was the middle of the cobblestone paving. He kept his head down, squinting vainly for guidance. He must have looked directly at that box-like obstruction. But he did not see it; did not know it was there until his toe caught it.

He was off balance, his weight was all wrong. That right foot, just starting its step, stopped short and the rest of him kept on going. One knee hit the paving first; then he went flat on the cobblestones and slid along on the camera which had caught under his chest. The bulky plate-case, slung around one shoulder, plopped down on the back of his neck.

It took Casey several seconds to collect himself. The complete suddenness of the fall seemed to aggravate the jar. The wind was knocked from his body and he had to roll off the camera before he could get his breath. Once he got it he began to swear.

He got to his feet, retrieved his hat and plate-case, and as he groped for the camera, his hand touched the box-like object responsible for his fall. Seizing this outlet for his outraged feelings with savage delight, he caught one corner of the box and knocked it to the side of the alley with a combined heave and sweep of his arm.

Again he groped for his camera, snatched it up; then, as he turned to continue down the alley, his foot caught a second unseen object.

This time he did not fall; he merely stumbled. But the shock was greater; a cold, nervous shock that yanked his muscles taut and made his breath stick in his throat.

The object was soft, yielding.

Casey pulled his foot back. The complete blackness of the alley defied him. He shrugged off the plate-case and went quickly to one knee, his left hand groping. Stiff fingers touched cloth, found the buttons of an overcoat and as he bent close the fumes of whiskey tickled his nose.

He said, "Oh, a drunk, huh?" and there was relief in his hushed tones. He let his pent-up breath out slowly and found a match.

The little burst of flame threw a weird orange glow at his feet, picked up the outlines of a man who lay on his side. The hat had fallen off and he saw the profile of a thin face, hair that looked reddish and tousled. He pulled the man on his back, said: "Jeeze! Shorty Prendell," softly.

The match went out. Casey tore another from the paper packet and his mind found temporary acceptance in a satisfactory answer.

Shorty Prendell was a photographer for the *News*, a happy-go-lucky fellow, an habitual souse, good-natured, well-liked in spite of his irresponsible character. Casey had saved him his job more than once by covering an assignment for him, when he passed out; apparently he was running true to form.

Casey struck the second match and again the feeble glow settled upon the inert form. This time Casey's peering gaze slid down to Prendell's overcoat, slid down as far as the chest and stopped; and he sucked air and forgot about the whiskey breath.

There was an irregular round stain in the worn fabric of the grey overcoat – a reddish stain with frayed threads showing in the centre.

For one brief moment Casey knelt there with his gaze riveted on the stain, and grappled with his thoughts while the stiff cold wind of the early March night swept the floor of the alley and tugged at his nerve ends. Then the match flame singed thumb and finger and he dropped it. Blackness wrapped around him, spurred him to action.

He left his case and camera, spun quickly and raced for the mouth of the alley, conscious of a dryness, a thickness in his throat.

There were three or four hundred people on Kaley Street, crowding the fire lines, hanging from windows, warming themselves and enjoying the blaze. There were firemen everywhere; but not policemen, not that Casey could see.

He found Wade right where he had left him. Wade was still dancing and he came up behind him and jerked him around.

Wade took one look at the white, grim lines of Casey's face and went wide-eyed and said: "What the—"

"Shorty Prendell," Casey flung out. "Shot. I stumbled over him in the alley. Get on a phone and—"

"Dead?"

"Call Logan!" Casey rapped, ignoring the question. "Tell him to bring a doctor. Save time. He oughta make it in five minutes." He hesitated while Wade battled his surprise, added: "Snap into it! I'm goin' back."

In the alley again, Casey moved cautiously forward until he reached Prendell's body. He struck another match, glanced at the thin face. Then he wiped a damp palm on his coat and reached for a limp wrist. He held his breath while he felt for a pulse; then he let it out in a silent blast and gently eased the lifeless hand back on the cobblestones.

Casey was hunched there in the darkness, sitting on his heels smoking a cigarette when Wade came into the alley. Casey called to him, directed his steps and Wade crouched beside him and said:

"Is he—"

"Yeah," Casey said wearily. "A slug in the chest."

Wade whispered an awed oath, fell silent, finally said: "Why? What's it all about? What—"

"How do I know?" Casey clipped and his voice was angry, irritable from reaction. "I stumbled over him – over his plate-case. Maybe he came back for the same reason I did. Maybe he came back to sneak a couple snifters out of his bottle. Somebody let him have it. Somebody might've had it in for him, or—" He broke off in a curse. "How the hell do I know?"

Wade said: "Jeeze. He was a swell guy."

"Yeah," Casey said. "And he's got a wife. And he was a souse and that made it tough for her. But he was a good guy. I'd like to get a crack at the punk that did it."

The two photographers were crouched there in silence when the police car jerked to a stop at the mouth of the alley. Two men swung to the sidewalk and became running silhouettes against the faint background of reflected light. A yellow cone from a flashlight swept the floor and sides of the alley, focused on Casey's face and Lieutenant Logan's voice flared: "Dead?" sharply.

Casey said: "Yeah."

The man with Logan, a vague, unrecognisable figure to Casey knelt beside Shorty Prendell, unbuttoned the coat, slid hands and fingers about in the semi-darkness."

"Shot twice," he said finally and stood up. "It's the examiner's job all right and he's still warm."

Logan said: "Thanks, Doc. Tell the driver to take you home and then come back here."

When the doctor withdrew Logan turned to Casey. "Let's have it."

Casey told him what he knew, and was bitterly conscious that he had but little to tell. Logan began a search of the alley.

"Well," Wade's voice was hesitant, guilty. "Er – hadn't we ought to get a couple pictures?"

Casey said, "Yeah," wearily. "With your box. I can't use mine till I look it over in the light."

Both ends of the alley were guarded by plain-clothes men. The examiner's physician had just finished his examination and he had but little to offer in the way of additional information.

"In the back," he said as he snapped his bag shut. "Looks like he was running, from the way he fell. One slug still in him; I'll turn it over to ballistics and give you a report tomorrow."

The little group around the body fell silent as the examiner left. Feet shuffled on the cobblestone floor and cigarette ends glowed and vaguely illuminated masklike faces. Logan spoke first and his voice was sullen, jerky.

"Not a thing. Not a damned thing but two empty shells." He turned to the lieutenant from the precinct house, and Casey whispered to Wade:

"You better beat it. The couple of shots I got of the fire ain't worth a damn alongside this. Take my case with you and—"

"But what're you gonna do?" Wade asked dubiously.

"Me?" Casey grunted. "Me – I'm gonna stick with Logan."

"Then why can't I—"

"Will you quit arguin'? You took the pictures – develop 'em. It ain't my job, is it? G'wan, now. Take my case. If they need my two shots, develop 'em. But they probably won't."

"All right, all right," Wade grumbled. He groped around in the darkness, shouldered the two plate-cases and started down the alley.

Logan said: "Listen, Flash, don't you know if Prendell was working on something that—"

"How would I know?" Casey hesitated. "Why don't you get those other *News* guys in here?"

"I will," Logan jerked out. And he did not have to go far. He found the men he sought trying to argue their way past the plain-clothes man at the alley's entrance, and brought them back.

With the help of the flashlights, Casey recognised them both. Beardsley, a photographer, and Kelly, a legman. Logan gave them a few seconds to get used to the atmosphere of death, then he said:

"Come on, now. Gimme a lead. We ain't got to first base yet. What was he workin' on?"

"Nothing that I know of," Kelly said. "The three of us came down here in a taxi. Shorty'd had a couple of drinks, and he still had the bottle. I didn't see him again after we got out of the cab."

"But wasn't he workin' on something else – before this, maybe?" Logan pressed. "Think, damn it!"

Kelly hesitated. Casey heard Beardsley opening his camera, and the *News* photographer seemed to do his work, instinctively, automatically. It was apparent his mind was elsewhere because he kept saying: "Jeeze!" Then, "What would they kill him for? He never hurt a fly. Jeeze!"

Kelly seemed to shake himself, spoke regretfully. "I don't know. He wasn't workin' on anything that I know of." He turned there in the darkness and spoke to Casey. "You know, Flash. He was a swell little guy when he was sober. But the bottle was gettin' him. He was slippin', never got any big assignments any more. I don't think he was working on anything."

"Well, hell!" Logan exploded. "Can't I get any co-operation? What am I, a magician or something? Somebody better know something or it'll go down in the books as a bust. A newspaper guy gets knocked off and every sheet in town'll yell its head off. But that's all. Yell and take it out on the department."

"We'll find something," Casey said and there was a certain grim conviction in his tone.

"Talk," Logan snorted. "You find him dead. With that fire nobody'd pay any attention to this alley. Nobody saw him come in here. How the hell—"

The fading wail of a siren stopped him. An ambulance lurched slowly into the alley, its headlights exploding light over the cobblestones. Two white-coated internes swung off the rear step with a stretcher, set it down beside Shorty Prendell.

Casey watched the thin form being lifted to the canvas and his fingers flexed and he became conscious of that tightening of the throat. A dull, gnawing resentment smoldered deep within him. A bitter sense of frustration, born under the goading of his helplessness, warped his thoughts.

Murdered. A harmless little guy like Shorty. But something would come to light that would help. There'd be a break some place. And Logan could weave the breaks together if anyone could. He watched the stretcher disappear, heard the doors slap shut. The ambulance backed down the alley and its bell clanged jarringly to clear a path across the sidewalk.

He turned quickly then spoke brusquely to hide his feelings. "You'd better take his camera and case when you go, Beardsley. And" – he hesitated, continued hurriedly – "if they take up some dough for his wife or anything, count me in."

Casey rolled over in bed, tucked his head under the covers for a moment, then stuck his nose out and blinked angry eyes at the insistently shrilling telephone on the bedside table. Each strident burst jarred the back of his head and in self defence he reached out, removed the receiver, dropped it.

He growled an oath, rolled over on his back. He stretched himself awake; for a second or two he enjoyed the luxury of a completely relaxed brain; then the thoughts of the previous night, and Shorty Prendell's death, flooded his mind and he sat up, scowling, at once troubled and resentful.

Reaching for the telephone, he pulled it over to his chest, fumblingly retrieved the dangling receiver, growled: "Yeah?"

The answering terse, incisive voice belonged to Blaine, city editor of the *Express*. This surprised him because he thought it was early and Blaine did not come on the desk until after lunch.

"What's the matter with you?" Blaine said.

"Matter with who?" Casey growled.

"You, dammit. Why didn't you bring that picture in yourself, develop it yourself, tell somebody about it?"

"What picture?" Casey said wonderingly.

"It looks like the biggest thing in months," Blaine went on crisply. "But that don't excuse you for running out on the job. Now, get down here – and in a hurry. Logan's waiting."

"Listen," Casey rapped, "what—" He listened, said "Hello," jiggled the receiver arm and finally slapped the telephone back on the stand and made noises in his throat.

Reaching under his pillow, he got his watch, saw that it was only ten after nine. He knew he was not due at the office for a couple of hours and he said, "What's eatin' him? What the hell picture is he squawkin' about?"

He swung his feet to the floor, ran thick fingers through a shock of curly dark hair that was streaked with grey at the temples. For a moment he sat there on the edge of the bed, scowling, his stiff arms angling out at his sides, propping him up. He reached for the telephone, then changed his mind about calling Blaine back.

"Now that he's got me up," he grumbled, "I might as well go down. Boy, what a job!"

He pulled his pyjama top off over his head, stood up and stepped out of the pants. For a moment he remained poised there, a big, naked, thick-chested figure, and grappled with Blaine's words.

He had gone back to the paper last night. Wade had the necessary pictures, and he, Casey, had stuck with Logan for an hour or so, until he saw that further developments in the murder case were unlikely until morning. It was nearly two o'clock then and he had stopped in an all-night coffee shop for sandwiches before coming home.

"Nerts", he said finally and went into the bathroom.

He took a quick shower and a shave. Within ten minutes he was fully dressed, and he had just picked up his ulster when the knock came at the door.

The knock annoyed him for some reason, and he put on his ulster and glared at the door without answering. The knock was repeated, vigorously, sharply.

Casey growled, "In a minute," then crossed the room, snapped back the lock and turned the knob.

There were two men in the hall. Casey knew one of them: a small, skinny fellow with a pale, wedge-shaped face and small shifty eyes. Sid Glasek. The other fellow, a thick-necked bruiser with a flat nose and scarred brows was a stranger.

Glasek pushed back his derby, said: "Hello, Flash," nodded to the thick-necked fellow and the two of them stepped across the threshold.

Casey frowned, stepped back, trying to figure things out. Glasek was a petty larceny politician, a punk and— He said: "I was just goin' out – and I'm in a hurry."

Glasek was warily apologetic. "It won't take a minute. He just wants to know if you got your camera and plate-case here."

"Yeah?" Casey's brows lifted sceptically and his voice got thin. "Why?"

The thick-necked fellow closed the door and put both hands in the pockets of his worn blue overcoat. Glasek shrugged, pushed his derby still farther back.

"We wanta take a look."

"You'd better beat it," Casey said and his brows came down. "I'm in a hurry."

Glasek's shifty eyes spied the camera on the centre table.

"There's no use gettin' tough about it. Show us the camera and case and we'll beat it."

"You'll beat it anyway," Casey clipped, "or maybe you wanta—"

"We wanta look around," the thick-set man cut in hoarsely. Casey glanced at him, watched the fellow take a heavy automatic from his coat pocket, deliberately turn it over in his hand and replace it so that the muzzle jutted threateningly forward. "And maybe you'd better pull in your neck while we do it."

Casey's eyes flared behind narrowed lids, but he made his voice disgusted. "Maybe you're right."

He stepped to the davenport, perched on the edge. The camera had nothing in it, was probably broken although he had not looked. And Wade had taken the plate-case to the office. The thick-necked fellow stood by the door and watched him, and Glasek searched the room, went into the bedroom, came back and spread his hands.

"Okey," he said, but he said it regretfully. "If it ain't here, it ain't here. You see? We didn't want any trouble." He moved to the door. "Nothing to get het up about. No hard feelings."

"Oh, no," Casey said and his lip curled. "No. Come in an' look around any time – any time you got some punk with a gun."

"Don't get smart!" the thick-necked fellow blustered.

Glasek said, "Come on," and opened the door.

Casey watched it close and he glared at the panels for a moment as he reached for a cigarette. "That kind of stuff burns me up," he fumed. "And I hate riddles."

He crossed to the two front windows, glanced up at the heavy, sullen sky, down at the bleak and sunless street. Glasek and his hood were just getting into a taxi. Casey saw that it was a Blue and White. He noticed the number – T36746 – and repeated it absently, half aloud.

Farrar, a rewrite man, was on the desk when Casey swung into the nearly deserted *Express* city room at nine-fifty, and he glanced up, said:

"Blaine's in Magrath's office. He's waiting for you."

"Yeah," Casey said. "I had an idea he was." He moved into a corridor behind the desk, turned into an office whose frosted glass panel said: T.A. Magrath, Managing Editor.

Blaine was sitting at the desk. Logan, opposite Blaine, turned and spoke over his shoulder before Casey got the door shut.

"You didn't hurry, did you?" he leered. Then, with a voice that snapped: "Hours we waste, you cluck. And all the time you—"

"Wait a minute," Casey barked. "What—"

"Sit down," Blaine said, "and listen."

Casey unbuttoned his ulster, made two more attempts to break through Logan's rush of words. Finally he muttered an oath, dropped into a chair beside the desk, and remained scowlingly silent, aware that some mistake had been made, but stubbornly unwilling now to try and explain until he heard the rest of the story.

Blaine, sitting stiffly behind the desk, his clothing immaculate, his grey hair smoothly parted, watched Casey and there was condemnation in his cold, grey eyes.

Casey watched Logan as he listened to his story and he saw that the lieutenant's handsome, smooth-shaven face was tense, a bit grim, that the black eyes were sharp and glaring.

"I don't know if it hooks up with Prendell or not," he was saying. "But this line we've got on Judge Ottleib is plenty hot."

Ottleib. Judge Ottleib had been missing for more than a month. The name jerked Casey's thoughts from Logan.

At first the police had gone on the theory that his disappearance was a straight kidnapping job. But there had been no ransom notes, no demands of any kind. The theory shifted. For a short time it was thought he might have been murdered by some criminal he had sentenced and who sought vengeance. Then some investigator turned up information that clouded the issue still further.

Judge Ottleib received a salary of 17,500 dollars a year. But in the past four years he had, in different banks, made deposits of nearly a hundred thousand dollars. And these deposits were almost entirely made of cash. With something to get their teeth into, the District Attorney's office began to unearth irregularities of other types. Certain criminal lawyers – Arnostein – Myers – Trask – had been thoroughly questioned. A record of cases tried under Ottleib showed a preponderance of decisions in their favor. Trask particularly had been fortunate in his verdicts under Ottleib.

But proof was lacking. And the disappearance of the Judge became a matter of personal opinion – that and nothing more. He was kidnapped, he was murdered, he intentionally disappeared.

"But I didn't have a lead," Logan broke in on Casey's thoughts. "No lead, no nothing; so I checked up on the guy that burned up in that tenement."

"It was straight, then, huh?" Casey said.

"Not so straight," Logan drawled sardonically. "But a guy burned up, yeah. The inspectors think the fire was set, but they can't be sure because the blaze wiped out everything. There's nothing left of this guy except bone ashes and teeth and a ring and a key – one of them law fraternity keys."

Logan grunted, stared at Casey and his eyes narrowed.

"The ring and the key were Judge Ottleib's."

Casey whistled and his eyes widened and Logan said: "We don't know how long he lived in that shack. Nobody in the neighborhood remembers him much until about a week ago. I showed 'em a picture of Ottleib. He's the guy that's been living there and the way it looks he's been there all the time. But he laid low at first when his picture was in the papers and everything, just started comin' out when the thing died down.

Logan pushed back in his chair. "The thing's a natural, huh? No mystery. The Judge hides out and gets burned to death. Only you and that bull-headed luck of yours run smack into a break again and knock the layout all to hell." Logan leaned forward. "Now, by gawd, I wanta know why you get a picture like that and then—"

"Wait a minute," Casey blasted, and anger flushed his face. "I'm gettin' fed up with these riddles. Where'd you get the picture?"

"Out of your plate-case," Blaine said and his tone was sarcastically polite. "Wade brought it in, but all he developed was his own stuff. That's about all I could expect from him. But you—"

"I've probably heard it before," Casey said caustically. "What's the rest of it?"

"Wade forgot about your shots. He didn't remember until early this morning. Then he called in about a quarter of eight and told Farrar maybe we'd better see what you had."

"That's not his fault," Casey said. "I told him he didn't need to bother with my stuff. I didn't have anything but a couple of routine shots that—"

"Routine?" grated Logan. "Why you held out on me, you louse."

Casey stood up. "Let's see this masterpiece of mine," he said quickly.

Blaine opened a drawer, took out a four-by-five print, handed it to Casey. The big photographer stared at it and his eyes went wide. He jerked his glance away from the

41

print, looked at Blaine, wet his lips. Then he looked back at the picture again and the eyes narrowed.

The camera had caught three men moving down what looked like an alley. All three men were back to the camera, but two of them, apparently attracted by some noise, were looking over their shoulders. Both faces were distinct. The man in the centre was Judge Ottleib; the big man at his right was Brad Shannon. The third man could not be recognised.

Logan's voice was harsh, accusing. "One of your friends gets knocked off and—"

"And," Casey clipped, "you think I'd have a picture like this and hold out on you? That's the kind of a punk you think I am, huh?"

"Well," Logan pressed.

"You took it, didn't you?" Blaine whipped.

"No."

"Then," choked Logan, "who—"

"I never saw it before," Casey said.

"Where'd it come from?" Blane exploded. "Who took it?"

"Shorty Prendell," Casey said grimly and then stared sightlessly at the picture and tried to figure out definite and logical reasons to substantiate his conviction.

Casey placed the telephone back on the desk and straightened up.

He looked at Blaine, then at the scowling and uncomprehending Logan. He took off his brown felt, wiped the sweatband, jammed it back on his head again.

"That's it," he said. "Beardsley says he tried to get me last night. There wasn't a single plate in my plate-case."

Logan took a deep breath and his nostrils dilated as he snuffed it out again. "He musta just taken it," he said thoughtfully. "He was tryin' to get away with it and somebody put the slug on him – twice. But I can't figure how—"

"Listen," Casey said and slid a thick thigh across the edge of the desk. "Suppose Shorty was out there sneakin' a drink. While he was standing there these three came along – came out of one of those back doors, maybe. Somehow he gets a look at 'em, recognises Ottleib. He knew what he had, and he took a flash of 'em and tried to run.

"Maybe he took a few steps before they got him. He went down on his face and the camera and case flopped out in front of him. Whoever shot him knew he had a picture—"

"Then why the hell—" Logan began.

"Because I musta come along," Casey said slowly, trying to visualise just what he had done the night before. "They were probably looking for the plate-case. I came along and they ducked into a doorway or something to wait until I went past. But I fell over the plate-case – Shorty's.

"And when I got up I knocked it clear over to the side of the alley. Then I found him. And I left my case right there beside him. They thought it was his. It's gotta be that way. They were there all the time and they opened my case by mistake, took out all the plates."

Silence greeted this. Blaine rubbed a lean jaw nervously, swivelled his eyes to Logan, back to Casey, "All right," he said. "What's the rest of it?"

"I can guess for you," Casey said. "Logan moved my case to one side. I told Wade to bring that case to the office. But Wade didn't know, or didn't think, about there being two cases besides his own. He picked up the first one – Shorty's – and brought it in. Beardsley took mine.

"I fell on my camera – would not risk using it. If it hadn't been for that I'd probably opened the case and then there would not've been any mix-up. But—" He broke off, continued as though talking to himself. "Shorty was good. He must've jerked that plate from his camera as soon as he snapped it; must've slipped it into the case as he ran and—"

Logan stood up with a savage grunt. "Talk about your breaks," he said. "I should've had this dope last night."

"You're lucky to get it at all," Blaine said. "If there hadn't been two cases, Ottleib would've got the plate and you'd still be thinking he burned to death."

Logan began to pace the floor, talking as he moved. "All right. We know why Prendell got it. One of those three guys shot him. We gotta find Ottleib or Shannon. And the hook-up between 'em fits."

Casey knew what Logan meant. Brad Shannon was the sort of private investigator who worked exclusively for lawyers. He could be found almost any day hanging around the City Hall corridors, or the Court House rotunda. On two occasions he had been forced to stand trial for jury fixing. And in one instance. Jim Trask had been implicated.

"Shannon used to work for Trask," Logan said. "And with this picture of him and Ottleib, we know which way we're going. I'll have a talk with Trask, too."

"He was at the fire," Casey said and told of the conversation.

"We'll get a story from him," Logan grunted. "Only it probably won't be much. Trask is plenty smart and he knows the law. Nothing but facts'll work with him. It's Shannon we want – or Ottleib."

"And Glasek," Casey said. He mouthed a curse, told of what happened at his apartment that morning.

"We got something," Logan said when Casey finished. "They know how they muffed the picture." He turned to Blaine. "Don't run it until I okay it. Let 'em worry about it and—"

"It's not ours, anyway," Casey charged. "It's a *News* beat."

"I'll take care of that," Blaine said coldly.

"Yeah?" Casey said. "Well, Shorty Prendell took it, and he oughtta get credit, even if it won't do him any good."

Blaine's eyes blazed. "If it hadn't been for you, and a pot full of luck, nobody'd have it. But at that, I don't steal pictures." His lips curled as he finished, and he reached for the telephone, asked for Murphy, managing editor of the *News*.

Casey thought about just one thing while Blaine talked: Shorty Prendell – and his wife. Casey had met Mrs Prendell and he recalled her now. A small, quiet, tired-looking woman who seemed to accept the negative lot life had cast for her.

Beardsley had not been quite right about Shorty. He had never harmed anyone maliciously, and he had the sort of personality that made you like him even when he was wrong. But he had harmed his wife. Irreparably, it seemed, by incessant drinking. She worked in an office to offset his expenditures on liquor. Casey brooded about all this, and more, before he finally remembered something that gave a new and hopeful twist to his reverie.

Blaine hung up, spoke sardonically. "It's okey with Murphy. We'll both run it. Satisfied, Casey?"

Casey stood up. "There was a reward, wasn't there?" he asked, ignoring Blaine's comment. "When Ottleib was first missing."

"There still is," Logan said dryly. "Twenty-five hundred." He looked curiously at Casey and there was an undertone of disdain, unusual in his relations with the photographer, in his voice, "Lookin' for your cut already?"

Casey caught Logan's gaze, held it as he moved to the door. His lips dipped at the corners and his eyes brightened and narrowed. "My pal, huh?" he grunted, and left the room.

Casey was slouched in a broken down chair in the photographic department a half hour later, his feet cocked on the desk top, a cigarette in his lips, when Wade came in.

The young photographer's guileless blue eyes were wide with interest and there was a breathless, eager quality about his stance as he stopped beside Casey.

"Hey," he flung out, "you know this guy Glasek that—"

"Yeah," Casey said.

"Well," Wade hurried on, "he and some hood come up to my place a little while ago and want to know about my camera and plate-case. They searched—"

Casey jerked erect in his chair, listened to Wade tell a story similar to his own.

"Now how the hell can you figure that out?" Wade wanted to know.

Casey stood up without answering, picked up his hat and shrugged into his ulster. "Come on," he said.

"Where?"

"Come on," Casey urged, starting for the door. "You remind me of an idea I've been too dumb to develop. It might be good."

"Yeah," Wade said, perplexed, "but where? Do I take the box or—"

"Why not?" Casey said. "We might need it. I want to check up on the Blue and White cab that carted Glasek and his hood around."

Casey and Wade were in luck. From the taxi office they found the driver had a stand on Providence and Boylston; and he was parked there when they reached the intersection. All this took but twenty minutes, and ten minutes after that they stood on Marlborough Street surveying the ancient vine-covered facade of a four-storied structure that had the appearance of a private house which had been remodelled into small apartments.

Casey had related the incidents of the morning, had told about the mix-up in plate-cases. Wade made brief awkward apologies for his failure to pick the right case and to develop Casey's supposed plates the night before, and, reassured by Casey's manner, promptly forgot about everything but the job at hand.

"It's a break the driver remembered where Glasek went," he said.

"There was nothing to it," Casey said. "He went from my place to yours, and then here. Let's have a look."

They went up worn stone steps, flanked by a stone railing, stepped into a gloomy vestibule. There were more than a dozen name cards tacked over mail-boxes along the wall, cards which identified the house or both a residential and business place, furnishing studios for two music teachers, an artist, an interior decorator.

Casey looked at the names twice, grunted disgustedly: "All we draw is a blank."

Wade looked glum, "What do you want to do?"

"I want to find out who lives in each one of these apartments."

"You don't know any of 'em, do you?"

"My gawd," Casey growled, "do you always give your right name?"

Wade grinned and said, "Oh," and then went out to the top step, stood there a moment while Casey took out a cigarette. When he lighted it and inhaled, he said:

"Go down to that drugstore on the next corner and call Logan. I oughtta pass him up after what he said, but I don't trust some of those Headquarters guys. You give 'em a tip and they freeze you out on the pay-off."

"What'll I tell him?" Wade asked dubiously.

Casey sighed wearily and shook his head. "What the hell do you think? Tell him to get down here. Let him dope up a way of going through the building."

Wade was gone about five minutes. The frown on his round, good-natured face told Casey the answer before he said:

"He ain't there. Just stepped out."

"Yeah," Casey stormed. "Stepped out with his foot on a rail." He scowled, looked up the facade of the building. "I don't want to take a chance on anybody else."

"Why don't we go through the place ourselves," Wade said.

"Sure," Casey sniffed. "And tip our mitt if anybody recognises us."

"Well," Wade scratched behind his ear and his brows knotted, "then why don't we get your car, park it across the street and watch the place. We could get a pint and—"

"Lay off," growled Casey. "You're wearin' me down." He flipped his cigarette away. "What we need is somebody to—" He broke off in a grunt of satisfaction and the scowl vanished as an idea caught in his brain, began to blossom. He said, "You wait across the street," and ran down the steps.

At the corner drugstore, he walked to the telephone booths, called the *Express* and a minute later was talking with Gowan, the City Circulator.

"Mac – Flash Casey. You got any solicitors in the office? Yeah, the guys that go around from house to house and ask if they want to take the *Express*. Yeah. Well send one to—" Casey gave the Marlborough Street address. "What? No, nobody wants to subscribe, dammit. I just want the guy to go through a house for me. I might get a lead on the Prendell job. If I do the circulation department might peddle a couple extra sheets. And listen, connect me with Jerry – in the morgue – our morgue. I'll have him bring some pictures down to this subscription guy."

The circulation solicitor was a hoarse-voiced, red-faced fellow with a faded black coat, a dusty derby and glasses.

Casey said: "Did you bring the pictures I told Jerry to give you?"

"Yeah. What do you want I should do?"

"Take a good look at those pictures," Casey said and waited while the fellow took them from his pocket and studied the faces of Ottleib, Shannon and Glasek. "Then go through this house just like you was selling subscriptions. If you see any of these guys beat it back here. I wanta know if—"

"How about orders?" the man wheezed. "I work on commission and if I can sell a coupla names—"

"Sell 'em, then," snorted Casey. "But shake it up and don't stop to gas with everybody in the building."

The man looked dubious and shook his head from side to side. Then he took a folded copy of the *Express* from his pocket and stepped through the vestibule and into the hallway beyond.

Wade, top-heavy with admiration, said: "Hey, Flash. That's a swell idea."

Casey said: "Sure," and stepped down in the areaway under the steps.

All through the noon hour they waited and the stiff, March wind swept the street and whirled and eddied about the areaway. Casey stamped his feet in a monotonous rhythm, and kept his hands in the ulster pockets, hunched the collar around his ears. Wade sat on his plate-case and hugged his overcoat, and pulled his neck in like a turtle.

Traffic in the street was swift, sporadic, flowing and ebbing with the signal light on the Avenue. Some time after one, two young girls with brief cases ran up the steps, giggling. A long-haired man with a flowing black tie came out.

A small truck with *Quinn's Trucking* lettered on its side pulled up to the curb. Two men got out of the enclosed cab. As they came up the steps one of them saw Casey in the areaway. He said "Hi, Flashgun."

Casey grunted, "How's it, Spike?"

The two men came out a few minutes later, carrying an old-fashioned, squarish trunk. Casey cursed softly, said: "I'll bet that subscription guy's sellin' the whole building." He stepped out on the sidewalk and lit a cigarette as he watched the trunk being loaded on the truck.

"This ain't so soft as drivin' a hack, Spike," he said.

Spike Largo, a former second-rate boxer who had put on weight and drifted to taxi-driving, and then to trucking, grinned at Casey, said:

"But I'm gettin' three squares now, son. I'd starve, hackin' in these times."

Heels clicking on the steps behind Casey checked a reply. He turned, saw the red-faced solicitor and forgot Spike Largo. He said, "Who'd you find?"

"Him," the man said, and showed Glasek's picture. He sucked at his teeth, grunted and spoke in an injured voice. "This is gettin' to be a tough racket. There was another guy in the room; I didn't get a chance to see him because this first guy acts like he's got a grudge against me, or something. I ask him, does he want to take the *Express* and he—"

"Where?" chafed Casey.

"Apartment 3-D."

"Here." Casey thrust a dollar bill at the fellow. "Here's some expense money. I'll tell Gowan you're a wizard."

While the man stood there looking at the bill, Casey grabbed

Wade's shoulder. "Listen," he ordered. "Go back to the drugstore. Call Logan again. If you can't get him this time, get Judson – or Orcutt. But get somebody, tell 'em where to come; then come back here and wait."

"What're you gonna do?" Wade argued.

"I'm goin' upstairs and—"

"You ain't gonna try and take those guys by yourself?"

"Hell, no. But I'm takin' no chances of their slippin' out the back way, either. I'm goin' up in the hall and wait there until Logan or somebody comes. But if Glasek *should* come out I can throw a bluff and—" He broke off. "Oh, hell! Will you quit givin' me an argument?"

Casey shoved Wade, watched him hesitate, then break into a reluctant trot, the place-case banging his hips. He climbed to the vestibule and went into a dim entrance hall that seemed strangely hot and stuffy. Opposite doors opened from the hall in front of the stairs, and adjoining this was a corridor which stretched to the rear. In one of the lower rooms, someone was banging out an exercise on the piano. From above came the muted shrill of a soprano trilling up and down a scale.

Casey climbed the carpeted stairs, unbuttoning his coat as he went. The practicing soprano became steadily louder, formed a background for thoughts that were expectant, yet apprehensive.

He did not know just how much good he was doing by following up his hunch and tracing the taxi; he was not sure what Logan would find when he went into the apartment. But it was at least a lead. The police would look for Shannon and Ottleib through the regular channels. This was on his own. And action, any kind of action, was better than sitting around and thinking about Shorty Prendell with the slugs in his back and a red-hot picture in his plate-case.

At the third floor landing the soprano was much louder,

but still above him. Casey moved slowly along the corridor, found Apartment 3-D was about halfway down. He stopped in front of the door, leaned close to listen. But the soprano defied him and he scowled at the ceiling, cursed softly.

He moved to the opposite wall, leaned against it and lit another cigarette. It was probably an unnecessary precaution, his coming up here. But after this much trouble, there was no use taking a chance. Logan – and he hoped to hell it would be Logan – should be here in another five or ten minutes and—

A lock clicked. Casey's eyes jerked to the doorknob of Apartment 3-D, saw it turn. He stuck the cigarette in one corner of his mouth, wiped his palms on his coat. The door opened. Then he stepped forward so that, as the door swung wide, he met Glasek in the opening.

He stepped back, acted surprised and uncertain. But his eyes shot over Glasek's shoulder and got hard and shiny as they fastened on the big, overcoated figure beyond, Brad Shannon.

Glasek's surprise was genuine. He stammered, "Why – what"

Shannon grunted and stepped forward, brushing Glasek out of the way. Then Casey saw the gun in Shannon's hand and he blinked, said:

"Hey. What the—"

Shannon stepped aside, motioned with the gun. "Come on in."

Casey moved into the well-furnished living room and closed the door by backing against it. He kept his eyes on Shannon, kept them wide and surprised.

Shannon watched Casey for a moment in silence. He was a big man, as tall as Casey and just as heavy; good-looking in a gross, swarthy way, he had a pointed moustache and hard, metallic eyes that seemed too small for his face. At the moment the eyes were suspicious, speculative; and his low voice had a snarl in it.

"Nosey, huh? Well, speak your piece."

"I was lookin' for Glasek," Casey said flatly.

"You wouldn't kid me, would you?"

"I was lookin' for Glasek," Casey went on and glanced at the little man's wedge-shaped face which was still over-written with surprise. "He busted in on me this morning and I wanta know the set-up."

"How'd you find this place?" Shannon said slowly.

"Taxi-driver."

Shannon seemed to accept this, but with the acceptance, the eyes narrowed and his moustache drew back against his teeth. Reaching into his coat pocket, he took out a blackjack, weighed it in his palm, slipped the gun into the pocket.

"I'm gonna enjoy this," he muttered. "I'm kinda hot; maybe you know it. And this Glasek gag won't rub. There's a picture out that's put the pressure on me. Right now I got only one out. I gotta run for it till I find out where I stand. And you're the guy that got me in the jam."

Shannon moved slowly forward. "I should've let you have it in the alley last night. Then there wouldn've been any picture. But we made a mistake. You've got nothing on Glasek; but me – I'm spotted. So for hornin' in last night – and now"

Shannon came forward swiftly, his left fist doubled, the right hand holding the blackjack, cocked.

Casey said: "Now wait—"

He knew what to expect; he shifted his weight and got ready for Shannon. And he had time to think that perhaps this was a good break, that the more time he could waste, the better it would be; and he was glad now, that he had taken the precaution to come up to the third floor hall and wait.

He poised on the balls of his feet, put up his hands. Shannon jabbed with his left, slashed out with the blackjack. Casey took the left, on his hunched chin, kept his eyes on Shannon's right, blocked the swing and stepped close, hooking his right. Shannon grunted, clinched, began to swing with blackjack as his left arm hugged Casey close.

Casey took two glancing blows – painful, but not too damaging – to the shoulder before he could counter. Then he got his chin over Shannon's shoulder, gained momentary safety from the blackjack, and slammed away with both hands; short, powerful punches that ripped into Shannon's stomach and solar plexus.

Shannon could not stand up under such an attack. Lacking the cast-iron stomach muscles of a fighter in condition, he doubled, gasped, fell back. Casey jabbed him away with a left and then whipped over a right to the face. The punch missed the jaw by an inch. Shannon went over backwards. Casey followed him. Then Glasek was at his back, raining blows on the back of his head and neck.

Casey cursed, spun angrily. Glasek's eyes mirrored fear and he jumped back with catlike quickness as Casey lashed out. His left was short, and he took a step forward to follow up; then Glasek yelled:

"No! For gawd's sake, no!"

Casey froze at the almost hysterical tone; saw that Glasek's wide-eyed gaze was not on him, but to one side. He glanced over his shoulder and went cold. Shannon was on his knees, his swarthy face a mask of hate. The gun was in his right hand and the trigger finger was tensed.

Glasek saved his life. Casey knew that. But he had no feeling of gratitude then; it was all over in two or three seconds, and his only sensation was one of surprise and stark, momentary fear, followed by relief as Glasek wheezed:

"The noise! You can run for it if you don't spoil it!"

Shannon's pitiless gaze shifted to Glasek. That did it. The gun hand seemed to relax, and he got to his feet.

"Okey," he said. "This can wait a while." He picked up the blackjack, cocked one eyebrow, moved around behind Casey and said: "If you turn around, you get it anyway."

Casey half turned in spite of the warning. Then the blackjack crashed on his head. His legs sagged. Pain exploded in his brain, in his ears, and he went down on his hands and knees. He did not entirely lose consciousness, but he was helpless for a long minute while he rocked there on his knees, his head hanging between braced arms.

When he got to his feet again, Glasek had a length of rope. Shannon, grinning now, covered him with the gun while Glasek tied Casey's wrists behind his back.

"This'll do," Shannon said. "Hands and feet. By the time you get loose I'll be on my way and before I go I'll give you something to remember me by."

Casey fought the panic in his head, glanced about the room and wondered about Logan. He did not know how much time had elapsed since he had left Wade, but in another couple of minutes it would be too late. Once Shannon and Glasek left the house, there would be small chance of finding them again. His glance stopped on the suitcase at the end of the davenport. He had not seen it before and it served to verify his contention: Shannon had a definite plan of escape.

Glasek stepped from behind Casey. Shannon said: "Down on your belly now while we get the ankles."

Casey hesitated. Shannon started for him. He did not repeat the command and he took but one step, because in the next moment a loud knocking shook the apartment door.

Casey stiffened. Glasek gasped audibly and Shannon

glanced wildly about the room, back at Casey. His gun came up then, and he stepped close, whispered:

"I don't stop now. I ain't got much to lose. Grab this and by gawd I'll let you have it." He looked at Glasek. The knock was repeated. Shannon prodded Casey with the gun. "Say, 'Just a minute'."

Casey repeated the command in a thick dry voice; then Shannon pulled him to the door, stationed him two feet in front of it. He motioned Glasek to one side.

Shannon flattened himself against the opposite wall, lifted the blackjack in his right hand and covered Casey with the gun in his left. He motioned again to Glasek, who reached forward and slowly opened the door, keeping behind it.

Lieutenant Logan, one hand making a suspicious bulge in the pocket of his new-looking Chesterfield, said: "What the hell were you doing?" and stepped into the room.

Casey's teeth clicked together. His hands clenched behind his back and he shook his head wildly in spite of his danger. Logan sensed the mute warning, but there was not time enough to do much about it. Shannon's blackjack slammed down on his grey felt before he could turn and he took one more step and folded over on his face, his hat rolling out in front of him.

Logan pulled himself to his feet three or four minutes later and said: "What'd he hit me with?" He rubbed the top of his head gingerly and his handsome face twisted in a scowl. "I'll bet you got a kick out of it, too, you louse."

"Nerts!" rapped Casey. "I got a lump behind my ear I'll stack up against yours. If my hands hadn't been tied I might've taken a chance." He hesitated. "But he was hot – and he knew it. He had the gun on me and if he started to blast – and he would if he got cornered – he'd 'a' got us both."

Logan punched his hat back in shape, cursed bitterly. "That part's all right," he grated. "I can take it. But he's clear again. How the hell we gonna pick him up? What the hell kind of a set-up did you frame?"

Casey said: "Untie my hands," and told the lieutenant what had happened.

"Why didn't you wait for me?" Logan said.

"How'd I know they wouldn't go out the back way? I had to stall 'em, didn't I? Why weren't you in when Wade called you the first time?" Casey rubbed his wrists when Logan untied them, turned as a new thought struck him. "Hey. Where's Wade? I told him to wait outside."

"He was outside," Logan said. "He followed me in and I told him he'd better wait downstairs."

Casey muttered an oath, jerked open the door. The hall was deserted and he ran down the stairs. At the front door he saw a police sedan at the curb and went to it, spoke to the driver.

"You know Brad Shannon?" The driver said he did and Casey continued: "He didn't come out?"

"Would I be sittin' here if he did?"

"Where's Tom Wade?"

"He went in with Logan. I ain't seen him since." The driver, a young, ruddy-faced fellow, pushed over on the seat. "Say, what the hell's up? What—"

"Plenty," Casey clipped and ran up the steps. He went through the lower corridor to the back door, looked out into the little courtyard. He stood for a moment, grumbling to himself, then went back upstairs. The soprano was still practicing the same scale on the floor above.

Logan was on his knees in the centre of the floor, inspecting a dark spot in the middle of the light brown rug. The spot was about three inches across and as he stepped close, Casey saw that it had a reddish cast.

Logan said: "That's blood just as sure as hell." He looked up at Casey. "It ain't yours." Casey shook his head. "Did Shannon or Glasek look like they'd been bleeding?"

"No."

Logan stood up, rubbed the lump on his head again, scratched his nape thoughtfully. When he spoke his voice was sharp, jerky.

"I don't know how old that stain is, but if it's fairly new, if it was made today—" He broke off, gave Casey a steady, narrowed glance. "The way I dope it, there's four guys mixed up in this act. Whose blood is it?"

Casey's brow drew down but he did not answer and Logan said:

"It ain't Shannon's, it ain't Glasek's; it ain't Trask's because we had him down for questioning and I only left him a half hour ago. So who does it leave?"

"Ottleib?" Casey wheezed. "Hell, you mean—"

"I don't know what I mean," Logan said grimly. "I'm just askin' myself questions. If—"

The sudden shrill ring of a telephone stopped the sentence. Casey and Logan both turned towards the instrument on the little stand near an opposite doorway. Casey reached it first, swept the receiver into his hand.

The voice was Wade's, and even in his present tense state, Casey sensed the excited, breathless quality in the tone.

"Where are you?" Casey flashed. "Where'd you go?"

"I was in the downstairs hall," Wade said hurriedly. "I heard somebody running down, so just for fun I ducked under the stairs. It was Glasek and Shannon. They went to the front door, saw the police car and ran out the back way.

"I didn't know what had happened to you and Logan, but I thought I'd better follow 'em. So I did. They went over to Newbury, to a garage. I went down to the corner and got a cab. When they came out in a car, I followed 'em—"

"Where?" Casey cut in excitedly. "Where the hell are you?"

"In a drugstore on Westland. Glasek went up in an apartment house; Shannon's hiding on the floor in the back of the car. I ain't seen a cop and I thought I could call you and—"

"We'll be right over," Casey rapped. "Stick—"

"They're comin' out," Wade gasped. "Gasek – and Jim Trask."

"Wait!" Casey shouted. "Wait and—"

"I gotta go," Wade said. "They're gettin' in the car. I gotta go. I gotta follow 'em, ain't I? Call you back."

Casey slammed down the receiver as the line went dead. "Call me back," he jeered. "How the—" He straightened up, knocked his head against Logan's who was standing over him, trying to get the gist of the conversation.

Casey told him what Wade had done and Logan said:

"Wait? Wait, hell! We can't wait. You said they took a suitcase. They'll blow out of town and—"

Casey didn't hear the rest of the sentence. One word stuck in his brain, flashed a driving association. Suitcase. In the stress of action he had forgotten an incident that might possibly be important – damn' important. Grabbing for the telephone directory, he pawed through it, found a number and again scooped up the telephone.

"Quinn's Trucking?" he bellowed a moment later. "Police business. Lieutenant Logan speaking. You had a call for a trunk at – Marlborough. Spike Largo was drivin'. What apartment number was it?"

He waited, thumping one heel against the floor. "Yeah?" he said a few seconds later. "Where were you supposed to take it? Where? Okey. Okey."

Logan grabbed Casey's arm and jerked him around as he hung up. "What've you got?" he clipped. "You been holdin' out again? You know where they're goin'?"

"Yeah," Casey said and told about seeing Spike Largo and the trunk. "That trunk came from here," he finished bitterly.

"Where's it goin'?"

Casey started to speak, checked himself as a sudden calmness settled over him and he found room amid his racing thoughts for a new and forgotten perspective.

He put his fists on his hips, sweeping the tails of his ulster aside as he did so; he leaned forward slightly and took special pains with his words.

"Maybe you and I are workin' on different angles. Shorty Prendell was a friend of mine. I don't give a good – damn about Judge Ottleib, except for one thing. There's a reward out. If we get lucky and pull something out of a hat, I wanta be damn' sure Shorty's wife gets it all."

"You're not sure now, huh?" Logan asked caustically. "You think maybe I'm chiselin' in on widows now, huh?"

"You made a sweet crack about it to me this morning," Casey said. "I want to get you straight on it."

For a moment Logan's dark eyes snapped their irritation and resentment. Then he seemed to relax and a wry grin tugged at the corners of his mouth.

"Just when I think you'd like a slap in the mouth for yourself, you pull something that makes me like you. You want me to write out an assignment now, or can you wait till we earn the dough?"

"I'll wait, and we'll earn it. That trunk went out to the Norwell airport. We oughta make it in time."

It was past mid-afternoon when the driver kicked the motor of the police touring car to life. Logan sat in front, and Casey braced himself in the middle of the seat and hung on to a door with one hand, his hat with the other.

They went through traffic which was normal and not yet snarled by the five o'clock home-going parade.

Outside of Dedham they were doing seventy and Logan hunched over and said: "Shake it up, Eddy."

"We're doin' seventy," Eddy said.

"Sure," Logan said. "But we're in a hurry. Step on it."

Casey held on. The chilled wind whipped in on him from both sides.

He let go of the door and leaned over on the back of the front seat. This was better and he wiped his eyes and watched the road. He saw the approaching truck about a mile this side of Norwell, had time to get a fleeting glance of Spike Largo in the cab.

"That's the truck," he yelled in Logan's ear. "Comin' back."

Logan nodded, yelled something in the driver's ear. The car held its pace for another minute, then braked suddenly and swung into a macadam feeder road in a dry skid. They roared up a half mile rise, reached the level ground again, and the landing field spread out before them under the dull and low-hung sky.

A heavy-looking cabin plane stood a hundred yards or so from the office, its wheels blocked, its propeller idling. Opposite the office, on the road, was a black sedan; a quarter of a mile behind this, a taxi crawled along, seemed on the verge of stopping.

Three men got out of the sedan as Casey watched. A figure stepped out of the office and walked to meet them. Even at a distance of a half mile Casey recognised the three men from the sedan. Faces were but vague ovals in the dusky light, but the figures – Glasek's, the towering Shannon, the burly stockiness of Jim Trask – furnished identification.

Casey yelled in Logan's ear again and the lieutenant pulled his coat open and reached for his gun. Then Glasek saw the onrushing police car; it was evident from the way he pointed.

For an instant all four men stared. The police car whipped past the loafing taxi and Casey saw Wade's face pressed to the side of the window. The man in the helmet started to run for the plane; the other three followed and strung out behind him.

Ten seconds later the police car slammed to a stop, its rear end yawing towards the ditch. Momentum slapped Casey against the front seat and he bounced back on the floor. By the time he got the rear door open, Logan was twenty feet in front of him with Eddy at his heels.

The taxi squealed to a stop. Casey saw Wade pile out and start to run and he yelled: "Stay back," and then set out after Logan.

The pilot was about ten yards from the plane. Glasek was about twenty yards behind him, Shannon followed, and Trask was still farther back, only fifteen yards ahead of Logan.

The lieutenant yelled a command, then Casey saw his right arm come stiffly up. His wrist kicked upward and the wind swept back the report of the shot.

Trask turned, stopped abruptly and whipped up his arm. He and Logan fired together; the police chauffeur fired. Logan went down as though one leg had been cut from under him. Trask staggered, fired again wildly; he went to one knee, pulled himself to a crouch, then fell over on his face.

Shannon fired over his shoulder, but kept running and the pilot had reached the plane, was tugging at the cabin door. Logan was trying to get to his feet when Casey raced past without slowing down. Then Eddy fired again; so did Shannon who was still ten yards shy of the plane.

Casey, weighted down by his bulky coat, was wheezing and puffing by the time he reached Trask's crumpled form; then he saw the automatic on the ground beside the outstretched fingers, and with no preconceived idea, he stooped, snatched it up without breaking his stride.

As he straightened, he saw Shannon jerk to a stop and spin about. Ignoring Eddy, who was five feet closer, Shannon swung his automatic towards the photographer.

Casey dropped to one knee as Shannon fired – and missed. He was close enough to hear Shannon's curses, close enough to see the desperate, twisted expression on the swarthy face, to see the black hole of the muzzle as Shannon brought the automatic down after the recoil of the first shot.

This time Shannon aimed deliberately. So did Casey. And a curiously fleeting thought of Shorty Prendell helped him, as he squeezed the trigger, felt the slap of recoil at his wrist an instant before he saw Shannon's automatic jump.

Two shots, Shannon's and Eddy's, roared out a fraction of a second after his own. Shannon's big body jerked sideways. Casey did not know whether it was his shot or Eddy's which had found the target, and he held his gun steady, waited stiffly on one knee.

Shannon's arm came down, hung limply and he took a step to brace himself. The gun slipped from loose fingers. Casey stood up and started forward, the police chauffeur moving at his side.

Death was streaking Shannon's swarthy face before Casey reached him. He seemed to crumple and go over backward, as though he were trying to sit down in a chair which had been jerked from under him.

Casey yanked his gaze away. At the side of the plane, Glasek and the pilot stood stiffly erect, their arms stretched rigidly perpendicular.

*   *   *

Logan limped to the side of the plane and Casey said: "You scared hell out of me. You went down so damn' quick I—"

"In the thigh," Logan said thickly. "I thought I lost a leg." He pulled his coat aside, glanced down and felt the side of his thigh where red was staining the blue fabric of his trousers. "It'll be okey when it stops bleeding."

Wade, who had run up and was standing at Casey's shoulder, whispered: "I'll be right back," and started across the field.

The police chauffeur had searched Glasek and the white-faced pilot and Logan said: "Where do you fit?"

"I don't know," the pilot said and his shaky voice sounded convincing. "That fellow" – he pointed to Glasek – "hired me to take him and two other guys to Richmond."

"What'd you run for?"

"Somebody yelled, 'Run' and I ran. I was rattled and—"

"It's gonna be tough for you if you can't prove it, buddy," Logan said.

He turned to Glasek. "You wanta talk?"

"I wasn't in on it," Glasek wailed. "I didn't know a thing about it till this morning. Trask told me to hire a plane, told me to see if I could turn up that picture and—"

"You didn't know about Prendell, maybe," Logan said. "But you damn' well knew about Ottleib. He couldn't stand the gaff and Trask couldn't either if Ottleib was caught. So the Judge hid out, doped out the plan to get himself burned to death. Who was it that got burned?"

"Shannon got somebody to claim an unidentified man in the morgue – some guy that drowned and was about Ottleib's size."

"And Ottleib," Logan went on grimly, "or maybe Trask – he was there – set that tenement on fire. Ottleib yelled from the window for a fake and beat it down the back way. Then what?"

"I tell you I wasn't there," wheezed Glasek. "How do I—"

Logan limped forward a step and slapped the fellow in the mouth so hard he knocked his hat off. It bounced on the frozen turf and Glasek yelped, staggered. He put his hand to lips that welled blood.

"Maybe you weren't there," Logan leered, "but you know."

"Shannon and some other guy was waiting in a place down the street. Ottleib beat it around there and when the fire got going good they sneaked out the back way to get a car and—"

"Prendell saw 'em," rapped Casey. "And he had guts enough to try a picture – and they shot him in the back." He stepped forward, cocking his wrist.

Logan grabbed him, said: "Lay off, I'm doin' the slappin' on this job." He pulled Glasek towards him. "What happened to Ottleib?"

Glasek's face went dead white and a fit of trembling seized him. Logan said: "He had a run-in with Trask or Shannon, huh?"

"He went all to pieces when they killed Prendell," Glasek whimpered. "Murder scared him. He said he'd give himself up and say Trask had him kidnapped. He tried to fight himself out of the Marlborough Street place." Glasek's voice became faint. "Shannon shot him."

Glasek's head came up and his voice got sharp. "But that was early this morning. I wasn't there."

"You could be right," Logan said. He hesitated, pressed his lips together, looked at the plane, then at the pilot. "The trunk loaded in there?" The pilot nodded nervously and Logan said: "Well, I suppose we gotta take a look," grimly.

Casey knew what Logan meant. He'd had the same idea in the back of his head all the time, but other things had kept the thought submerged.

"Come on," Logan snapped. "You" – he pointed at the pilot – "and you, Flash."

They lowered the trunk to the ground.

Logan found it locked and the police chauffeur eventually found the key on Shannon.

Logan opened the lid, sucked in his breath. Casey took one quick look. That was enough to see that the body which lay face down inside, was tightly wedged with wadded newspapers, that there was quite a bit of blood, that the legs did not seem to be in the right place. He looked away and wiped cold sweat from his face as Logan slammed the lid.

"What were they gonna do with it?" Logan asked the stiff-lipped pilot.

"I don't—" the fellow said and Glasek interrupted.

"They were gonna dump it in the ocean – way out. Shannon was goin' to Miami, get a Pan-American to Trinidad. Trask was comin' back if it worked – you had nothin' on him."

Logan looked steadily at the pilot. "What a break for you, son."

Wade stumbled up then, fell over his plate-case as he slipped it from his shoulder.

Casey had forgotten that Wade had taken the camera with him from the office. Now he said: "You been luggin' that thing all this time?"

"Sure," said Wade, opening the camera and fooling with the shutter and focus.

His pop-eyed gaze fell on the trunk. "You find Ottleib? Is he in there?" Casey nodded and Wade said: "Then open it up and let me—"

Casey and Logan said: "No," together. Wade looked hurt.

Then his tone brightened. "Ain't there a reward or something for finding Ottleib?"

"Yeah," Casey said. He looked at Logan, who met his gaze with steady eyes and nodded slowly; then he added: "There's a reward, but it's all sewed up. And don't give me an argument," he growled, but the hint of a smile in his eyes belied the growl. "Just get busy with that box. Get pictures enough for both of us and I'll take you in to Steve's and buy the drinks."

"Hah," Wade said. "I knew there was a reward in it some place."

SCOTLAND YARD

(BBC, 1955–1957)
Starring: Edgar Lustgarten, Russell Napier &
Ken Henry
Directed by Jack Greenwood
Story 'Forbidden Fruit' by Edgar Lustgarten

It was perhaps no surprise that the first popular crime series on British television should feature Scotland Yard. In 1954, the headline-making career of the great thief-taker Inspector Robert Fabian was adapted by BBC TV for a series entitled *Fabian of the Yard* – with the commanding character actor Bruce Seton in the title role – and the 30 minute, pre-filmed episodes quickly built up a large UK audience before being syndicated with similar success in the USA. *Fabian* was still on the air when the noted criminologist and author, Edgar Lustgarten, became the host of *Scotland Yard* (also known as *Case Histories of Scotland Yard*) which fictionalised real cases from the Yard's huge files of robberies, blackmailings and murder. It featured as regular characters Inspector Duggan (Russell Napier) and Inspector Ross (Ken Henry). Arthur Mason who appeared as the gruff Sergeant Mason was something of a prototype for Sergeant Flint (Arthur Rigby) who in 1955 co-starred with Jack Warner in the classic Bobby-on-the-beat series *Dixon of Dock Green* which has subsequently become one of the benchmarks for all police shows on television. (Hard on the heels of these series in 1956 came *Charlesworth* with the authoritarian Metropolitan police officer, Chief Detective Inspector Charlesworth, played initially by John Welsh and later by Wensley Pithey, which also ran for over two years.)

The landmark show, *Cases of Scotland Yard*, remembered for its many scenes of police cars, bells clattering, rushing from the Yard into the streets of London, was produced by Jack Greenwood, but the driving force behind the success was undoubtedly Edgar Lustgarten (1907–1978) who combined a profound knowledge of crime with a gift of oratory which he had begun to develop while at Oxford University.

Born in Manchester, the son of a prosperous lawyer, he naturally enough entered the law and graduated to the bar in 1932. Although he was soon running a very successful practice, Lustgarten was also keen to write and in the mid-Thirties began to contribute short stories to magazines and plays to radio. After working with the BBC in counter propaganda during the Second World War, he started broadcasting on radio himself and made the transition just as easily into television when the BBC began transmitting once again in the late Forties. His book *A Case to Answer* (1947), a novel about the sordid murder of a Soho prostitute, was a best-seller and led to a string of other novels and works of non-fiction all dealing with crime and criminals. He was a natural to front *Scotland Yard*, and such was his success at describing murders and mysteries by making full use of his hooded eyes and sepulchral voice that he became widely known by the epithet, 'Mr Murder'. Following the success of the *Scotland Yard* programme, he appeared in several more series with similar themes and titles like *Prisoner at the Bar, Accused in the Box* and *Famous Trials*. 'Forbidden

Fruit', the story of a young man's infatuation with a beautiful model and its tragic outcome, written by Lustgarten in 1953, was daring for its time and serves as an excellent reminder of the man who helped to pioneer the crime series on British television . . .

The very first moment he came in last night I guessed from his face exactly what he had to say. Only a half-wit could have missed it. He's not a bad old stick, quite soft-hearted in his way, but I'd swear he only wears that particular expression – as if he were nursing some secret sorrow of his own – in circumstances such as those that made him visit me.

I wouldn't admit to myself, though, that the look of him told me all. There are mental defenses one keeps manned to the last. I quickly thought up some other possible reasons for his coming: my mother was ill, or a message from friends, or pure humdrum routine. For a split second I even half kidded myself that he'd brought good news, that everything was okay. Then he turned his eyes towards me, and I let that idea drop.

"I'm sorry, Holt," he said.

"Yes," I said, fatuously.

I realize now I was trying hard to detach myself from the scene, to escape being emotionally involved in what would follow.

"I'm sorry, very sorry indeed," he said.

We had been playing dominoes when he arrived. I fixed my gaze on the double-blank, the last piece I had played.

"It's my duty," he said, and hesitated, "my unhappy duty—"

That got through all right. My defenses cracked on the instant, and I met reality.

I knew then for certain that a reprieve had been refused. I

knew then that mortal power could do no more on my behalf. I knew then that the day after tomorrow I should hang.

It is only now, though, when those shocks have been in part absorbed, that I also realize there is no longer any reason why I should not tell, in these last hours of my life, the whole truth about Marian and me . . .

The first time I actually set eyes on Marian I had gone to her home as a reporter to get an interview. She had recently been voted Top Model of the Year by one of the countless panels that bestow suchlike distinctions, and it was reckoned she would rate a couple of pars on an evening when we were running short of West End stuff. I always got what the Features boys thought not quite worth their while, so this assignment was a natural for me.

When the office gave me her address I remember querying it, and as I pressed the doorbell I still wondered if they had it right. I am not sure exactly what sort of set-up I expected, what sort of background I pictured, for the Top Model of the Year. A flat, I suppose, in a fashionable district; on the small side, possibly, but up-to-date and chic. Certainly not an old-fashioned house with French windows and a garden, tucked away at the foot of a cul-de-sac with a railway running by. It couldn't have been more than a one-and-sixpenny ride from the bright lights, but it was the sort of place that made you tell the taxi-man to wait.

I wasn't kept long in doubt, though. She opened the door herself.

Our picture editor had already had her photographed, and I had judged from the pictures that she was quite a dish. I was ready for the great dark eyes, the mass of raven hair, the faultless curve of the slightly pouting lips. What the pictures didn't – couldn't – catch was the light in those dark eyes, the soft coils of that hair, the provocation in that pout.

She stood still, as if waiting to be admired. I admired her.

"Bob Holt's my name. *Evening Post*. You're expecting me, I think?"

"Of course," she said. "Come in."

She led the way across a middle-class hall to a middle-class sitting-room where the colorless domestic comfort stressed her vividness. It was like seeing a bird of paradise in a hen run. I concluded she must still be living at home with Mum and Dad.

She took a bottle and a glass out of a cupboard and poured me a stiff Scotch without so much as asking; I could only assume she recognised the type. As she passed me the drink I noticed how slender her hands were and how her long pointed nails resembled delicate red almonds.

"Sorry to make you come so late in the afternoon," she said. "I've been working all day. Only got back at five."

"It would be a pleasure to see you any time," I said, and meant it. "Aren't you drinking?"

She slapped her waist. "Would never do," she said. "Now, tell me, what do you want to know?"

She curled gracefully up in the armchair opposite while I put her through the stock questionnaire. Her answers were invariably brisk and businesslike. She was 25; started modeling at twenty; had always been a freelance, liked it best that way; enjoyed her work, and specially her occasional jobs abroad; wouldn't be specific about her annual earnings, but admitted she was very nicely paid. Ambition? . . .

This was the first time she paused before replying. "I think I'd sooner keep that to myself," she said at last, and momentarily a curious look came into her eyes – a look that suggested we were about to share some intimate secret.

I never worked harder to stretch out an interview. I did my best, but of course I couldn't keep it going forever. Presently it began to grow dark, and she turned on a lamp in a way that somehow pronounced the interview at an end. But I still wasn't willing to part with her. I tried another tack.

"Have you any engagement later on tonight?" I asked.

"Why?"

"Because if you haven't, I'd be delighted if you'd come out with me."

It was only one step better than a pick-up. She might have felt bound at that point to have given me a brush-off which there could be no possible question of going back on, and then I should have been loafing around Fleet Street at this moment instead of sitting here in the condemned cell at the Scrubs.

She might or she might not; that I shall never know. For I had hardly uttered the words before I heard a sound outside – the unmistakable, characteristic sound of the key turning in an automatic lock.

Marian heard it too.

"That'll be Jim," she said.

I don't know why it startled me so to discover she was married. Nothing had been said to imply that she was not. She wore no wedding ring, but girls in her line seldom do. And a husband would account for that house as well as a Mum or Dad.

But I had taken it for granted from the outset – so much so I didn't even bother to inquire – that Marian was entirely without strings and unattached. Somehow her personality created that impression, and to clinch it there was that curious look that I had glimpsed – not an invitation, mark, it fell far short of that, and anyway invitations hardly form an acid test – but a look that simply didn't go with a girl who had a husband. I couldn't then have told you why. I could do better now . . .

Jim turned out to be a commonplace bloke, older than Marian by twenty years and shorter by two inches. When my errand was explained to him he fairly glowed with pleasure, poured me a fresh drink, and refused to let me leave. There was so much, he said, he could tell me about Marian which, he knew, she would never tell herself.

Had she told me that when they married, seven years ago, nothing had been further from her thoughts than modeling? No. Had she told me that she had never had a lesson? No. Had she told me that she had reached the top at one bound? No. Had she told me how success had never turned her head, how they still lived in this house he had bought before their wedding, how they were just like any other contented married couple?

I glanced at Marian – and saw that look a second time.

"How, then, did she get the chance of modeling?" I asked.

"Through me." He made a deprecating gesture. "I'm in the gown trade. I had to beg her on my knees, mind. But look where she is now."

It was Jim, not Marian, who made me stay for dinner. It was Jim, not Marian, who did the talking afterwards; half the time, as I recall, she wasn't in the room. It was Jim who walked me to the gate, slapped me on the back, and said he knew for sure I'd write up Marian real good.

I had exchanged barely a word with Marian herself since my interrupted and unfinished pass, and she had given no clue to what she felt about that, if indeed she felt anything at all.

Next morning I wrote about her. Then I thought about her. When I'd thought long and hard enough, I dialed her number.

"So you're not working today?" I said, when eventually she answered.

"Who's that?"

"Bob Holt."

"Oh," she said. "No."

"Good," I said, "because I've got stuck in the draft of my article." I called it an article to make it sound important. "There are one or two points I'm not quite clear about. If you don't mind, I'd like to go through the draft with you in detail."

"All right," she said. "Read it to me."

"No good trying over the phone. I must see you," I said.

"What was that?"

I plunged.

"*I must see you*," I said, and put all my meaning in it.

There was a longish silence, but I could tell she had understood me, and I almost held my breath.

She broke the silence with a laugh – whether of triumph or of amusement or of scorn, I couldn't say.

"I suppose what must be, must be. Come round today at the same time."

"Not till six o'clock?" I said. "But you're at home this afternoon."

She laughed again.

"All right then, make it five."

I was there at half-past four. And I forgot to take the draft.

I was never at any time under any illusion about how and why I wanted Marian. After all, I was thirty-five; I'd knocked about a bit, and even if I didn't know that much about the world, I knew nearly all there is to know about myself. I wasn't inspired by romantic love or by genuine affection; I never even liked Marian very much.

It was a simple case of biological attraction from which all other elements were utterly excluded. I'd had the symptoms far too often not to recognise them – but I also recognised they were exceptionally severe. Marian recognised it too. That was the cause of all the trouble.

Looking back, I can see clearly enough that, even on this plane, Marian didn't really go for me. It was all, I'm certain now, an accident of timing. She had reached an acute stage in a self-suppressed rebellion against her husband and the life he symbolised; the alternative outlet for that rebellion must be a secret lover; I happened to come on the scene and made a play for her; she didn't find me repulsive, and so she took me on. For this inner conflict was positively obsessive.

As we lay in each other's arms, she would intersperse her love talk with bitter attacks on Jim: his stupidity, his unimaginativeness, his lack of elementary social *savoir faire*, and, above all, his stubborn refusal to move from a house and neighborhood which mocked her success and which she had out-grown.

These diatribes had me puzzled; I couldn't see why she didn't walk out on him if she wanted to, and said so. It wasn't as if she need depend on any man to keep her. But she retorted that you couldn't go on for ever modeling; and added that Jim was a very much richer man than I might think, that his will and his insurance policies favored only her, and that she didn't intend to pass them up by being a bloody fool.

This gave me my first inkling of that tough cupidity which I learned later was Marian's ruling passion.

Everything made it an easy affair to manage. Neither of us had any hard-and-fast working hours, and when we were both with a job immediately on hand I would slip up during the daytime to the house. Jim never returned from business until half-past six or so – it turned out he was boss of quite a big concern – and it didn't seem to worry him even when he found me there (as we thought it wiser that he sometimes should). We told him I was working on publicity for Marian, and that satisfied him; he was not the suspicious sort.

Marian fussed much more about her neighbors; they were a nosey lot, she said, always ready to start gossip, and it would soon be noticed and commented on if I regularly ran the gauntlet of the cul-de-sac. So, more often than not, I would use quite a different route, which took me across the railway line on the blind side of the house, over the garden fence which crowned the low embankment, and through the French window of the sitting room – a window normally left unlatched except at night or when nobody was in. This route not only screened me from prying eyes; it also heightened the flavor of forbidden fruit.

Things had been going on that way for the best part of three months – and I was still content they should go on that way forever – when Marian suddenly made the first big move in her campaign.

That afternoon – it was high summer, and I remember the hot sun beating on our bodies – she pulled unexpectedly out of an embrace.

"It can't go on like this, Bob," she said.

"Like what?" I said.

"The three of us," she said.

I wouldn't give her another lead. I just lay quiet and waited.

"I don't sleep any more for thinking," she said presently. "And I know I'm right, Bob. It's either you or Jim."

I was shocked at this transformation in her attitude, which threatened to destroy the nice soft option I had won. I started handing her the arguments she had handed me; think of the money, I urged, the insurance, the will.

"It'll all go by the board," I said, "if Jim divorces you."

"I wasn't thinking about divorce," Marian said.

*   *   *

It would be drawing it mild to call it an unusual experience. Not one person in a million – I should hope – ever in their lives faces a situation where someone they thought they knew as well as they know themselves, someone they'd always credited with normal human instincts, displays the will and purpose to contrive cold-blooded murder. I've had that experience, and I can tell you this: it doesn't work out exactly as you would expect.

Perhaps just because the idea is so shocking, you don't – or, at least, I didn't – get an instantaneous shock. At first you take it for granted that the whole thing is a joke – a grim piece of humor, but humor all the same. Only slowly do you tumble to the fact that it isn't a joke to them – they have a vehemence that doesn't go with jokes; you then decide it's temporary rage, a way of blowing off steam, and that they themselves would be horrified if it ever came to the point.

And when you fail to talk them out of it, and you stand on the brink, you don't draw back as you could and should and meant to, because you can't now without appearing a coward and traitor – and, in my case, without losing what I knew I had to have.

Marian must have thought over her plan to murder Jim for a long time before she ever mentioned it to me; otherwise she couldn't have explained it in such detail. Mind, I wasn't given these details all at once – only bit by bit, spread across a week or more, as, I suppose, she judged I was in proper shape to take them. But I soon grasped the broad lines on which the plan was based; the scheming should be hers, the action should be mine.

Her idea was for me to do it in the house, under conditions which would point to common robbery, which would enable me to come and go entirely unobserved, and which – if, notwithstanding, suspicions turned our way – would provide us *both* with a cast-iron alibi.

How shall we make it look like robbery, I asked, and I laughed, with a peculiar catch in my throat; I was still thinking it a rather ghastly game.

That was the easiest one of all for her to answer; she'd tell him she'd be home in the evening, and she wouldn't be; I'd drop in casually, as he'd quite got used to; after I'd done it, I could turn out his wallet – he always kept a fair amount of money on him – and take away, and lose, one or two valuables from the house. Coming and going unobserved? Didn't I do it already? Wasn't there the railway?

My heart sank as she grew more insistent. I was conscious of nerves around my eyes that I didn't know I had.

"You get hanged for murder," I said.

"If you're caught," she said.

I paced up and down, my thoughts whirling.

"You talk," I said, "as if he would sit quiet and let me do it. And *how* am I supposed to do it anyway? Shoot him and have the bullet traced to my revolver? Strangle him and have the scratches noticed on my hands?"

Marian gave me a rather pitying smile. Then she came up close so that I got the scent of her.

"You'll do it with a mallet."

"You must be raving mad."

"Remember the Rattenbury case? That's how Stoner did it." I remembered something else then – the number of crime books that she'd lately had out of the library. "They'd never have been arrested if she hadn't gabbed. It's the easiest thing coming up behind somebody's chair; if they know you're about the house, they're not going to turn round."

"So it's easy, is it," I said, "for me to come up behind Jim's chair with a mallet?"

"We've a mallet in the tool shed. I'll leave it tucked away in the hall. You have a few drinks with Jim and make an excuse to leave the room. You know both the armchairs have their backs to the door. You come in again. With the mallet."

"And this alibi," I said weakly. "Who's our alibi?"

She pressed her parted lips against my mouth.

"We shall be each other's alibi," she said.

We picked the evening with the utmost care; we had to. It was nearly three months more before all the circumstances favored us. Meanwhile I'd gone around like a man on whom the doctors have passed sentence of death, but who can't believe it simply because he's still alive. Even when we actually reached the day itself and the preliminaries were already under way – when I heard Marian make the phone call we'd rehearsed so often ("Jim, I'm being kept late . . . Back about 10:30, dear . . . Promise you'll be in . . . You know I hate coming into an empty house at night") – when I watched her hide the mallet under the cupboard in the hall – when I fetched her little traveling-case and she crammed it with her night things . . .

We registered at the hotel shortly after seven. I purposely cracked a joke or two with the reception clerk, and Marian asked him some question which he answered civilly. I signed us in as Mr and Mrs Robert Holt, and added my address; I used my natural handwriting.

We were shown up to our room, which we had booked in advance for its position (we liked the first floor and the bathroom and the view, I had explained); on the way there I cracked more jokes with the bellhop. We had dinner upstairs and we both chatted with the waiter. After dinner we undressed, got into bed, rang for the maid, and gave her instructions to bring early morning tea.

The moment she went I got up again, drew the bolt across the door, and took out of my suitcase the only apparel besides pajamas I had brought – my old reporter's props, my battered evening clothes . . .

It seemed hours that we stayed taut and silent, listening for the cue. In the banqueting chamber immediately below, a well-known anglers' club was holding its annual stag party, perhaps two hundred strong. We could hear, though greatly muffled, the shouts of the toastmaster, sudden gusts of mirth, billows of applause. The speech-making went on and on, and I suppose the fish they were describing got bigger and bigger; certainly the noise grew steadily in volume. I kept looking at my watch, and then across at Marian; in another twenty minutes, fifteen, ten, we'd have to pass it up.

Then, as I started to feel frustration and relief in equal measure – relief at putting it off, frustration at not getting it done with – from the banqueting chamber came a sound of scraping and of shuffling, immediately followed by the strains of Auld Lang Syne.

Without a word or even a glance exchanged between us, I slipped out and gently closed the door behind me.

I met no one in the corridor. Had I done so, I should have turned back; the project would have failed. As it was, the place might have been cleared for my convenience. I walked down the staircase – naturally, I didn't use the elevator – and straightaway got caught up with a seething mass of anglers.

Nobody saw us leave – saw us, that is, as individuals. We were just an amorphous mass; we were The Banquet Breaking Up. The swing doors swung for us; the porters said "good night"; but not one of us meant any more to them than the faceless silhouettes they use to illustrate statistics.

Immediately outside the door, I made towards a taxi; then deliberately allowed some thrusting chap to win it from me. I moved forward towards another, which I similarly lost. I moved forwards once again, and this time gained the street.

I was out . . .

It was still only September, but quite cold enough at that hour to justify me keeping my coat collar turned well up. I walked as briskly as I could do without drawing attention. I can't remember feeling any emotion, even fear; I was far too busy going over all I had to do, as I might put a story into shape while walking to the office.

Within half an hour I had the back of the house in view, and I could see a light in the sitting room which showed that Jim was home. I crossed the railway line, and as I came over the dark garden I could see him through the partially drawn curtains – a decent, harmless chap patiently waiting for his wife. I noted that impression, without feeling it any concern to me.

I didn't dare go to the front door, with a street lamp opposite. Jim didn't know I ever used the garden route, but I could always say that I'd been ringing and he hadn't heard, and that I'd walked round to see if anyone was in. Jim wouldn't put two and two together – and even if he did it hardly mattered now.

I gave a pretense of a knock at the French window, and walked in.

"Hello, how's tricks?" I said.

I read it myself on the tape in the office shortly after lunch.

The daily woman had called the police as soon as she arrived. They found him lying on the sitting room floor. His skull was broken. A mallet lay nearby. His wallet had been rifled. The pathologist's report would not be available till later, but obviously death had occurred several hours before.

I studied these details with intense concentration but curious detachment. I had no feeling of guilt, no pangs of remorse, no sense of what had happened in terms of life and death. I had one thought only – *Shall we be found out?*

Everything was assessed and measured solely in this context, and, far from flinching at the record of my handiwork, I praised myself afresh for pushing his body to the floor so that it might suggest there had been a struggle with an intruder. It was the sort of precaution that could make all the difference.

Though we were over the biggest hurdles we'd foreseen – like my re-entering the hotel with the cabaret customers, and those breathless seconds on the stairs when I gambled on my luck – there were still the statements we would have to make that afternoon. For we had agreed that, immediately the story reached the papers, Marian should go from the hotel straight to the police and tell them with whom and where she spent the night. And that would naturally bring them round to me.

There was nothing much to worry about so long as we kept our heads, but the more it looked like straight robbery, the less we should be asked.

They came to the office about six – Inspector Gorman and a sergeant. Plainclothes men, of course, but you can never fail to spot them, and I got some ribbing from the chap who told me they were there. Murder will out, he said; murder will out, old boy.

I took them to a little room we used for interviews. The Inspector said who they were, and that they were inquiring into the murder, and that Marian had got in touch with them. Would I be willing to answer a few questions? Certainly.

"She says she stayed last night at the Grand Hotel with you."

"That's right," I said.

"I understand from her this is the first time that it's happened – the first time that she's stayed with you all night, and not gone home."

"That's right," I said.

"We know definitely that death took place after ten o'clock last night." The Inspector looked at me affably. "And not later than two. So it's routine to account for the household in between those hours."

"I understand," I said.

"Then they can be eliminated from the investigation."

"We were in bed before ten," I said. "You can ask the chambermaid."

"We have asked her," the Inspector said. "Did you both stay in bed for the remainder of the night?"

"Until they brought tea at eight."

The Inspector went on looking at me affably. "How long has your affair with this lady been going on?"

"Six months."

"Did the dead man know of it?"

"No."

"What sort of terms were you on with him?"

"Excellent," I said.

"When did you last see him?"

I should have been ready for that one, but it very nearly threw me.

"Oh, earlier this week," I said. "I saw him quite often."

"A terrible end for him," the Inspector said.

"Terrible," I said.

"Well, thank you, Mr Holt."

When they left I got the impression they were satisfied.

I didn't see any more of them for the next two or three days. Marian did, of course, but only on formal matters. We behaved as we supposed they would expect from an erring wife and her paramour. Marian stayed on for the time being at the hotel. I slept at my flat. While there was no point in trying to disguise the fact that we were lovers – that had indeed become our ultimate safeguard – we felt that discretion required we should not flaunt it until we could be certain that the inquiries had been closed.

So I was alone that evening when my bell rang, and I opened the door to Gorman and his sergeant.

"Robert Holt," the Inspector said.

I went, as they say, quietly. They could put me on trial if they liked, but I had a cast-iron alibi.

My counsel decided to call the alibi witnesses first. There was a sporting chance, he said, that the jury might want to hear no more, and then the trial would be over without my having to go into the box.

Certainly the prosecution hadn't been so hot. It was a thin case of identity, depending on an elderly couple who lived in the house next door. It had turned out that my secret visits to Marian hadn't been so secret; this pair could see me cross part of the garden from their window, and, scenting an intrigue, they kept up something like a watch. They knew me as well by sight, they said, as one of their relations; they'd seen me coming and going scores of times these last few months. And they had seen me come and go on the night of the murder too; came about eleven – that was most unusually late – and go less than half an hour afterwards, apparently in a rush.

Wasn't it dark? asked my counsel. Yes, but light shone from the window. Wasn't it past their bedtime? Not at eleven o'clock. But at half-past? Well, they stayed up purposely. To spy? Yes, if he wished to put it so. But on *this* they couldn't be shaken – they were sure that it was me.

Still, as my counsel said in opening my defense, it's the

easiest thing in the world to make a mistake of identification. I saw a juryman nod his head in obvious agreement. It seemed as though one good push now would do the trick.

The evidence from the hotel came out nice and smoothly. It fixed me in bed there at ten to ten that night, and in bed there again at eight o'clock next morning. The prosecution hardly challenged that. The only question was: did I go out in between?

My counsel called Marian.

There was a bit of a sensation when she entered the courtroom – a tribute to her loveliness, her mild celebrity.

"I shall be as brief as possible," my counsel said. "You remember the day you learned of your husband's death?"

"Yes."

"Where did you spend the previous night?"

"At the Grand Hotel."

"With anyone?"

"With . . . Mr Holt."

Her hands were trembling, and she didn't look at me.

"What time did you go to bed?"

"Early. Before ten."

"Did you have breakfast in bed together in the morning?"

"Yes."

"Did Mr Holt ever leave you at all during that night?"

Marian shook her head.

"Just give your answer aloud, please, for the purpose of the record. Did he ever leave you that night?"

Marian shook her head again, and finally whispered, "No."

This wasn't at all the Marian I'd been expecting. She had come to see me in prison a few days before the trial, and no one could have overlooked her air of confidence. Now apparently her nerve was failing her. Luckily she hadn't a lot to remember – or forget; so long as she just kept repeating that I'd never left her, there wasn't much that anyone could do.

Prosecuting counsel seemed of the same opinion. He began to cross-examine Marian in a half-hearted style, as if he was resigned to getting absolutely nowhere.

"Are you a heavy sleeper?"

"Not very," Marian said.

"Have you an idea what time you fell asleep that night?"

"Late," Marian said, and a young reporter grinned.

"Before or after two o'clock?"

"After," Marian said.

"So if the prisoner left you before two, you would be bound to know?"

"Yes," Marian said.

It had been drummed into us over and over again that two o'clock was the latest hour at which Jim could have died. The prosecution had arrived at a dead end.

"And you swear he was with you in that hotel bedroom without a break from ten o'clock till two?"

He couldn't think of any other line to take. He was drawing his gown back, ready to sit down. She had only to say one more word to clinch my alibi.

But she didn't say it. Her mouth worked a little, but she didn't speak. Her hands trembled more now. I watched her, helpless, with an uneasy foreboding.

"Do you swear that?"

The prosecutor was on to it too. He'd perked up, and had let his gown fall back again.

"Do you swear that he was with you in that hotel bedroom without a break from ten o'clock till two? *Without a break* – do you swear that on your oath?"

He was pressing without a clear idea of what he was

pressing for. He simply recognised the symptoms of a crackup, and went on hammering hard and hopefully.

"You have not answered my question. Do you swear that on your oath?"

Marian's trembling was painful to behold. Nothing had gone wrong, she hadn't been caught out, she'd never even come under any real fire. But here she was bordering on collapse.

Mechanically I gripped the rail before me with both hands, then realised that Marian in the box was doing the same. She had taken off one glove, and irrelevantly I wondered if my knuckles were showing as white as hers.

"*Do you swear that, madam?*"

The whole court waited in an agonizing silence.

"I won't swear," she said in a muffled, strangled voice. "I don't know. I can't remember."

Then she crumpled, and dropped her face into her hands. The judge said something I didn't catch, and they led her out of court.

The vital hours of that night lay unaccounted for. My cast-iron alibi had gone straight down the drain.

It was no longer a question of whether I could hope to escape the witness box. It was a question of whether I could hope to escape the rope.

My solicitor and my counsel had both pointed out to me the dangers inseparable from an alibi defense. If it flops, you can be left much worse off than you were before. For instance, they said, if you *admit* going to the house that night, but maintain that when you left Jim was alive and well, you will stand a reasonable chance of being acquitted; it's just conceivable that somebody came in and killed him later.

But if you call witnesses to prove that you weren't there *at all*, and those witnesses do not convince the jury, they will be disposed to think you are lying when *you* say you weren't there, and, moreover, *to infer you've only one reason to lie*. So you must be very sure, they said, about an alibi.

But I *was* sure of mine, I told them, absolutely sure; and I wanted to be on a cert, not on a reasonable chance.

And the result? I had my back right up against the wall, and the knowledge that in the last resort my only hope was me.

I understand that I gave my evidence well. I felt conscious at the time that I wasn't yielding ground. Maybe prosecuting counsel didn't amount to much; maybe I got a bit of extra lift from desperation. Anyway, I could see his attempts to catch me from a mile off, and I had an answer for every single one.

I did best of all, I think, when he referred to Marian – a reference that he must have saved up for a parting shot. We were engaged in a passionate love affair, were we not, he asked. Spending our very first illicit night together? Could I think of any reason, in those circumstances, why Marian couldn't remember whether I stayed with her or not?

"Of course I can think of a reason." I started pulling out the stops. "It doesn't need an awful lot of imagination, either. We were in love with each other, don't you understand? You can say it was morally wrong if you like, but in fact we weren't hurting anyone; up till then it had been something private and sacred to ourselves."

"I didn't invite you to make a speech," said prosecuting counsel.

"You asked me for a reason why Marian went blank in the box, and I'm giving you a reason. She was the only one who could vouch for me that night, because we were alone together, because we were making love. To prove my innocence she had to reveal that publicly, to turn a part of her intimate life into a public shame. Do you wonder it was more than a woman's nerves could take? If I could stand my trial over again, I'd let it go by default rather than put her to such torture."

That had a good effect. I could tell from the prosecutor's shrug as he sat down, and from my solicitor's expression as I went back to the dock. At least, the latter conveyed, we're in the running again.

But though I may have solved the Marian mystery for others, I was still far short of solving it for myself. Possibly it made sense to them; it didn't make sense to me. Marian wasn't the nervous kind, and she wasn't bashful either; you can't be a Top Model without an exhibitionist streak.

What had destroyed the jaunty self-assurance that she still possessed when she last visited me in jail? Was it perhaps going back to live in the house she'd shared with Jim, as she told me she had done on the day before that visit? Had it got her down?

I couldn't see any reason for it; and when Marian said something vague about expense I couldn't forget the news with which she'd opened the visit – that her money from Jim totted up to £30,000. She need not, should not, have gone back. But would she let it get her down – and if it did so, would she have stayed?

Whatever it was, I owed to it the fact that even now I'd barely a fifty-fifty chance of getting out . . .

The jury retired in mellow afternoon sunlight. Night had fallen before they reappeared . . .

I dodged everyone. I wouldn't even stop to say more than a single word of thanks to my defenders. I wanted Marian, and when I heard she had gone home I followed.

Automatically I took the route that had become habitual . . .

The light glowed dully through the drawn curtains. The garden stretched out darkly as it had done that other night.

I wondered whether the French window would still be left unlocked.

I tiptoed up to it, intent on surprise, and grew aware of an intermittent voice inside.

I couldn't pick out any words, but I knew it to be Marian. She was obviously speaking to someone on the 'phone, and in tones of such urgency that they stopped me in my tracks.

Very gently I pressed the latch. The French window yielded. I opened it an inch or two, just enough to hear.

". . . doesn't matter how," Marian was saying. "It's not *my* fault, goodness knows . . . All right, all right, but there it is, the fools have let him off . . . Dear darling heart, don't let's argue, there's no time . . . He'll be here before we know where we are, and then what's going to happen? . . . No, listen, honey, bring the car to the usual place . . . I won't have a bag at all, I'm leaving double quick . . . Brighton or somewhere, so long as it's away . . . Yes, dearest boy, in half an hour; my dearest, dearest boy."

She made a noisy, silly, kissing sound – the noisy, silly, kissing sound she used to make to me.

I gave a pretense of a knock at the French window, and walked in, as I had walked in that other night weeks ago.

Her head jerked round and her jaw dropped in the ugliness of horror. She slammed down the 'phone but kept her hand on it so that the black receiver set off her nails, like delicate red almonds.

"Bob," she said. "Bob."

"Hello," I said, "how's tricks?"

You may call it rough justice. But I don't feel that way. I do feel some remorse now over the man I murdered. But I feel no remorse over the woman who murdered me, and I shall go to the scaffold cursing her lovely, broken corpse.

PERRY MASON

(CBS, 1957–1967; 1985–1993)
Starring: Raymond Burr, Barbara Hale &
William Hopper
Directed by Sam White
Story 'The Case of the Howling Dog' by
Erle Stanley Gardner

From a real-life lawyer introducing a series, it was only a small step to a programme in which a lawyer was the star – and the overwhelming success of *Perry Mason*, based on the novels of Erle Stanley Gardner about a brilliant defence counsel, which CBS first screened in September 1957 and ran for the next decade, has had a profound effect on TV crime drama. In its stead have followed several other series about men of the law including CBS' *The Defenders* (1961–4) featuring a father and son team played by E.G. Marshall and Robert Reid (in the pilot episode, the stars were actually Ralph Bellamy and William Shatner – later of *Star Trek* – with Steve McQueen as their client!) and Thames TV's *Rumpole of the Bailey* (1978–) with Leo McKern in the continuing cases of John Mortimer's droll barrister. Most recently there has been *Kavanagh QC* (1994–) with John Thaw, fresh from his role as Inspector Morse, playing a barrister who is notorious for his rapier-like cross examinations, and the pudgy, balding Theodore 'Teddy' Hoffman (Daniel Benzali) the top LA defence lawyer in

Murder One (1996–). Perry Mason, of course, originated from the pages of the novels which Erle Stanley Gardner started writing about him in 1933 with *The Case of the Velvet Claws*, and he had already been featured in movies in the Thirties played by Warren William and a decade later on radio by John Larkin before being taken up by TV. But it was the television series which made Perry an icon and the man who played him, Raymond Burr, into a household name. Burr's death from cancer in 1993 was mourned by fans all over the world. The actor had, in fact, only just completed work on a new Perry Mason TV film, *The Case of the Killer Kiss*, the last of two dozen television specials in a second series which had commenced in 1985. However, but for a twist of fate, Raymond Burr might never have played Perry Mason at all: for when the series was first auditioning actors in 1956, he read for the part of District Attorney Ham Burger, but on an impulse also asked to play a scene as Mason. The rest is history.

Erle Stanley Gardner (1889–1970) had himself been a lawyer in California where he specialised in championing hopeless cases where penniless defendants were at the mercy of authority or big business. Later, to augment his funds, he decided to make use of these experiences in fictional form and began contributing to the crime pulp magazines such as *Black Mask* and *Detective Story Weekly*. But it was with his first Perry Mason novel, *The Case of the Velvet Claws* – which was actually rejected by several publishers before being taken on by William Morrow – that he created a hero who was to feature in over 80 more novels as well as being adapted for all the entertainment mediums. Today, quite a number of the novels are still in print, while the movies are regularly rerun on television as are the two series of

made-for-TV productions. 'The Case of the Howling Dog' which Gardner wrote in 1934 and was filmed that same year, was also adapted for the small screen in the third season of *Perry Mason* in 1960 and is here presented in an adapted version prepared by the author for *TV Guide*.

Perry Mason was admitted to be the cleverest criminal lawyer in the city, but he was more than that. He was a great counsel, either for the prosecution or the defence, though Perry himself always preferred to save a man than to get him sentenced. A fine, handsome man in the early thirties, he was as big a success in Society as he was in the courts. He entertained lavishly, and in other ways spent money as fast as he made it.

Della Street, his pretty confidential secretary, who was also his fiancée, reminded him of this one morning.

"A cheque for three figures would send the old bank balance on the wrong side," she said, showing him his pass-book.

"So bad as that," said Perry, pushing the pass-book back. "Well, we'll have to put the brake on, I guess. Thank goodness the business is good."

A little while later Della announced Arthur Cartwright. It was Perry's invariable custom to look his clients over carefully while they were doing the talking. From this observation he often got more information from them than they gave him by their words.

The first thing Perry noticed about Arthur Cartwright was that he was in a terribly nervous state, and he knew the cause was neither drink nor drugs.

"It's about a dog that howls all through the night," began Cartwright.

"I'm sorry," said Perry. "But I can't be bothered with such a paltry case."

"But there's a will as well," said Cartwright. "A will involving quite a lot of money."

"Let's hear about that first," said Perry.

"Is a will valid no matter how a man dies?" asked Cartwright. "I mean if he died by hanging or anything like that."

"If the will was all right in other respects it would stand," Perry assured him.

Cartwright seemed greatly relieved.

"All right, then," he said. "I want to leave all my property to Mrs Clinton Foley, of Milpas Drive."

Perry glanced at Cartwright's visiting card.

"A neighbour of yours?"

"Next door. Just one other thing. Supposing that Mrs Foley isn't married to Foley but is living with him as his wife?"

"That could be made clear and legal." said Perry. "You simply state in your will that you leave your money to the woman now living at the address you name and who is known as Mrs Clinton Foley."

"Thanks. I'll send you the will some time to-day. Now about this howling dog."

Perry waved a protesting hand.

"I have already told you I cannot take such a case."

Cartwright threw down a bundle of notes.

"There's a sum to recompense you, and more if need be," he said. "I'm quite sane, and there's more in this howling dog than you think. However, the will is the first matter to consider. I'll send it to you."

Cartwright picked up his hat and walked out.

Perry Mason sent for Della and told her what had happened.

"He's in a shocking nervous state," he said. "He may be eccentric, but I'm sure he's quite sane."

The next morning the will arrived, and Perry got a shock. Instead of leaving his money to the woman 'known' as Mrs Clinton Foley, Cartwright had left it to 'the real Mrs Foley, the legally wedded wife of Clinton Foley'.

"The will is perfectly drawn up," said Perry to Della. "Cartwright is sane enough, as I told you. But I'm curious to know why he changed his mind overnight. It's not a question of old age and doddering. The fellow can't be over forty."

That, so far as Perry Mason was concerned, was the beginning of what he afterwards set down in his records as 'The Case of the Howling Dog.'

The next move was made by Clinton Foley, who came to the district attorney with a statement that Arthur Cartwright was insane, and that he wanted a warrant issued to that effect.

Foley's complaint was that Cartwright had made himself objectionable by continuous observation of his house.

"He looks at my place through a pair of field-glasses," said Foley. "The nuisance has become so great that my servants have left me, and I am getting into a state of nerves myself."

Perry, who had been sent for by the district attorney, smiled.

"And Cartwright complains you are driving him frantic by keeping a dog that howls all through the day and night."

"Nonsense!" exclaimed Foley. "My dog never howls."

"Suppose we all go over and see your dog," suggested Perry.

He said nothing of a mysterious message he had received from Cartwright, which read: "I know now why the dog howls. I appoint you to represent the beneficiary under my will and fight for her interests."

Perry had already told the district attorney this. That was why he was at the conference.

Perry had quickly decided that he did not like Foley.

The man was good-looking enough, about forty, and well mannered, when he was not angry, but he had a blustering way which irritated the lawyer.

When they arrived at Foley's house they were met by Lucy Benton, whom Foley introduced as his housekeeper. She showed a note to Foley, and when he had read it he passed it to the others. The note read:

> 'A few days ago I found out who was living next door. I know now that I have always loved him and not you. We are going away together, and I know we shall be happy again. – EVELYN.'

"Then the so-called Mrs Foley must be Cartwright's wife," thought Perry. But he said nothing.

Foley was tearing up and down like a madman, threatening what he would do to Cartwright.

"He must have forced her to go away with him," he shouted. "She would never have gone willingly. She hated him. That's why she left him."

Perry focused his attention on Lucy Benton. There was something strange about the woman.

She was young, and would have been pretty had she cared to make the most of her looks, but she had not done so. Her hair was arranged in a most unattractive way, and her dress was old-fashioned. It was strange to find a woman who did not want to look her best. Perry noticed her right arm was bandaged, and he asked her about it. She told him the dog had bitten her, but hastily added that it was not his fault because he was ill at the time.

Perry's attention was next called to a building that was being erected.

He asked Foley what it was.

"I'm extending my garage," replied Foley sharply.

Perry went back to his office and started his staff on making inquiries.

Information came through about the Foleys and the Cartwrights.

Two years before the two families had been living in Ventura on very friendly terms. Then Foley had run away with Evelyn Cartwright. Mrs Foley had not taken any steps to get a divorce, nor had Cartwright. Mrs Foley still lived in Ventura, though she travelled a lot, and Cartwright had gone from place to place until for some reason he had taken the house next to Foley.

Perry ordered Dobbs, one of his best men, to watch Foley's house and put the others on to trace Cartwright and his wife. But all inquiries drew a blank. Neither could be found. Baffled in this direction, Perry decided to have another go at Foley. He rang him up and asked for an appointment. Rather grudgingly, Foley made an appointment for eight o'clock that night. As he approached the house, Perry saw Dobbs watching it from a vantage-point across the street, but he did not speak to him.

He rang the bell, but there was no reply.

Perry tried the door and found it open.

Calling Foley by name he entered.

An uncanny stillness pervaded the house, and Perry felt a sense of disaster as he walked through the hall into the library on the right.

His fears were confirmed. Clinton Foley was lying on his back, dead, and a short distance away was a police dog, also dead.

Both had been shot.

Perry telephoned the police, and then rushed across the street to Dobbs.

"Better make yourself scarce," he said, when he had told him the facts. "The police will want to question you if they see you."

The lawyer went back to the house, and presently a number of police cars came along.

In the first were Claude Drumm, the district attorney, and Detective-sergeant Holcomb. Perry told them of his appointment with Foley and of his discovery.

"Cartwright must have done it," said the D.A. To this the lawyer made no reply.

Perry rushed back to his office where Dobbs was waiting for him.

He had plenty to report.

Shortly after seven o'clock Lucy Benton had left Foley's house in a motor-car, accompanied by a man. A few minutes later the real Mrs Foley had arrived at the house in a taxi.

She sent the driver to the Cartwright house, and while he was knocking at the door Mrs Foley entered the Foley house. A minute later there had come from the Foley house a blare of radio.

"I guess it was the radio and the driver's pounding at the Cartwright's door that prevented me from hearing the shots that must have been fired," said Dobbs. "Anyway, Mrs Foley drove away, and soon after that you came along."

Dobbs had taken the number of the taxicab, and it was an easy matter to trace it.

And from the information given by the taxi-driver they traced Mrs Foley, who was living under an assumed name at a quiet hotel.

The taxi-driver had told Perry's assistant that he could certainly recognise his fare again. He described her appearance and the fur coat she was wearing. Moreover, he had noticed a very fragrant perfume that had come from a handkerchief she had left in the car.

Della Street was with Perry when the report came in.

"We've got to see Mrs Foley at once," he said to Della. "That woman has left a trail that even the dumbest cop could follow. Come on. We've not a second to lose."

Della did not ask any questions. She knew that when Perry Mason was working at high pressure he wanted quick action – not talk.

As they drove to the hotel a glimmer of an idea began to focus in Perry's brain.

He knew nothing of the real Mrs Foley, and had only the photographs his staff had collected of her to imagine what kind of a woman she might be.

But he had decided that he liked her face just as strongly as he had disliked the face of her husband.

On the drive he kept looking closely at Della.

"Might be done," he said to himself.

On arriving at the hotel, he pushed his way past all who asked his business and made his way to the room occupied by Mrs Foley.

"There's no time for talk," he said to Mrs Foley. "I'm Perry Mason, and I've got an order to look after your interests. I want that fur coat you wore to-night and a lot of your scent."

"Perry Mason," said Mrs Foley. "I'm so glad you've come."

"Get the coat," said Perry, "and the scent."

But Della had already got the fur coat and the scent-bottle.

"Miss Della Street, my secretary, and the smartest girl in the city," explained Perry. "She's going to get back the handkerchief you left in the taxicab. Big mistake leaving things in taxis."

He turned to Della.

"You know where to find the driver of the taxi. Dobbs told you. You've got to be the woman who drove to the Foley house in Sam Kerr's taxi. You've come back for the handkerchief you left in the cab. Got me?"

"I got you a good two minutes ago, great chief," said Della. "It will be easy. Mrs Foley and I are both very pretty and resemble each other quite a lot."

She waved a hand and disappeared.

"Now tell me all that happened," said Perry to Mrs Foley. "I know when you arrived at the house, and I got there a bit later to find Foley dead – shot. There was also a police dog, also shot dead. I may tell you that the police also know this."

Mrs Foley shivered.

"Hurry," warned Perry. "There's not a second to lose."

"I did go there," said Mrs Foley. "I went there to see my husband. But instead of listening to me he set a dog at me. As the animal leapt at me shots were fired. I saw the dog drop, and then my husband. I was horrified, and rushed from the house. The taxi was waiting. I came here. That's all."

Perry looked at her closely.

"You're in a bad jam, Mrs Foley. You can't afford to lie. Why don't you trust me. I'm your lawyer."

"I've told you the truth," said Mrs Foley in a weak voice.

"All right," said Perry. "But don't tell that truth to the police. It's not convincing."

"The police! Do you mean they're going to arrest me?" cried Mrs Foley.

"They'll be here any minute," said Perry. "But don't get frightened. I'll be here as well. All you've got to remember is you don't answer any questions."

Perry was about to add some more instructions when there came a heavy pounding at the door.

"The cops," said Perry laconically, as he smiled at Mrs Foley. "Leave everything to me. Don't answer a single question."

He opened the door and let in the police. They were not pleased to see him there, but they respected him as much as they feared him when he was against them in a case. Perry could not prevent the police arresting Mrs Foley for the murder of her husband, but he did prevent them from questioning her by warning them that any attempt at the now notorious third degree would result in something that would make the police of the city an object of public derision.

The big thing that worried Perry after the police had taken Mrs Foley away was where were Arthur Cartwright and his wife. They must know something about the shooting of Clinton Foley. But all the efforts of his staff failed to discover the Cartwrights.

As for the real Mrs Foley, Perry had failed to convince her that if she wanted him to save her life she must tell him the whole truth.

She stuck to her original story as she had told it to him on the night he had first seen her.

Perry knew she was not telling him everything. He wanted to save her because he felt sure that she was just as good a woman as Clinton Foley had been a bad man. But he was helpless in the face of her determination not to confide in him. The case worried him so much that he began to show signs of a nervous breakdown, and that sent Della Street into a state of great anxiety.

"You've done all you can," she said to him one morning, after he had been down to the court and once more succeeded in getting the trial postponed.

"No," cried Perry, "I've not done all. There's something I've missed. And that something is the link I want."

Three days later Della came down to the office to find Perry his old self.

"I'm ready for the trial now," he told her.

"What has happened?" she asked.

"Don't ask questions," said Perry, pinching her cheek. "You know I am a bit theatrical. I like to keep my big surprise till the last act – even from the one I love so much."

"That's all right with me," said Della. "I feel in my bones you're going to do something great, but my big joy is that you're better yourself."

"Never fitter, never fitter," said Perry, arranging his tie with that exactitude that showed his mind was at rest. "I've fixed it up with the D.A. that the trial shall open to-morrow. Here's your piece, little sweetheart, and don't forget it."

In the opinion of the public Mrs Foley was as good as convicted when she stood before the judge charged with the murder of her husband. But that was not the opinion of some of the reporters who had become wise from experience of Perry Mason.

"He's sure going to drop a bomb," said the 'Herald' man to his rival on the 'Recorder'. "When Perry smiles like he's smiling now there's going to be wailing from the other side."

The district attorney put his case with a clearness that not only carried conviction to the people in the court, but was also sufficiently strong to carry a conviction of sentence of death from the mouths of the jury.

But Perry Mason was in no way perturbed. He scarcely seemed to listen when Sam Kerr, the taxi-driver, swore that Mrs Foley was the woman he had driven to the Foley house on the night of the murder. He identified her positively.

"Your witness, Mr Mason," said the district attorney, resuming his seat with a quiet smile of triumph.

"Della Street," said Perry, in a voice that was quiet in tone but which thrilled the court. "Stand up in court, Della Street."

Della stood up.

Perry turned to the taxi-man.

"Look closely at this lady and tell the court if you have ever seen her before."

The taxi-driver's face was a study in surprise.

"Did you return a handkerchief to this lady – a handkerchief she had left in your cab?" thundered Perry.

"Well, it certainly looks like the lady. Yet the other one—"

Sam, the taxi-driver, broke down and looked helplessly at the judge.

"Go on," said Perry. "Tell the court the truth. That's what you're here for."

"I don't know. I can't say which was the lady I drove," admitted Sam.

"That will be all," said Perry, as he sat down.

The next witness for the prosecution was Lucy Benton.

She swore she had seen Evelyn Cartwright, who had lived with Clinton Foley as his wife, leave the house on the morning of the day when Foley was murdered.

Perry did not attempt to cross-examine her. Instead he put an amazing proposition before the court. He asked that the proceedings be transferred to the Foley house.

"It is essential in the interests of justice," he pleaded with the judge.

The amazing fact of a court moving from the recognised seat of justice to the scene of a crime was then carried out.

The court was reconstructed.

The judge took a chair, and Lucy Benton took another chair in lieu of the witness stand.

From outside came the noise of hammering, so insistent, that the judge complained.

"If I am to hear evidence," he said to Perry testily, "you must see that that noise is stopped."

"In a moment, your Honour," said Perry.

He faced Lucy Benton.

"You have sworn that you saw Evelyn Cartwright leave the Foley house on the morning Foley was murdered," he said.

Lucy Benton paid no heed to him.

"Stop that hammering!" she screamed.

Perry smiled.

He turned to the door of the library.

As though at a signal from his eyes Dobbs rushed in.

"It's right, sir," he said, breathing heavily. "We've just found the bodies of Mr and Mrs Cartwright under the cement in the new garage. Both have been shot – murdered!"

Perry turned to the judge.

"I shall bring medical evidence to prove that the unfortunate Evelyn Cartwright was murdered some days before this witness says she saw her leave the house. And she was murdered by Clinton Foley. This woman here, Lucy Benton, has sworn false testimony. That is for another court to deal with. In regard to my client, I can say this. The prosecution have admitted that whoever shot Clinton Foley, also shot the dog. That dog was an Alsatian, or a police dog, as we call them. He was my client's dog, her servant. He was one of the best of his breed and could not possibly have attacked his mistress. Some hand shot down Clinton Foley and the dog, but it was not the hand of Mrs Foley."

Perry sat down, and the jury did not even move from their chairs before returning a verdict of 'Not guilty'.

In his office the next morning Perry saw a thankful Mrs Foley.

"I don't know how to thank you, Mr Mason," she said.

"You don't have to thank me, Mrs Foley," said Perry, placing his arm round her. "I just did my best."

Later, Della said to Perry:

"What is the real inside story?"

"I know this much," replied Perry. "Cartwright was right about the howling dog. He did howl. He howled on the night Foley murdered Mrs Cartwright. Cartwright found out the truth, challenged Foley – after altering his will to give the real Mrs Foley his money – and Foley murdered him. You see, dear, knowing his wife was dead, he had nobody else to leave his money to except the real Mrs Foley, who had suffered from Foley's brutality and double-crossing as much as he had. Lucy Benton lied because she wanted Foley to marry her, and doubtless was an accessory to the murder of Evelyn Cartwright. But that is for the D.A. to deal with."

"But the howling dog?" persisted Della. "Why didn't he howl afterwards, when you went that morning?"

"Because he wasn't there. Foley took him to a dealer and changed him. These Alsatians are pretty much alike."

"Then you lied when you said Mrs Foley couldn't have killed her husband and the dog. You said it was her dog."

"Sure I did," said Perry, taking a cigarette and lighting it with a smile.

"Well, what about Mrs Foley's story, about somebody shooting both Foley and the dog?" said Della.

Perry smiled once more.

"Mrs Foley's story is her own. I don't want to hear it now I've got her acquitted. After all, if she did kill Foley, he deserved it, and I could have brought it in as self-defence. But I don't *know* exactly what happened. Now, what about a little dinner? I've been working terribly hard lately – and so have you."

NAKED CITY

(ABC, 1958–1962)
Starring: John McIntire, James Franciscus &
Leslie Nielsen
Directed by Paul Wendkos
Story 'Down The Long Night' by William F. Nolan

Naked City has been deservedly described as a milestone
in TV production – being the very first crime series to
have been filmed on location in the streets of New York
where many of its stories were set. It's success with
viewers was also very influential, inspiring a number of
later cop shows such as the tangled lives of the *87th Precinct* (1961–1962) with Robert Lansing and Norman Fell
based on the novels of Ed McBain; the soap opera-like
storylines of *Hill Street Blues* (1981–1987) starring Daniel
J. Travanti and Michael Conrad; and most recently
the controversial *NYPD Blue* (1994–) featuring David
Caruso and Dennis Franz which was actually banned
by some of the smaller US TV stations for alleged
excessive violence and 'soft core pornography' and, not
surprisingly, became the most popular TV cop series in
the rest of the nation! All of these series had at their heart
the theme of a close relationship between two central
characters – a concept that had begun in *Naked City*
where the veteran Detective Lieutenant Dan Muldoon
(John McIntire) and rookie Detective Jim Halloran
(James Franciscus) formed a partnership of mutual

107

respect and affection that enabled them to get through any situation and week by week lived up to the show's famous closing line, 'There are eight million stories in the Naked City . . . this has been one of them.' The episodes all featured different guest stars and among the young hopefuls who earned early breaks working on the crowded streets of the Big Apple were Robert Redford, Martin Sheen, Gene Hackman, Jon Voight, Peter Falk and Dustin Hoffman. For some viewers, the city itself was the star of the show, and it certainly added a gritty realism to the stories in which the cops were as likely to have faults as the criminals were to have redeeming features. Spectacular car chases were another feature of the stories which regularly delighted in the oddest titles such as 'The Man Who Bit A Diamond in Half', 'The Well Dressed Termite' and 'Make It Fifty Dollars and Add Love to Nona'!

Naked City drew the material for many of its episodes from the work of leading Hollywood writers and novelists such as William F. Nolan (1928–) whose novels have included the classic SF story of a future where growing old is a crime, *Logan's Run* (1967) – which has been filmed and made into a TV series – as well as numerous scripts for television specials and series. Recently, Bill has begun an ingenious and entertaining series of novels recreating the days of the hardboiled detectives of the Thirties in which the men who wrote those stories – Dashiell Hammett, Raymond Chandler and Erle Stanley Gardner – are themselves the sleuths. The series began with *The Black Mask Murders* in 1994. 'Down The Long Night' was adapted from Bill's short story by Charles Beaumont for *Naked City* in November 1960 and starred Nehemiah Persoff, Geraldine Brooks and Leslie Neilson, the cult hero of the recent *Naked*

Gun movies. It serves as an ideal reminder of a landmark crime series which deserves to be rerun more often than it is . . .

The ocean fog closed in, suddenly, like a big gray fist, and Alan Cole stopped remembering. Swearing under his breath, he jabbed the wiper button on the Lincoln's dash, and brought the big car down from fifty to thirty-five. Still dangerous. You couldn't see more than a few yards ahead in this soup. But he said the hell with it and kept the Lincoln at thirty-five because he wanted this mess over in a hurry, because he wanted to hold Jessica in his arms again before the night was done.

Above the damp Santa Monica pavements, looped tubes of neon glowed coldly, like colored seaweed; but there were no other cars. Cole shot through a blinking amber eye.

Actually, he thought, I should have turned him down flat. I should have said, Look, Paul, last week you ripped it. Period. So I don't give a good goddamn *what* kind of trouble you're in.

But then he heard Paul Bowers' anxious voice again, hard and metallic: "*I've got to see you, Alan.*" And he knew that, despite everything – even the way the guy had been acting since Jess had given him the shoulder – he did care. Why?

Nearing Ocean Pier, he thought about the telephone call, attempted to form an attitude. What would he say? For Godsake, how do you talk to a man you've called a loser and a phony and a coddled neurotic?

It had come just after lunch. Cecile couldn't say why she'd put it through against his instructions, except to remark that it sounded important. Of course it had to be Paul. After that screwball telegram from San Francisco, which didn't even start to make sense, Alan had been expecting the call. A big play to get in as a 'friend of the family', no doubt. A well thought out pitch on how sorry he was that he'd blown his stack and, needless to say, he wished them both the best of luck, and would they please forgive him – maybe even invite him to the wedding?

Except it didn't turn out that way . . .

Cole punched loose a cigarette, lit it, and went over the conversation for the umpteenth time, searching for clues.

"I've got to see you, Alan."

"No go. They're shooting this scene tomorrow, and I can't—"

"Alan, listen – I'm in trouble. I need your help."

"Like hell. You don't need anybody's help – unquote."

"Wait – Look, I know I said a lot of stupid things last week. But if our friendship ever meant anything to you, for the love of God listen!"

"Paul, I said I'm busy. I meant it. Let me give you a ring tomorrow."

"Tomorrow is too late." The pleading voice had seemed to crawl from the receiver. A pause. Then: *"The police are after me."*

"You're kidding."

"I swear it! Meet me at the pier when you get off work. Crazyville, the funhouse – you know. And don't laugh. It's the only safe place. I'll be waiting for you, Alan. Don't fail me. It may mean my life . . ."

And then the sharp click as Paul had hung up. Damn him, and damn the day they ever met!

Still, Cole thought, unaware that the Lincoln was wavering on the wrong side of the double white lines, still – it was through Paul that he'd met Jessica. They were engaged then. At least, that's what Paul thought; the poor guy couldn't see how bad he was for the girl. She had been impressed with him, at first. Then, like everyone else, she became disenchanted. And, like everyone else, she had a hell of a time pulling loose.

Was it *my* fault, Cole demanded of himself, that the two of us hit it off so well? I didn't take Jess away from Paul. He'd lost her a long time ago . . .

He spotted a parking place and nosed the car in, cut the engine, sat a moment, quietly, then opened the door.

Chill air went into his throat; it tasted of brine and heavy salt and fathoms. As he locked the automobile, turned and started to walk down the deserted street, Cole remembered how he had always hated this cold, which had nothing of winter in it; and how Bowers had always loved it. As usual, they disagreed. Over the years their likes and dislikes had seldom coincided. Bowers the social lion, the studied Bohemian – to all outward appearances sophisticated and intellectual; and Cole the recluse, the quiet one, the guy over there in the corner. How, Alan wondered, could two such people ever have formed a strong friendship? And was it really that?

Up ahead, the pier stretched, fog-draped and empty. Only the frozen spokes of the ferris wheel and the rotting wooden lacework of the Hi-Boy rose above the pressing blanket of gray.

Alan moved down Marine Street toward the pier, watching his image ripple and flow past streaked shop windows.

What was it with Paul, anyway? What the devil had he done? Robbed someone – no, that was hard to take, not Bowers' long suit. Or—

He passed a window filled with photographs of wild-eyed matted men in silk trunks. Lord Perkins; The Boston Bull; The Strangler.

—murder?

No.

Another window promised salvation to the penitent, damnation to the wicked.

Hotels, shops, missions – all empty and silent. As they had been a million winters ago, when he and Bowers and Jess had walked this street the last time.

Where are the people? he had wondered then. He wondered it now.

Maybe there aren't any people. You never see them moving behind glass. Maybe—

Alan shook his head. Ease off. You're just nervous. Paul's in trouble of some kind, so you're nervous. This place is nothing more than an amusement park, shut down, closed for the season; and that's all. So knock it off, Cole. You're a big boy now.

Yet, Alan felt a slow fear building in him – an uneasiness. With every step, years were peeling away, stripping off in layers. A few moments ago he was Alan Cole, thirty years old, a moderately successful screen writer and not anxious to be anything else. Now . . .

Marine Street flowed into the wide concrete length of Promenade. Alan hurried across, listening to the thin cries of circling gulls and to the lonely night beach.

Taking a final drag on his cigarette, he ground it underheel and turned into the amusement park.

Again the sense of something amiss. Partly Paul and also, this place. As if only a moment before, every stand had been open, every ride spinning and whirling and rolling in colored movements, the walk itself alive with people. And as if magic fingers had been snapped, causing all the people and the movement to vanish instantly.

Passing the roller coaster, Alan could almost hear the chant of the bored, slick-haired ticket seller:

"The Hi-Boy! The Hi-Boy! Don't miss it, folks! It's safe! It's exciting! The Thrill of a Life-Time!"

He glanced at the sheeted train of wooden cars, waiting in coiled silence on their tracks, and hurried past.

His stomach felt light. Dizziness had returned with memories. ("Jess, I'd like you to meet an old buddy of mine, Alan Cole. Alan, this is my gal, Jessica Randall. Isn't she a doll?") He quickened his step past the closed concessions, endless rows of shabby canvas curtains; past the rifle range and the Whirlagig and the Caterpillar; past the arcade where you can watch a thirty year old strip-show and then leave, wondering how the dames look today.

A hundred yards ahead, on the tip of the pier, he could see the fog-buried angles of Crazyville.

Paul would be waiting there. And it would all be over soon.

He'd see to that, by God.

The ticket booth was a gigantic smiling head. Within its mouth between the plaster teeth, a sign read: CLOSED.

Alan paused at the wicket gate and glanced back along the walkway. It was empty.

He vaulted the gate and peered across the yard. A tiny, twisting path marked LOONEY STREET horseshoed around mad wooden building fronts.

Gravity seemed missing here; it was a force that belonged entirely to the outside world. The houses convoluted above the cobbled walk, gables and roofs and walls leaning at impossible angles, one upon the other.

Alan cupped his hands about his mouth. Softly, he called: "Paul."

No answer.

He swore. He hadn't changed; not a bit. This idiot place was supposed to make you dizzy, so – he was dizzy.

And where the hell was Paul?

He moved toward the bat-wing doors which opened to the black maze of damp tunnels. Beyond this point lay a man-made night so intense and so impenetrable that, once inside, you could no longer imagine day.

"Paul?"

He hesitated, glanced up. A ragged, toothless crone sagged drunkenly from a second-story window. Her throat had been carefully saw-cut; her eyes protruded in dumb disbelief.

Bloodied faces peeped from every window, each with a name and a history. Paul had once claimed that they were his only friends, these plaster nightmares, the only ones who truly understood him.

Standing in the silent yard, Alan felt the familiar horror of the funhouse engulfing him again. The death-figures seemed to writhe just beyond the perimeter of his vision: he could almost *hear* their frozen cries.

He drew a deep breath, pushed open the doors, and hesitated there, divided squarely between the interior shadows and the solid reality of the outside.

"Paul – you in here?"

Like a huge sounding-box, the wooden tunnels bounced the words along, echoing, finally lost.

Then: "Alan?"

"Yeah!" He wiped perspiration from his palms. "Come on out."

A pause. "I can't." The voice was faint.

"What do you mean, you can't?"

"Too dangerous. I might be seen."

"There's nobody around for miles."

"I – can't afford to take the chance."

"All right, all right. God! Where are you?"

"Just follow the tunnel. First room."

"All right, but – this better be *good*."

Alan stepped into the long night of the tunnels; into a colored blackness that danced before his eyes in a million tiny specks of light. The walls, damp and slippery beneath his groping hands, smelled of the sea; the odor of soaked and rotting wood seeped up from the floor. Far below hidden waters sloshed against tired pilings.

The walls began to narrow as he moved forward. The ceiling lowered gradually. He was forced to crouch, turn sideways.

The walls ended.

Alan extended cautious hands, encountered nothingness.

"Okay, so I'm out of the first tunnel. What now?"

"You're fine." The voice was much closer. "Keep coming."

"I can't see a damn thing."

Alan remembered his lighter, got it out, thumbed the wheel. It sparked feebly, failed to ignite. Another spin. A tiny guttering flame this time.

He shielded it with his left hand and peered ahead. A cleated platform led upward. He slid his feet over the cleats and reached a wide opening.

"In here, Alan."

The light flickered. "Well, turn on a flashlight or something, will you! I'm going to fall flat on my ass."

Of course, he realized, Paul must know this place as a blind man knows his own bedroom. Always running out here to 'think'. Or to bang quail. Or – what?

Alan advanced carefully, tapping. A heavy object brushed his shoulder; he hissed, leaping back. The lighter clattered to the plank flooring and winked out.

Total darkness.

"Paul?"

"Over here."

"Over *where*? What am I, a goddamn cat or something?" There was a scrabbling, a fast padding, "Look, buddy, this routine is getting old at a rapid clip. In fact, the hell with the whole thing. I'm getting out of here."

He patted his handkerchief pocket, removed a matchfolder. He struck one.

The object that had brushed against him was, he saw, a body – swinging from a thick rope.

No – not a body. By adjusting his eyes to the feeble glow, Alan saw that it was a scarecrow. One of many. The room seemed filled with hanging straw corpses, all revolving in submarine slowness on their corded lengths of hemp. Scarecrows . . . papier mache trees . . . Now he remembered the room. Horse Thief Hall, or something like that.

The flame bit into his finger.

Blackness.

He lit another match, dropped it, tore the last one out savagely. "Okay, kid, you wanted to talk – here I am."

Silence.

He swung the match in a slow arc above his head, knowing, suddenly, that it was useless, knowing that Paul Bowers' entire phone conversation had been another fake. The sincerity and the pleading and the desperation: all fake. Part of a final, elaborate practical joke. Paul didn't need help; what he needed was a long overdue kick in the teeth!

"Fun's over, Cole catches on!" he called.

Silence.

The third match burned out. Alan turned to retrace his steps, thinking about Jessica's probable reaction to a stunt like this. Maybe he oughtn't to tell her. The less said about Paul in her presence, the better.

It takes a certain talent, he thought bitterly; a certain

definite talent to be a perpetual fall-guy. Drop the hook, I'll bite!

He'd almost reached the doorway when four naked green bulbs, one in each corner of the room, bloomed into silent life.

Alan blinked, the pale glow burning into his eyes. He scrubbed at them, realizing, vaguely, that Paul had found the central control box and activated a switch.

The swinging scarecrows came into focus. Alan's fist knotted. His head jerked about the room. "Listen!" he shouted, "I'm going to walk back out of here, Paul. Don't try anything cute. Because if you do I swear I'll break your damn neck. Is that clear?"

He started for the opening. Another scarecrow bumped against his shoulder. He wheeled, buried his fingers in the mouldered straw, and pulled, furiously. The figure tore loose at the neck, collapsed to the floor with a wet, pulpy sound.

Soft laughter from the tunnels.

He was about to push his way through the hanging figures when he paused.

Everything inside him paused.

Sensation became thought: *Scarecrows are made of straw.* And the object that had just touched him was *solid!*

Alan turned, and jammed a fist against his mouth.

Hanging there, swaying amid the rotting scarecrows, was Jessica Randall.

For a long moment, Alan could not move. His body was incapable of movement; every muscle locked tight.

His mind tried to reject what his eyes saw.

She was naked. And cold. Her flesh, once warm and vibrant, carried now an icy chill; and her eyes, though unseeing, were open.

Her sheer silk stockings had been knotted about her

throat and about a ceiling beam, and supported her slight weight easily.

"Jess!"

Alan put a trembling hand to the girl's breast, and then he knew she was dead.

Jess was dead. And Paul had killed her. He knew that, too. Because she had fallen in love with someone else. Paul had done this, just as he'd promised in that crazy speech he'd delivered to them. They hadn't believed him, or taken him seriously, because Paul Bowers had always been a lot of talk, a thin red-faced clown full of empty promises and emptier threats. And they'd been wrong.

Alan saw Jess's clothes, her red blouse and white skirt, her undergarments, her black leather ballet-shoes – all folded and placed neatly in a corner on the floor. And he knew a hate and a fear, then, that he had never dreamed of.

Run! he thought. Try to stay calm and get out of this place. He wants you to panic. Don't panic. Just get out, quickly – then wait and get him.

He pulled a shutter in his mind that closed off the reality of Jess and what had happened to her. Out, the same way, he thought; but it wasn't so easy. He'd turned so many times that he had lost all sense of direction. Three separate doorways opened on the room of scarecrows and only one of them led back to the first tunnel: the others were phony. And he couldn't be sure which was which.

He'd taken a single step forward, aware now that the laughter was mechanical, not human, issuing from the cracked lips of a plaster fat man, when the ceiling lights blacked out again. Paul was still at the switch and that meant he had little time. Hurriedly, he knelt on the plank flooring and groped for the fallen lighter. Without luck.

Okay, so you move in the dark – but by God you move!

He touched one wall of the room. He moved along, tapping the rough wood: he would have to try one of the doorways and hope it was the right one.

He thought of Bowers, at home in the darkness, gliding through the looping maze of passageways like a swift fish in green waters, perfectly at ease, perfectly in command.

The funhouse was Paul's world.

Abruptly the wall ended, but not in emptiness. He'd fumbled himself into a corner. A corner— Without knowing exactly why, he reached up and touched a light bulb. It was still warm. He unscrewed it in quick short motions and dropped it into his pocket. Then he followed the next wall and reached one of the doors.

Careful to walk slowly, he entered the tunnel. And walked head-on into a pocket. Wood on all three sides.

Alan groaned softly, his throat went dry. He tried to swallow and couldn't.

All right, you missed. Now turn around and go back to the next one. Move, damn you, move!

He re-entered the still black room and groped numbly along to the second doorway. At least this one would lead somewhere. Alan stepped out onto the cleated platform.

This must be it! It seemed to possess the same dank odor, the same narrow twistings . . .

He pressed forward.

A buzzing, a whirr of turning machinery, and the blackness blazed into light. Far off, the laughter again. Within a niche in the wall directly to Alan's right, a huge gorilla raised its fists, swiveled its savage head back and forth, snarling.

"You son of a bitch, Bowers! I'll kill you."

The apparition faded behind him. He was running now, knowing that this tunnel led deeper into the funhouse. Toward Paul's voice?

Six explosions, deafening, somewhere in the dark. Gunshots. Paul had a gun. But why waste bullets?

To let you know he's armed. To let you know he's waiting . . .

Alan ran on, constantly aware that in order to get Bowers, he would have to get into the open, into *his* world. He stumbled, barking his knuckles on trick partitions, pushed himself forward, his face sweatsoaked, legs weak and trembling.

A dragon sprang into colored life. It lay on painted rocks, a fat reptilean creature, its green-scaled head nodding, forked tongues licking in and out.

Sudden shrill gusts of wind hissed up from the floor.

And the infernal laughter, mocking him, following him wherever he went—

He ran on, crouching, sometimes on hands and knees, blundering forward, knowing, even as he ran, that he was close to death. A bullet or a knife would meet him in the darkness; and he wouldn't have a chance.

Then he saw light – faint, but only moments away. Only a few more steps!

The floor dropped away beneath him. Alan felt himself plunging downward; he thrashed his arms, clutched at shadows and blackness.

The trap-door closed.

The room was full of people. Frightened, angry, staring people, all seated at the bottom of a long slide.

A memory clicked into place for Alan Cole. The Mirror Room – where you spend an hour, alone, trying to find your way out.

He licked his dry lips and wiped the perspiration from his hands.

He listened. Footsteps.

You're unarmed. Move!

Jerkily, he thrust himself into the corridors of glass. He saw his image reflected in a thousand bright distortions as he slammed through the maze, bumping, cursing, moving, moving.

He reached another glass tunnel. A tall, freckled, crewcut man faced him.

Himself. He caught his breath. Everywhere, mirrors. A small skylight above for ventilation. But no exit that he knew of.

"Alan?"

He narrowed his eyes, located the voice, found that he was staring down a dark corridor that could not have existed.

A figure stood there, motionless. Something glinted in the figure's hand.

"Writers should never run," the voice from the darkness said. "It makes their faces turn red. Take a good look at yourself in one of these mirrors, Alan. You've no idea how ridiculous you look!"

"You lousy bastard!"

Alan's perspective had melted; now, suddenly, it reformed. Until this moment he had not been entirely able to connect the man who had murdered Jess with an ineffectual guy he'd bummed around with. Sure, Paul Bowers had been a whiner and a loser and a neurotic; but, God, not a killer. Killers were what he wrote cheap movies about. Yet—

Alan recalled a book he'd once read for research. A study of criminology. It postulated that every human being on Earth was a potential murderer, needing only the right set of circumstances, the right personal motivation, to turn killer. A world full of dynamite sticks, waiting to be sparked. His engagement to Jess had sparked it for Paul, had set the fuse burning. And it had been burning for a week.

Kid-gloves, boy. He's nuts now. You read books on

psychology, okay, be psychological. Or, brother, you're dead, too.

"Paul, listen – can't we talk or something?"

The figure did not move. "Clear the air, you mean? Get it all tied up in a neat package?" A small chuckle, like a tapped siphon.

Alan recognized the words, the same words he had used when he gave Paul the straight goods that night. "I didn't mean everything I said. Honest. Is that it?"

"Part of it, Alan."

The blackness stirred. A shape took slow form.

Paul Bowers stepped out of the tunnel, smiling. He was, as always, impeccably dressed. His charcoal gray suit tailored to make him look heavier than his 175 pounds; his shoetips gleaming; his pale, bony face clean-shaven and smelling of lotions. Across his high forehead, the fine blond hair was neatly, perfectly combed. "By the way," he said, "don't try anything dramatic. You're much too clumsy."

He looked white and businesslike and totally unlike a killer, except for his hands. They were powerful and bright red, ending in thick fingers; the hands of a longshoreman or a mechanic – or a strangler. In one of them, held firmly, was a twelve-inch blue-steel hunting knife.

Alan looked at it.

"Ugly monster," Bowers said. "But a hunting knife seemed appropriate for the occasion. Borrowed this one from you quite a while ago, if you'll remember. And I thought, 'Now *there*, by God, would be a touch!' And so it is. At least give me that."

Alan's blood grew hot. "Why did you kill Jess?" he blurted, before he could stop the words.

"The old story, pal. You know: 'If I can't have her, then by the Holies, no one—' Etc. Besides, I wanted to see if I had the nerve. Sort of practice, you might say. For you."

"Paul, listen."

"Of course."

"What do you want me to do? Do you want me to beg for my life, is that it?"

"That would be kind of fun, I must admit. But to tell you the honest to God truth, I'm getting a little tired of the game." Bowers stepped closer, smiling. His eyes were misted over. And the laughter still echoed down the halls.

"You're sick. You know that, I suppose."

"Oh, yes. Mad as a March hare." It was the Party Paul, the bored intellectual who built his words and rolled them out on oiled casters. "I would describe my illness as Acute Reaction to Prolonged Injustice. The prognosis is fair, however; fortunately, I know the cure. Jess was part. You, Brother Rat, will complete the treatment."

Alan's throat moved convulsively. In all his films, a man with a knife was a pushover. You kicked it out of his hand, or rushed him before he could use his arm, or bluffed him. But that was the movies. In real life, it worked out differently. A man with a knife was a man with a formidable weapon. If he knew how to use it – and Paul knew – you might as well be in front of a .45 or a cannon.

"Paul, you'll be caught. The police will investigate sure as hell, find we were all friends and track you down wherever you go."

"You really think so?" Bowers lowered the blade, as if bemused by the thought, and Alan stepped forward; but then the knife was up again, and Bowers was laughing. "Alan, you don't give me any credit. You never did, of course." His voice rose in pitch. The smile had become fixed and deadly. "Exactly how long did you think you could go on kicking me before I kicked back, anyway?"

An auto horn bleated out beyond the pier. A strange sound, part of a different world.

Alan remembered the skylight, was very careful not to look up. Was it possible that he could reach it? No. Too high, too small . . .

"I gave you friendship, Alan, and what did I get in return? Betrayal. Oh, I didn't expect you to break your neck trying to give me a little help, but I thought at least you'd appreciate what I'd done enough to stand by me. Not say, 'Thanks, Paul' – no, not that – but maybe show a little loyalty." He was trembling. The hunting knife jumped in short darting flashes in his hand. "Always take, take, take, and never give. Never a helping hand. No; it's good-bye, Paulie, I'm a big man now. Lots of money. Lots of fame. Too busy to help a two-bit loser like Paul Bowers – after I pushed you to the top with my bare hands. Do you deny it?"

"I—"

"Do you deny that it was I who got you in at the studio, introduced you to Kay, almost forced him to hire you? And who was it that stayed up till four every morning helping you to make that lousy script acceptable?"

"I don't argue that you helped me, Paul. I'm grateful for it."

"Grateful!" The thin man drew his lips back. He breathed heavily. "I guess that's what accounts for your aceing me out, playing along with the rumors about, 'Poor old Bowers, all washed up!' And I guess it was the final expression of your gratitude to turn Jess against me?"

"That's a lie, Paul. I – damn it, Jess just fell in love with me. I couldn't help that."

Bowers' jaw muscles twitched. "I believed that for a

124

while, Alan. Felt that maybe I really *was* the oddball you said I was. But then I started checking around. And I found out a few things. For instance, who it was that talked Kahn into giving me the sack. And who it was that got me blackballed right afterwards." He stepped forward. "I know you pretty well, Alan, enough to know you probably still think of yourself as a noble guy in an embarrassing situation. Those shutters in your mind. They won't let you remember the filthy things you've done."

"It's not true."

"The convenient little shutters won't let you face the fact that you've been scared of me ever since we met. Scared spitless. You know I'd got you in solid at Galactic, so your ego forced you to get rid of me. And it was easy, because I trusted you. I trusted you with Jess, too. All the time you were filling her mind with dirty lies about me, *I trusted you!* And I didn't wake up for a long time. When I did, it was too late. But not too late for me to spoil your little play—"

Bowers raised the knife.

At that instant, Alan grabbed the light-bulb in his pocket and hurled it to the floor with all his strength.

The explosion whipped Bowers' head around. In that split second, Alan leapt for the skylight. His fingers closed over the heavy beam; held. Hidden sacs seemed to burst and flood strength through him. A single surge pulled his body up and over the edge. He could feel hands clutching at his legs, slipping, gathering the cloth of his trousers. He kicked, viciously, at the hands, and swung his ankles against the wood. Bowers' hold loosened. He kicked again. The weight fell away.

Alan drew his legs up swiftly, pivoted, and stood up on the slate roof.

Cold bit into his skin; the fog, a wash of wet mist,

billowed and pressed in upon his eyes. He balanced there on the slippery roof a brief moment, breathing.

Take it easy, he thought. Try to run and you'll end up cartwheeling off the edge headfirst.

The roof was an iced pond, impossible to run across. Alan squinted. If he could only see! How far down was the pavement, anyway? Where was the edge? He was on a slat island, surrounded by moving gray tides.

And now Paul Bowers' hands were closing over the beam.

Alan crouched above the opening, braced himself and lashed out with his foot. The blow tipped Paul back, forced one hand off. Alan lifted his right foot, prepared to send it heel-down on the strained white fingers.

Something grabbed his ankle, jerked.

He caught a glimpse of Paul's face, grinning, blazing red, as though every blood vessel had ruptured and tendriled out.

Then Alan fell.

With a grunt, Bowers heaved through the skylight, landed nimbly, and took the knife from its belt position.

Alan struggled up, his eyes on the long blue sweep of steel in Paul's hand.

"Shutters open, Alan? Or do you still think you're a hero?"

Now!

The blow caught the side of Paul's head, sent him reeling back. Alan felt his muscles go cold: bright color fireworked in his mind. He struck out again, blindly, throwing his entire weight into the blow. Soft inner nose cartilage crunched beneath his hand.

He had not fought for a long time, but now hate activated him, put strength into his arms, goaded him. But even as he swung, he knew that he could never win out against Paul and

126

the knife. Perhaps the blade had already entered his body – they say you don't feel a knife thrust right at first – and his life was, even now, ebbing away.

"Go ahead, Alan, fight! You're doing fine!"

He aimed his fist, drove for that grinning red face. Bone and flesh yielded. But the fury of the lunge pulled him forward. He stumbled, slid, his head striking a ledge of plaster at the roof's edge.

More fireworks. He tried desperately to shake them away. He tried to shake away Paul's burning words, the image of Jess . . . *Was it true?*

Paul Bowers glided toward him, smiling, calm, the knife poised high.

All over now. Done. Finished. He closed his eyes. *In a second now. Another second.* He waited, his breath in a bottle and the bottle sealed. He could smell the honed steel and the rough leather handle; he could taste the metal in his throat.

A strange sound, then. Like the last drops of water draining from a sink – a short bubbling indrawn scream.

Alan opened his eyes.

Paul had slumped to his knees, teetering, making thin dry noises and staring, staring.

Then he toppled, spilled sideway to the roof, and lay there. His fingers spasmed on the wet slats like the overturned legs of two giant spiders.

Then he was quiet.

In his chest was imbedded the long steel of the hunting knife.

Alan rose, shakily. The roof listed, heaved, settled. A sharp wind from the ocean had cleared some of the fog. Without trying to understand, he located the roof edge again and the pavement below. Less than ten feet.

He jumped. The ground was made of needles and electricity. It buckled his knees. He fell against the rusting ribs of an ancient trolley, and leaned there, trying to swallow.

He began to walk. He listened to the sound of the sea washing in on the beach, and the gulls cloaked high in night, and his footsteps.

Is it true? That was all he could think. He knew that Jess was dead and that Paul was dead and this was no nightmare, no bad dream, but something real; yet, he could only think: Is it true? Did I do those things to Paul, actually, turn Jess against him, actually—

The sky revolved: Alan felt that it had suddenly shaken loose. The peppermint striped shroud covering the Caterpillar began to shimmer and twist darkly; the towering wooden immensity of the Hi-Boy swayed and separated into bright pieces and showered soundlessly down upon him.

He staggered on, out of the amusement park, down a street, to an all-night cafe.

He lifted the receiver off its hook. "Give me the police," he said, in a soft, tired voice.

It was 10 a.m. when they knocked on the door. He'd fallen into a pit of black exhaustion, not bothering to wash or change clothes and getting out of the pit was difficult. When he awoke, he didn't question that the night had been real: his hand ached and his head throbbed and he still felt the numbness.

"Just a minute." His mouth was sour. He could barely remember talking to the police, waiting while they checked his story, staggering out of the squad car.

Alan Cole opened the door. A large man in a brown double-breasted suit stood there. He was flanked by two cops in uniform.

"Yes, what is it?"

The large man stepped inside the room. "A good yarn

you told us, Cole," he said. "Mighty good yarn. We swallowed it."

Alan shook his head. This was the man he'd spoken to last night. Captain Boylen, Homicide. But now he looked different.

"What do you mean?"

"Cole," the man said, "you can make it easy, or you can make it tough. It doesn't matter much."

"I—" Alan sat down on the bed; his senses began to swim. "I don't know what you're talking about."

"Then I'll tell you," the man said. "Your story washes out. Point one: We found six bullet holes and a 32.20 at the funhouse. Pistol registered under Paul Bowers' name. We examined the knife. It's yours—"

"I know. I admitted that, didn't I?"

"Then I suppose you know that rough leather won't take prints."

"So what?"

The policeman removed a cigar, skinned off its cellophane wrapping, lit it. "Guy was pretty well armed, wouldn't you say? Gun *and* a knife."

Alan sat quietly, trying to understand.

"Point two," Boylen went on. "We got a report from the medical examiner. It's his opinion Bowers didn't commit suicide. Man decides to kill himself with a knife, Cole, he stabs within an area of a couple inches, like this—" The policeman made stabbing motions against his chest. "There were *four* wounds in Bowers. One here, in the ribs; and here – and here – and finally the one that got him. All spread out. Suicides don't do that, Mister. Care to say anything?"

Alan remembered Paul's telling him of the criminal medicine course he'd taken in Zurich – a course for student lawyers and insurance investigators, the purpose to show the difference between a murder victim and a suicide . . .

"Keep talking, Captain."

"Point three." The policeman removed an envelope from his breast pocket and tossed it over to Alan. "It's been photostated," he said. "Read it."

Alan removed the letter. Flawlessly typewritten, with thick margins. From Paul, addressed to the police.

"Mailed sometime yesterday afternoon, late," Boylen said. "Downtown got it. Sent it over to me early this morning. Go on, read it."

But even before he began, Alan knew. Everything fell instantly into place. The screwy telegram from San Francisco, (*'Sorry it turned out this way. The best man lost. Paul.'*); the shots in the dark and the pistol (to make it appear that they had struggled); the borrowed hunting knife.

He forced himself to read, knowing what the letter would say, knowing fully.

Homicide Div.
LA Police Department
Los Angeles, California

To Whom It May Concern:

I hope that this letter will end up in your crank files and that I'll wake up tomorrow feeling pretty ridiculous about the whole thing. But record – just in case.

I have reason to believe that Alan Cole, an employee of Galactic Pictures, Galactic City, Calif., is preparing to do harm to my fiancée, Jessica Randall. Cole and I have been friends for years, and I know him well. He was engaged to Miss Randall up until two weeks ago, at which time Miss Randall confessed that it was I whom she loved and wished to marry. Cole pretended to take it well. But this morning he called Jessica, asking her to have one last drink with him at a little bar they used to frequent, across from Ocean Pier, Santa Monica – Bisco's. I tried to dissuade her from going, but she likes Alan and doesn't feel there's anything to it.

Maybe there isn't. But, as I say, I know Cole. Somewhere inside him, there is definitely a strange and vicious streak. He is a man capable of almost anything.

It's likely nothing will happen. In that case, I'll phone tomorrow. If not, and if this fear of mine turns out to have any justification – contact Alan Cole. But make sure you're armed.

Sincerely,
Paul A. Bowers

Alan folded the letter and put it back in the envelope and handed it to the large man.

"You want to tell us about it, Mister Cole?"

Alan thought of Paul's words, of shutters that would not close inside his mind; of Jess and the clever lies he had told her, unconsciously. The lies he had told everyone, including Alan Cole . . .

Hell of a script, he told himself. Who's the hero? Who's the villain?

"Sure," he said, thinking this was *one* job he wasn't going to ruin for Paul. "I'll tell you about it."

Then he started laughing, and it sounded like the mechanical man at the funhouse. Only he couldn't turn it off.

SOFTLY, SOFTLY

(BBC TV, 1966–1976)
Starring: Stratford Johns, Frank Windsor & Norman
Bowler
Directed by Leonard Lewis
Story 'Equal Status' by Elwyn Jones

In Britain, the Sixties opened with another ground-breaking crime series that remains famous more than thirty years later: *Z Cars*. At one fell swoop, the series changed forever the image of the British policeman as he had become epitomised by Dixon of Dock Green and let viewers into the much tougher world of policing a fictional patch called Newtown which was clearly modelled on an area of Liverpool. The officers of all ranks were seen warts and all – and from the young PCs like Bert Lynch (James Ellis), Jock Weir (Joseph Brady), 'Fancy' Smith (Brian Blessed) and Bob Steele (Jeremy Kemp) via the Desk Sergeants Blackitt (Robert Keegan) and Twentyman (Leonard Williams) right up to Detective Inspector Charlie Barlow (Stratford Johns) and his assistant Detective Sergeant John Watt (Frank Windsor), these were quite clearly policemen drawn from life and their cases soon became essential viewing in British homes every Saturday night. The realism of the series in terms of bad language and the occasional rough treatment of suspects, brought complaints from some members of the public and a number of senior police officers – but with its penny whistle signature tune and excellent scripts, *Z Cars* ran for 667 episodes until 1966. Thereupon Barlow, Watt and Blackitt were all promoted to their own series, *Softly, Softly* concerning a regional crime squad based at Wyvern which was said to be near Bristol. The irascible Barlow (now a Detective Chief Superintendent) and long-suffering Watt (a Detective Chief Inspector) proved as popular as ever and the new series ran for the next ten years with a total of 264 episodes. Some viewers believed it to be a superior programme to *Z Cars* – and certainly more memorable than its successors, *Barlow at Large* (1971–1973) and *Barlow (1974–1975)* in which Charlie was promoted yet again to work for the Home Office.

The mastermind behind the success of *Softly, Softly* was Elwyn Jones (1923–1982), a television scriptwriter who had joined the team working on *Z Cars* and proved very influential in the development of the series and its characters. He was then instrumental, and perhaps even more crucial, in the devising of its sequel. Welshman Jones had been a staff writer for Odhams Press in London in the years immediately after the Second World War before working on *Radio Times* from 1950–1957 which gave him an entrée into the world of television. Here he joined the BBC Drama Series and, thanks to a lifetime interest in crime and mystery stories, slipped easily into scriptwriting for *Z Cars*. Later he became producer of *Softly, Softly* and pioneered the introduction of police politics into a crime series – previously a taboo subject – as well as writing some of the programme's most memorable scripts. 'Equal Status' was written for the 1973 season and co-starred Clive Merrison as David James and Clive Roberts as Daniel Owen.

One of the Wyvern files had pasted inside the back cover a copy of the front page of a morning paper. John Watt recalled how he'd been sitting at his desk in the Wyvern office reading that paper, when a small explosion reached his ear from the far end of the corridor. A few moments earlier, Barlow had galumphed along there in the direction of the washroom. The explosion which followed was the raising of his voice in angry protest. John Watt allowed himself the shadow of a smile. He knew what had angered his boss; he knew too that he had the answers to a number of questions that Barlow had not as yet asked. He quietly folded over the front page of the newspaper and sat back in his chair as Barlow stormed into the office.

"John, d'you know what! I just went into the washroom to freshen up . . . turned on the tap . . . and all it did was spit at me."

"Good morning, sir." Watt politely reproached his boss for the unceremonious entry.

"You what? Oh . . . good morning." But Barlow continued to glare at him, as though the insolence of the plumbing were his fault. "So what's happened to the water?" he demanded.

"I'm not the caretaker," said Watt, "but I do read the papers." He unfolded the one in his hand for Barlow to see the headline. 'BOMB OUTRAGE' it read, in thick black type.

Barlow took the paper and quickly scanned through the paragraphs below. It told him of an act of sabotage the previous night upon the main pipe line bringing the water supply for the Wyvern area down from the Welsh hills. The details were sparse, but imagination filled in the picture: the dark-clothed figures treading soft-footed through the sleeping darkness towards the gleaming curve of the newly installed water main; the deft hands taping the explosive charge to a riveted joint where it would do the greatest damage; the hastily retreating figures leaving a length of trailing fuse behind them; the sudden flare of the match, and the line of fire running thinly across the gorse towards the packed joint, where it suddenly erupted in a sheet of flame; the belly-rumbling explosion that made the distant cottagers turn in their beds several miles away; and then the waste of waters pouring from the jagged hole in the pipe over the hillside.

"Why, John? Why?" Barlow demanded.

"They don't want us to have their water."

"Us? . . . Them?"

"The Welsh over there, and us over here," Watt patiently explained, though he knew that Barlow was fully alive to the protests that had been voiced, in English and in Welsh, over the flooding of some of the most tranquil valleys in Wales to provide water-supplies for the increasing thirst of the industrial Midlands and West of England. But protests being of no avail, action had followed, violent action, explosive action, of which the sabotage of the previous night had been the eighth incident in rapid succession. And Watt had heard a whisper, passed on to him by Jim Cook, the Squad's Intelligence Officer, that the Wyvern Regional Crime Squad was going to be asked to assist in finding the terrorists.

Barlow stared when Watt told him this. "Thanks," he said. "I'll bone up on the background." On his way to the door he hesitated.

"John . . ." Barlow's heavy early-morning look had already lightened, and a blandly ingratiating smile was beginning to lift the corners of his mouth. John Watt knew what was coming, but he didn't look up. Barlow cleared his throat. "Er . . . John . . . er . . . what's your analysis of this little explosion?"

Crafty old fox, thought Watt. He's not done his own homework, so he's hoping that I have. But his response to Barlow was an innocent, "Me, sir?"

"You're our political expert now," Barlow was laying it on thick, ". . . since you sorted out our local red revolutionary at the aircraft works."

"Who turned out to be a very confused little night watchman," Watt reminded him, ". . . so afraid of being alone in the dark that he set off those security alarms just so's he could get someone to come running along and keep him company."

"Ay . . . well . . ." Barlow wasn't giving up, ". . . but our Mr Gilbert was impressed with your political grasp . . . told me so himself."

John Watt relented. "All right, sir. What do you want to know?"

"This Welsh Nationalism . . . what's it all about?" Barlow pulled up a chair and sat down. "It's not just about water, is it."

"It's about patriotism, sir. Local patriotism. Like you and I feel about Lancashire. Finest place in the world."

"Widnes is," Barlow said, confining this Lancastrian patriotism to his own home town.

"Widnes . . ." and there was just a hint of questioning in Watt's voice as he went on to murmur, ". . . where no birds sing."

"That's right. But so what?" Barlow demanded.

"So why shouldn't the Scots be local patriotic as well," Watt reasoned. "Or the Welsh."

"They can be as local patriotic as I am. But I don't go blowing things up to prove it."

"You don't need to," Watt told him, "since nobody's stopping you talking the way you want."

"You mean the way I've always spoken?" Barlow's

usually subdued Lancastrian tones became unusually promi-
nent. "Why should anyone object? I've not heard objections
to the Welsh accent either, though this part of England is
busting with it."

"It's not busting with the Welsh language, though," Watt
pointed out.

"I should hope not," said Barlow. And went on to ask
slyly, "How much Welsh do they speak in Wales?"

Watt contrived to make his answer sound casual as he
trotted out the hard facts. "About a third of the population
of Wales speaks Welsh. Only half of that number thinks
Welsh."

Barlow was impressed. "Expert," he murmured.

"Not really . . ." Watt's modesty was genuine. A very
modest man, John Watt thought himself, which was still no
reason for hiding lights under bushels. "As a detective, I try
to understand motives."

Barlow was incredulous. "You think you know what
makes these bomb fellows tick?"

"I understand a bit of their attitude . . . what they're
on about. I've got it written down somewhere." Watt's
neat little pocket book fell open naturally at the last
page written on, which was taken up with only two
words printed in large block capitals; strange words to
Barlow's eye, being made up of double ds and ys and
odd combinations of consonants unpronounceably lacking
in vowels. 'DDILYSRWYDD CYFARTAL' was what
it spelled out, though Watt's careful pronunciation of it
was more like 'Thilisrooth cavartal.' "And that," said
Barlow, "doesn't sound anything like what you've got
written down."

"Easy really." Watt explained. "Double d is like th as in
'thick'. F is always v as in 'vanity'."

"And then what the hell does it mean?"

Watt translated: "'Equal validity'. They want the Welsh language to be equal to the English language."

Barlow was magnanimous. "They can have that, as far as I'm concerned."

"And as far as Whitehall's concerned, in theory." Watt's voice hardened. "But only in theory. I'll give you an example. The birth of a child can be registered in Welsh; but only if the local Registrar understands it. Otherwise your ardent Welshman has to journey umpteen miles to find a Registrar who does understand Welsh, and then gets fined for registering outside his own district."

Barlow tut-tutted at this bureaucratic injustice.

"So they protest." Watt reached the inevitable conclusion.

"By blowing up water mains?" There was little doubt of Barlow's abhorrence of such a form of protest.

"That's the violent fringe." Watt shot a hard look at Barlow. "And whether we accept it or not, the fact is that there haven't been many political successes without violence."

Barlow's voice was as caustic as the effluent of the Mersey. "You sound like a public relations man for a bunch of crooks."

Watt explained himself. "It helps to know what we're up against."

"You are against, are you? I was beginning to wonder."

Watt angrily exploded, "Don't be so . . . !" And then hastily caught himself up. The boss was always the boss, and police discipline had to be observed. "I'm sorry, sir." Barlow nodded his acceptance of the apology. And having both cooled down after their brief spat, their faces were sombre as Watt went on to say, "Of course, I'm against violence. I'm against the destruction of property, public or private. And we both know that it doesn't stop there.

Because this lot will kill somebody one of these days, whether they intend to or not."

They were both silent, aware that beyond the abstractions of politics were the harsh realities of death and destruction which they as police officers were pledged to prevent.

Detective Sergeant Hawkins had already gone to the site of the previous night's explosion where he noted, almost with admiration, the skilful way that the amount of explosive and the placing of it had been so exactly judged as to cut a large enough hole for the purpose, without raising so big a bang that every copper in the valley would come racing to the scene to find out what was amiss; noting as well that one unexploded stick of gelignite bore the printed lettering which would enable its source to be traced, and that several detonators, which were also traceable, even after they'd been fired, had been found among the debris.

But what might have been a couple of helpful leads turned out to be more of a confusion, for the gelignite had come from a quarry in North Wales, while the detonators were traceable to a colliery in the South.

The Special Branch Officer who confirmed this came back with Hawkins to meet Detective Chief Superintendent Barlow and Detective Chief Inspector Watt, who had now been officially requested to assist in tracing the terrorists. Hawkins went in to prepare his bosses for the arrival of the Special Branch man. "I've brought Superintendent Evans with me, from the scene," he told them, discreetly lowering his voice.

Barlow looked up sharply. "Evans?" he queried. Hawkins nodded. "You mean . . . a Welshman?" Barlow asked, in total disbelief.

Superintendent Evans, waiting in the corridor, clearly heard this last, though it had been spoken in Barlow's softest tones, for he slipped past Hawkins to say breezily, "That's right . . . set a Taffy to catch a Taffy." Then, not a whit abashed by Barlow's fish-eyed look, he forced the introductions with a cheerful, "Good morning gentlemen! You'll be Mr Barlow." And when John Watt introduced himself, Evans responded with the same plump-fisted and over-sweaty handshake that Barlow had just been treated to, accompanied with a knowing, "Heard of you too, Johnnie-Boy!"

God help us, thought John Watt. Johnnie-Boy! We've got a right one here. And he exchanged a glance of sympathetic wariness with Barlow.

But despite his outward flabbiness, Superintendent Evans of Special Branch was brisk enough and hard enough when it came down to discussing terrorist suspects. "I've got a list, see," said Evans, making no attempt whatsoever to produce it for Barlow's information. "I've got a list of extremists, activists, and belligerents. It's not a long list."

"Is it accurate?" Barlow slipped in with a malicious twist to his lips.

Evans chose to ignore the malice and answer the question. "As far as we know, it's accurate, Mr Barlow. As far as we know. Can't say it's complete, of course. But every name on it is active, fighting, even extreme."

"So what do you do about them . . ." asked John Watt, not forgetting to say 'sir' to his senior in rank, who had so far failed to give this entitlement to Mr Barlow, who was senior to both of them.

"We watch them, boy," said Evans. "We watch our suspects . . ." and a far-away and somewhat pained look came into his eyes as he added, ". . . as far as we can."

Barlow quickly seized on this. "Which is not very far?"

"How can it be?" Evans's voice was plaintive. "It's not like watching a bunch of crooks. I've got names written down here"; he tantalizingly tapped his breast pocket where his list of terrorists was presumably kept. "I've got names of professors, librarians, even lecturers at Theological colleges as well as other Reverend gentlemen. These are not criminals. These are not thieves. These are respectable people; people of *status*."

If Barlow's eyes could have bored through the cloth to read that list they would have done so. As it was, he had to content himself with asking: "Were any on that list away from their homes last night?"

Evans hesitated before he answered, and Hawkins quickly came in with, "Those who live near either the colliery or the quarry where the explosive materials came from have supposedly been cleared."

"Five of them," explained Evans, "none of whom were away from their homes."

"How do you know?" demanded Barlow.

"I've checked," Evans told him.

"Did you ask them? Did you interview them?"

"Not all of them," Evans was as cautious in his answers as he clearly was in his investigations. He went on to defend this caution, "We've got to watch our step. There's one gentleman, very learned he is. I only have to be wrong about questioning him once more, and he'll have my head on the block."

Watt was thoughtful. "They can't all be so highly educated."

"Indeed no," Evans agreed. "Some of them are only students."

Barlow had picked up John Watt's line of thought. "Students . . . whose status is not so great."

"That is so."

Barlow threw a significant glance at Evans's breast pocket. "How many?"

"About seven."

"And have *they* been interviewed in connection with last night's explosion?"

Evans's reply was guardedly non-committal. "I can't guarantee that they all have."

Barlow and Watt were both sitting upright now, thinking together, working together; and though it was Barlow who kept throwing the questions, it was as though the two of them were speaking with one voice.

"Could you find us two youngish suspects who haven't yet been questioned over last night? Preferably linked in some way to either of the two places where the explosives came from, the quarry or the mine."

"Does it matter which?"

"No. I just need an excuse to call on them. A 'reason to believe' if you like."

Evans's hand crept to his breast pocket and slowly brought forth several closely spaced pages of typescript. Watt's eyebrows lifted as he exchanged a look with Barlow. Were there really so many Welshmen suspected of terrorism? But Evans had little difficulty in picking out of that number the one who fitted the bill for Barlow's devious purpose. "If you have in mind, sir, what I think you have in mind, sir, I'd suggest young Daniel Owen."

John Watt wondered at the sudden sly rash of 'sirs', and whether it had anything to do with Evans's astonishing alacrity in producing this one name. He'd hardly looked at his list to find it. Hawkins, who was more fully briefed on the morning's investigations, knew the reason why. "Daniel Owen is the one real lead, sir."

Evans explained, "Daniel Owen has a car. And whoever did last night's little job would need a car since the place is miles from nowhere."

"And a car was seen . . . ?"

"By a sergeant who noted a grey Morris 1100 in the early hours of the morning, about three miles from the scene of the explosion. He had no reason to pay it special attention, there was no road check on at the time; and if he did hear the bang, well it was just another noise. But he's a careful type, so any traffic he sees tootling around at four thirty AM he takes a note of. And the number he noted is this."

Evans placed on the desk a slip of paper with a car number written on it in thick black pencil. Watt stared at it; it was too good to be true. "That number can be traced to Daniel Owen?"

"Not quite," said Evans. "Daniel Owen does have a grey Morris 1100. But its number is this."

He produced another slip of paper with a typewritten number which he placed above the pencilled one. There was a one figure difference between the two numbers.

"The Sergeant could have made a mistake," said Barlow, jabbing at the pencilled registration. Evans did not disagree with this possibility.

"Has the Sergeant's report been checked?" Watt demanded. "Not with Daniel Owen," Evans told him. And then added, choosing his words slowly and carefully, "I was saving him for you."

Barlow looked up in surprise. "Why?"

"He's young, tough, and a bit wild," Evans told him.

"Are you frightened of him?" Barlow nearly said. But though he bit the words off half way, Evans caught at his meaning. "No, Mr Barlow, sir," he answered, with no apparent rancour at the imputation. "I'm not frightened of him. But neither is he frightened of me. He knows me too well. He's seen me too often."

Barlow looked at Watt thoughtfully. "But he's not seen either of us."

Evans ignored the inclusion of Watt, and said straight out to Barlow, "He's certainly never seen *you*."

Barlow sat back heavily in his chair. "And you want me to frighten him?"

"Certainly not," Evans said hastily. And then with a bland deviousness that was near the equal of Barlow's he carefully explained, "It's just that . . . well, I'd feel there were better hopes of a satisfactory outcome if someone of your status saw him."

Watt nodded his head in understanding. "Sefyllfa," he said slowly. Only it sounded like 'sevulva'. Barlow raised an astonished eyebrow. "Means 'status'," Watt explained to him. And Evans nodded admiringly. "They told me you were conscientious, Johnnie. You've been learning Welsh."

"Just a word or two," said Watt modestly.

"That's one of the important words," said Evans.

And Sergeant Hawkins, whose own lack of status pressed heavily upon him, uttered his sombre agreement.

Barlow, impatient of this mood of solemnity, broke their triple reverie. "Aye. Where does this Daniel Owen live?"

Evans wrote the address on the slip of paper with the typewritten car number upon it, and handed it to Barlow. "You remember the colliery where the detonators came from . . . it's quite near there."

The Crime Squad trio drove to the Welsh mining valley which was the home of Daniel Owen. When they came in sight of the pit-head that stood tall sentinel above the village they went separate ways, Watt going off alone to follow up a lead that Evans had provided on one of Owen's close acquaintances, while Barlow and Hawkins went straight to the terraced street where the young man lived. They parked the car away from the house and walked the last few hundred yards, but for all their efforts to obscure their arrival their brisk and confident march along the street was the tread of strangers in a place where men walked slowly to pass the time of day. Barlow slowed his pace to let Hawkins go ahead and beat a rat-tat on the gleaming knocker of number twenty-seven. For a long moment there was neither sound nor movement from inside the house. Barlow patiently shifted his weight from one foot to another; all his life he was used to waiting on doorsteps.

At last, the door opened slowly, reluctantly. The woman who stood with her hand upon the latch was all stillness, but it was the stillness of resignation rather than repose. In answer to Hawkins' enquiries she admitted nothing more than that she was the mother of Daniel Owen, that her son was in, and – after having closed the door on Barlow and Hawkins for a further few minutes – that her son did not wish to speak to them. Hawkins put his foot in the door before she could close it again. "We don't want a fuss, Mrs Owen, do we?"

"Why not then?" she answered, with spirit. "Our neighbours are used to the police coming here. Don't even bother to look out of the windows any more. Used to it, they are."

Barlow, who saw through this show of unconcern, asked her directly, "Are *you*? . . . used to it?" And Mrs Owen's bravado blew away like thistledown. "No," she admitted, and there was more sorrow in the single word than in a valley of tears. Barlow was gentle with her: "Don't make it harder for yourself. Let us in, or send Daniel out. We need a word with him – for his own good." And in a harder voice, pitched up for the benefit of the listener within, he said to Hawkins, "Imagine . . . a man of twenty-two sheltering behind his mother's apron."

This clearly upset Mrs Owen's pride, maternal and domestic, and the flash of spirit shone through again as she answered, "Why not then? Though I'm sorry about the apron." She removed it with neat dignity, already folding and smoothing it as she looked up at Barlow and told him, "There's no welcome for you in this house. I am *not* asking you in."

She went back into the house leaving the front door open. Hawkins would have slipped in after, but Barlow was not content with this minor victory. "Easy now," he said, holding back Hawkins's impatience. He was playing a bigger fish.

The young man who did come to the door, after keeping them waiting a while longer, had his mother's composure . . . but there was no resignation in it. He answered Hawkins' questions politely enough, except that the answers were in Welsh; it was only the nod of the head that indicated his acknowledgement of being the Daniel Owen they were seeking, and the gesture of invitation that showed his consent to their entering the house.

Barlow and Hawkins followed him down the passage and into the parlour, the neat domestic appearance of which was overlaid by the litter of books stacked in heaps everywhere. Barlow picked one up; the title on the cover was in that same strange consonantal mixture of ds and ws and ls that Watt had lectured him on the same morning; and when he placed it back upon the pile that stood shoulder high, he saw that they too were all Welsh. Barlow regarded them with astonishment; he'd no idea that there were so many different Welsh-language books. Well, if the lad wanted to do all his reading in that strange lingo, it was his look-out, but he had no right to go on answering Hawkins's questions in Welsh. At best, it was lack of courtesy; at worst, it was deliberate obstruction of the police in the execution of their duty. He warned the young man of this, making the statement quietly and in reasonable tones. If there was going to be any hot blood raised by this breakdown in communication, it would come from the young man's side, not from his.

Daniel Owen responded to Barlow's warning with the belligerent utterance of two Welsh words which Barlow immediately recognized from his discussion with Watt the same morning . . . Dilis-something-or-other. "You mean Equal Validity," Barlow snapped back at him. And Owen was so surprised at the Englishman's recognition of the slogan that he unconsciously answered in English, "That's right."

Barlow's lips twitched in a half smile; first round to him. Owen still insisted, though, "I don't do myself justice in English. I prefer to answer your questions in my own language."

Barlow shrugged at this. "Go ahead." And added with a hint of sarcasm that diminished the young man's heroic stance, "After which, you can translate your own reply. Take a little longer, but I'm in no rush."

Owen's response was an angry sputter of Welsh, the tone of which made the meaning clear without any need for translation. Barlow turned an amused look to Hawkins. "Funny how frightened men always get nasty."

Owen's need to deny the accusation of cowardice was strong enough to make him lapse into English for a second time. But in reply to the questions that Barlow then put to him, concerning his whereabouts the previous night, and the present location of his car, Owen once again retreated into Welsh. Barlow had had enough. With a word of warning to the young man first, he and Hawkins closed on him, ready to take him into custody, by force if necessary.

The parlour door opened quietly, so quietly that Barlow knew that Mrs Owen must have been standing outside clutching the handle, waiting for the necessary moment to intervene.

"You've asked the boy where he was last night," she said to Barlow. "He's told you, if you had the wit to understand. He was in his bed upstairs."

"How d'you know?" Hawkins demanded.

"I heard him go to bed," Mrs Owen told him. "I didn't hear him get up again until the morning."

Hawkins dismissed this as an alibi; Daniel Owen might have slipped out while Mrs Owen was asleep. She denied the possibility. "Mr Detective," she addressed him with firm dignity, "I would have heard. I barely sleep you see. Not at night. Not any more."

Barlow's head came up. He had the whiff of a trail that he knew he could pursue with success. And he would be gentle, ever so gentle in pursuing it. "Why don't you sleep, Mrs Owen?" he asked.

"Because I'm worried sick . . . !" Daniel tried to dam the overflowing of his mother's anxieties, but there was no holding them back. "I'm afraid for him. In and out at all hours. People coming and going at all hours. The police coming at all hours . . ."

"And last night?" Barlow gently led her on.

"Nothing last night. He was in his bed."

Barlow knew that she was speaking the truth, and he meant it when he said to her, "I'm glad." Turning to Daniel with studied politeness he asked him to write down the Welsh equivalent phrase for "I was in my bed" in the notebook which Hawkins held open for him. "I've a feeling I'll be hearing that phrase again," he explained. "And I'd like to be able to recognize it." Daniel smiled as he wrote it down. They certainly would be hearing it again . . . and again and again . . . He scarcely noticed what Barlow was saying to his mother, quietly and with great sympathy.

"I had a sergeant once, Mrs Owen. One of the old school. Tough but very human. He used to say that he was really sorry for only one thing. 'I'm sorry,' he used to say, 'for all the thieves' mothers in the world'." Barlow's voice was equally sorrowful as he went on, "I'm beginning to be sorry for the mothers of agitators. You bring them into the world, look after them, educate them . . . and that's a struggle for some folk – widows, for instance, as I understand you are Mrs Owen . . ."

Daniel rudely interrupted Barlow's sob story. "You'll bring tears to my eyes."

"Look at your mother's . . ." Barlow grated at him. Mrs Owen was sobbing quietly, making no attempt to wipe away the tears.

Hawkins took the opportunity of hammering at the agonized young man. "Where's your car, Mr Owen?" Before Daniel could half utter his expectedly incomprehensible Welsh reply, Mrs Owen had answered for him, "He gave permission to some friends to borrow it."

"I was afraid of that," said Barlow.

"Which friends?" Hawkins asked.

Daniel's terse outburst in Welsh was as good as a refusal to answer. Barlow guessed that Mrs Owen knew who had borrowed the car. Well, she was a sensible woman. It should be possible to persuade her to cough up for her son's own good. "Mrs Owen . . ." his tone was reasonable, ". . . last night a water main was damaged by explosives. You tell me that Daniel was in his bed at the time and I believe you. But a car was seen not far from where the explosion took place, of exactly the same colour and make as your son's, and with nearly the same licence number."

She seized upon this loophole in the case against Daniel. "Only *nearly* the same . . . ?"

Barlow nodded. "You see, I'm being straight with you, Mrs Owen. I'm admitting the possibility that it was another car altogether." Mrs Owen breathed her relief which Barlow gave her no time to enjoy. "It's also possible," he pointed out, "that it *was* your son's car, and the officer who saw it simply made a mistake, a very slight mistake, in noting the number. So we'd like to check on wherever Daniel's car is now."

Still Mrs Owen hesitated to tell him; Barlow drove home the final warning that would play upon her fears, and though his voice was gentle, his words conjured up a picture of bloody violence. "Last night, Mrs Owen, four and a half ounces of gelignite were used to blow that main. Nearly enough to blow up this house and half the street with it." Mrs Owen uttered a gasp of horror; Barlow pressed on, "There's more to it than that, and I'll be frank in telling you. Last night's job was an expert one. Is your son an expert in explosives?"

Mrs Owen's reply was in Welsh, but her face agonizingly said 'no'.

"I was afraid of that, too," said Barlow. "You see, these amateurs get hold of explosives, they don't know how to look after them, they keep them for months, maybe long after they've become dangerous to handle, and what's the result? I'll tell you, Mrs Owen. One of these days, or one of these nights, these bright boys are going to blow *themselves* up." And as he saw the shocked look come upon her Barlow quickly slipped in, "Who borrowed Daniel's car?"

"David James . . ." Mrs Owen's reply was that of an automaton, ". . . lives over in Ebenezer Street. Number thirty-one." Daniel's reproachful, "Oh mam!" was near to despair.

Barlow and Hawkins exchanged a quick look. Chief Inspector Watt, acting on information from Evans, Special Branch, was even then making enquiries about the man James, over in the vicinity of Ebenezer Street. "I'll get the message to Mr Watt, sir," said Hawkins. "He'll need to know about the car when he talks to James."

John Watt could see that David James was pleased with the way the interview was shaping. He'd been nervous at first, frightened of the contained man in the grey overcoat who didn't smile very much, though he didn't shout or bluster either. In fact, for a police officer, and an English one at that, Detective Chief Inspector Watt seemed to be very sympathetic – very understanding, and even approving of the different forms of civil action taken by the Welsh Nationalists to further their cause. John Watt had even expressed his willingness to sign any petition in support of maintaining the Welsh culture, the Welsh institutions, or the Welsh language, as long as it stopped short of approval of any kind of violent protest. But when John Watt tackled the young man on his own attitude towards violence, there was a hesitation in the lad's reply which Watt pigeon-holed for future reference.

In the meantime, and having persuaded the lad that no one was going to subject him to third degree questioning, Watt sought some answers on questions of fact. "Where were you last night?" he asked.

"In bed," David told him.

"Where?"

"Here, of course."

"Why 'of course'?" Watt didn't even try to conceal his astonishment. "At your age I quite often slept away from home."

David James nodded, "So do I." But he said it so solemnly that Watt wondered if the lad had caught his meaning. "So you slept at home last night." Watt pressed the point, "Can you prove it?"

"How?"

"How the hell should I know!" Watt was beginning to get irritated with David James. Wet, that's what he was. Couldn't even provide his own alibi. Did he want Detective Chief Inspector Watt to provide one for him? "You didn't sneak some little Welsh sweetheart into your bedroom?" he suggested.

David was shocked at the idea, which Watt didn't think so very implausible. The lad wasn't at all bad looking, and he'd already said that his parents were away on holiday, which would have made it possible, even easy, to sneak in a girl friend. But if he said he hadn't, well he hadn't. In which case, nobody could possibly have seen him in bed, which made it difficult – as Watt explained to the lad – for anyone to believe his story; managing to convey that he, John Watt, would like to believe it, if only young David could produce a scrap of substantiation. "What time did you go to bed?" he asked, with an underlying air of saying "let's try to tackle your alibi that way".

David had a ready answer. "About eleven," he said promptly. "Just after the Welsh telly news."

Watt shook his head at this, and his tone was that of regret rather than disbelief. "That reply of yours, David . . . it was just a bit too pat. Do you follow me?" And he leaned forward as though to share a confidence. "It's like the too clever thief who says: 'I was watching Panorama at the time, which was about the American Presidential Election'."

"It would be," said David.

Watt nodded his agreement, "Just so." And while the lad was still smirking at this shared insight, Watt shot the next question at him. "Where is Daniel Owen's car? Now, think before you answer, since you were the one who borrowed it."

David's jaw dropped open; and it wasn't all that firm when it was closed, thought Watt. He was glad that he had been given the information about the borrowed car before he came in to talk to David James; it was going to be the clincher in cracking the lad who was, God knew, close enough to cracking already. "It is true, isn't it, that you borrowed the car," demanded Watt. "Or are you going to call your friend, Daniel Owen, a liar?"

David stared in disbelief. "Did he tell you?"

John Watt himself never told a lie when he could avoid it. "Let's say he didn't deny that you've got the car," was his careful reply. "Which Daniel could have done. Except that he's got his own skin to save."

There was a fierceness about David's refusal to believe this imputation of his friend's disloyalty which Watt shoved in the same mental pigeon-hole as his earlier thoughts about the lad. But there was the matter of the borrowed car to clear up first. "Where is it?" he demanded. And went on to threaten the lad with arrest if he refused to answer, a threat which he had every intention and every right of carrying out.

David clearly had no stomach for taking his resistance that far. "The car's in the garage," he told Watt. "Our garage. My dad's garage."

"What's it doing there?"

David shrugged. "Better than out in the street."

"It's going to be looked at," said Watt. "A touch of the old forensics. Did you use it last night? Or anybody else?"

"I didn't. Nor did anyone else . . . to the best of my knowledge."

Watt shook his head . . . "That's another tricky answer. Never mind. When did you borrow it?"

"Two days ago."

"Why did you borrow it?"

"To go for a run."

"Did you go?"

"No."

Watt's ear had picked out a note of envy in the lad's last replies. "You've no car of your own?" he asked casually.

"No."

"Do you want one?"

"Of course."

Watt held the lad's gaze, like a snake fixing a rabbit. "You could get a car of your own, you know." He kept talking, spelling it out slowly, "By keeping your eyes open . . . And opening your mouth a bit . . . In a good cause."

David's gaping mouth snapped shut. "I would never betray . . ." he began, without saying just what it was that he held so sacred.

"Just consider who you'd be helping," Watt pointed out. "You lot are doing all right now. Every time you make a legal protest, you're winning. But if you mean to go beyond that, then watch it."

"We're not afraid," said David James. But his voice was not as firm as he intended it to be.

Watt's face was sombre as he told the lad, "I am afraid, David. Not *of* you, but *for* you. Somebody's already been hurt by these bomb protests, you know that. One of these days, someone might even be killed." Watt caught the shade of a tremor across the lad's face, and he pressed home the point. "You're like me, David. You get frightened. When you see a stick of gelignite, you want to run. I know that I do. I'm against gelignite."

"So am I," David said.

"Then make your own protest," Watt told him, ". . . against explosives." Watt took a pencil from his pocket, and while the lad watched him, he wrote a number in the margin of a newspaper that lay on the table. It was the number of the private telephone line at the Wyvern Crime Squad office, the line reserved for police informants. "I'm glad to have met you, Dafydd," he said, giving the name its Welsh pronunciation. "Any time you want to talk to me, just call that number. You could be doing everybody a favour. Your cause, your country . . ." hat in hand, Watt was already at the doorway; he turned to say as an afterthought, "And you'd be doing a favour for yourself."

"David James didn't do it."

"And Daniel Owen didn't do it."

The three Crime Squad officers had met up again with Superintendent Evans of Special Branch to compare notes on their investigations of the two young men. Barlow was convinced that Mrs Owen was telling the truth in claiming that her son was in bed at the time of the blowing up of the water main; while Watt's instinct told him that the other lad hadn't the guts to tell a straight-out lie about it. Moreover, the car seen on the road nearby . . . the car that looked like Daniel Owen's, was the same colour as Daniel Owen's, and had nearly the same registration number as Daniel Owen's, turned out to be a different car entirely, owned by someone else in the locality with a perfectly good reason for being out and about at four-thirty in the morning.

Barlow had a feeling though, that there was some purpose behind one of the lads loaning his car to the other.

"They were going to do something," John Watt agreed. "But I don't think that David James will now."

Superintendent Evans looked at the quiet self-contained man with a new respect. "Scared him off, did you?" he suggested.

"A bit." Watt's face was expressionless as he added, "I said we'd be interested in buying him off too."

Barlow and Evans responded with equal casualness to the possibility, sorting out in a moment that neither of them were likely to make a suitably soft impression on the young man, which left it to Detective Sergeant Hawkins to follow up John Watt's first sounding out. Watt noticed that Harry Hawkins' usually prognathous jaw jutted out even further as his senior officers discussed the method of approach. What's biting our Harry? John Watt wondered. It wouldn't be the first time he'd done a deal with an informant.

"How much are we going to offer?" John Watt raised the question as a practical issue; which Barlow followed up with an even more loaded question, directed straight at Superintendent Evans of Special Branch: "Whose funds will it come from?"

"There'd be no trouble about who paid, sir," Evans assured him. "We would." And then added hastily, lest Crime Squad should let their generosity run away with Special Branch's funds, "Keep it around fifty quid . . . for the first time anyway."

While Barlow and Evans went off to continue their higher level deliberations – over a shared bottle of whisky, Watt suspected – Hawkins stayed to splutter up his bubbling dissatisfaction to John Watt. "What a job you've landed me this time, sir! . . . Trapping a kid into betraying his mates."

"It's distasteful," John Watt agreed. But to Hawkins's impertinent "You can say that again!" he snapped back "And you can keep a civil tongue in your head." Cheeky young devil. And him only a Detective Sergeant, speaking like that to a Detective Chief Inspector. Still, the young 'uns had to learn, and some of the lessons weren't easy. Like this one of betrayal. It was distasteful, even creepy. But as he explained patiently, if somewhat wearily, to Harry Hawkins, "We shall never crack this bombing set-up without an informant. Not in a month of Sundays. But over in Ebenezer Street there is a potential informant. So go and recruit him. And discover there's more to police work than shouting."

*   *   *

Harry Hawkins needed a reason for calling at Ebenezer Street. You don't knock at a man's door and offer to buy his conscience straight out. So he presented himself to David James as a forensics expert, come to inspect the car borrowed from Daniel Owen, and confirm that it had not been driven about in the vicinity of the sabotaged water main within the previous twenty-four hours. James opened up the garage and stood looking on while Hawkins scraped bits of earth from various parts of the car's chassis and put them into labelled envelopes in what he trusted was a suitably scientific sort of way. And while he worked, he talked, letting the conversation hover, like a butterfly around a buddleia bush, round and about the subject of selling information. Soon Hawkins forgot his scruples and lost himself in the enjoyment of playing his 'snout' like a fish on the end of a line; baiting the hook with talk of sports cars and the kind that young David James wished he could afford to buy; casting it on the water with practical advice on how David could explain a sudden rush of wealth as a win on a Premium Bond; making a strike with a precise demand for information on where and when the next sabotage incident was likely to take place; giving the lad his head on a loose line while his conscience kept him dashing to and fro; then slowly reeling him in . . . closer . . . closer . . . ready to fall into the net. It wasn't so much different from playing a criminal snout, except that the cost of ideological betrayal seemed to be higher. "Fifty pounds . . ." Hawkins dropped into the conversation, going to the limit that he'd been authorized to offer; to which David James responded with a phrase in Welsh and a wry twist of his mouth.

"What are you on about?" asked Hawkins. And wasn't surprised when James translated the phrase as: Thirty pieces of silver. It was just the sort of melodramatic attitudinizing

157

that had got these crackpots up to whatever antics they'd been dallying with.

"You were going to do something, weren't you?" Hawkins put to him.

"He was."

"Daniel Owen?"

"Yes."

"But not you?"

James shook his head. Hawkins casually asked, "What were you going to do?" When James tried to hedge by pleading uncertainty of the plans, Hawkins brutally told him, "You're no good to us then."

David James's sallow face took on an even more waxen tinge. It was the crunch; he either had to talk to Hawkins now, tell all he knew; or forget about whatever hungers were driving him on to betraying his friends. He still seemed to be dithering as he stated obscurely, "His mother thinks I've got the car."

"She was right."

"He wasn't really keeping it a secret then," James pointed out. "Even you know I've got it."

Hawkins was puzzled. What was this leading to? James babbled on, "Daniel Owen . . . he's not stupid. He wants me to drive the car about . . . tonight."

Hawkins's back went rigid. Tonight! Christ, was it going to be as soon as that? Outwardly though, he was as casual as ever, as he prompted the lad, "Just drive it about?"

James explained, "He reckons you'll follow the car. Keep an eye on it anyway. And you'll see nothing. For I shan't be doing anything."

"But somebody else will?"

"Yes."

"Daniel Owen?"

James nodded.

"What will he be doing?"

"I'm not sure."

Hawkins was already translating promises into hard cash, counting out five one-pound notes from his wallet as he told the lad, "We could test your idea. If there's anything in it, we'd pay . . . just for the idea. Meantime, this is on account." He held out the cash; before James could even crook his fingers to take it, Hawkins drew it back, slowly, just enough to leave the fluttering notes within reach of a longer grasp, if David James would only stretch out his hand. "There's more for you, now," Hawkins promised, ". . . if you tell more now."

James was really caught. The plan, of which he clearly knew every detail, spilled forth from his lips. "Daniel's coming here at seven. We drive around a bit. Perhaps have a drink or a bit of supper somewhere. I drop him back home by nine."

"And then we follow you?"

James nodded. "He reckons you'll do that as long as I'm driving his car."

"While he slips out on foot?"

"Out of the back of his house. He's counting on your not watching it back *and* front . . ." He faltered in the telling of the plan. Hawkins added five more one-pound notes to the five already in his hand. "Keep on talking."

James drew a deep breath. "He'll be meeting two others . . . going by bus to the rendezvous . . . *9.23* from the bus station."

"Where to?" Hawkins demanded.

"Hir Deitho."

He could just as well have said Llanfair . . . whatever it was, for all that meant to Harry Hawkins. "What's at this place . . . ?"

"Hir Deitho? It's where there's a water main."

Another one, thought Hawkins, like last night's. These jokers are not kidding. "Does the bus go all the way there?" he questioned. And when James retreated into a sideways glance, he demanded, "Come on! Come on!"

"He'll be getting off two stops before the Hir Deitho terminal . . ." the words were tumbling out now in his eagerness to void the last bitter-tasting residue, ". . . there'll be a car waiting to pick him up. From then on I don't know . . . I don't know . . . I don't know."

Hawkins was already adding another five to the ten one-pound notes in his hand, having satisfied himself that he'd got from the lad all that he had to tell, when a sudden creak of the garage door made him turn and brought a gasp of alarm from David James. It was Watt, with a word of caution for James. "Your voice pitches up, you know. I heard some of that. Not that I'm saying it to frighten you. Just speaking the truth . . . as I hope you were."

"I was," James assured him.

Watt nodded. "In which case . . . you'll be driving Daniel Owen about for two hours this evening before you go your separate ways. Two hours of just you and your friend together, with him not knowing about this chat, and you not letting on. Do you think you can keep it up?"

"Oh yes." There was a half smile on David James's face, and all the half hints that Watt had previously pigeon-holed suddenly fell into place as he said, "You see, I don't very much like Daniel Owen."

The trailing operation that evening was carefully set up, even to the extent of laying on a rather too conspicuous car-full of plain clothes men to continue following David James when he drove away, alone, from Daniel Owen's front door. A more discreet observer checked Daniel into his own house and out of it again – after a brief but far from reassuring word with Mrs Owen – by the back door.

Meanwhile John Watt was making his way to the bus station to catch the *9.23* bus to Hir Deitho. A quiet man in a grey overcoat who looked as though he might be an insurance collector out on an evening round as he boarded the bus a few seconds after Daniel Owen and settled himself a couple of seats in front of the lad. The bus whined its way along the quiet roads, up and down the sides of the valley, through the villages already half slumbering, climbing towards the crouching hill top; and in its wake a small car meandered gently, sometimes close enough for the driver to read the destination board 'HIR DEITHO', but more often so far back that the bus was no more than a faint glow around a bend of the valley road. Hawkins's hands on the wheel of the car were relaxed, now that his earlier qualms were submerged in the need for action. This was something he understood; the hard-grinding, patient, solitary existence that was so much a part of Crime Squad life; watching, waiting for the crime to take place or at least be attempted; being almost disappointed when it didn't happen, which was more often than not; but getting that adrenalin kick of satisfaction on the rare occasions when one of the 'big ones' was caught and put inside for a stretch that would confound his knavish tricks for a long while to come. These bombers now; true enough, they weren't criminals, but a quantity of 'gelly' going off was a nasty business, no matter who it was that was doing it or for what reason. Bombing was dangerous; people got killed.

Daniel Owen didn't look like a killer as he got off the bus at a deserted wayside stop and turned about to head back the way he'd just come. John Watt saw him go, watching the lad's reflection in the side window as the bus started up again to carry him on to the next stop. A pleasant young man who looked as though he cared; if he'd only channel his caring in a more sensible direction . . . and the others mixed up with him in the whole silly business.

The two young men in the car that picked up Daniel Owen a few moments after he got off the bus were very much like him, young, alert, eager-looking. Hawkins saw the pick-up take place and nodded his satisfaction; so far the James boy's information had proved accurate; if they stopped the car now they'd likely find the gelly on board and be able to take the three lads on a charge of unlawful possession of explosives. But they needed more, they needed evidence of intention, which meant letting them get a bit closer to the water main before dropping on them. Anyway, picking the right moment was something for Mr Watt to decide.

Watt got off the bus at the stop after the one where Daniel Owen had alighted and walked briskly along the road like a man with somewhere to get to and no time to be lost in getting there. The car with the three young men in it passed him, and if Daniel Owen did feel a flash of alarm at once again seeing his fellow passenger on the bus, his fears must have been allayed by the rear view sighting of the grey-coated man being rapidly left behind as their car turned the corner. A moment after their tail lights disappeared, Hawkins's car stopped to pick up Watt and swiftly followed at their heels.

The two cars were now approaching the village at the HIR DEITHO bus terminal, above which was the water main now under threat from the saboteurs. Two side roads led up towards the water main. The car containing the three young Welsh lads and perhaps the sticks of gelignite slowed down as it neared the first of these side roads. Hawkins automatically speeded up and passed it; follow-the-leader was a dead give-away in the trailing game; better to go past and then turn round and come back again. No fear of losing the quarry with other police cars lying tucked away in the vicinity, waiting for the radio call that would bring them roaring up to their rendezvous with the bombers.

Nervous and edgy were these three bombers as their car stopped within sniffing distance of the water pipe-line. Daniel Owen got out and took from the back seat a bundle that looked like a number of dirty greasy candles bound round with black insulating tape. Sweaty they were in his hands, and sweaty was he himself, feeling the trickles soak his skin and then turn icy cool in the night air. The car howled and moaned as it made a three point turn on the rough lane, manoeuvring to face the way it came from for a quick get-away. The wheels spun on a patch of loose earth as the driver wrenched at the steering wheel in the darkness that was suddenly, blazingly lit up by the headlight flare of two cars approaching at speed, two police cars, the one a patrol car with two uniformed men, the other the small saloon with Hawkins and Watt; all four police officers already out and running across to where the two young men still sat in their car, held there by the paralysing headlight glare. But the third man, Daniel Owen, already out of the car and on his feet, with desperation to drive his heels, sprang for the covering darkness and fled like a fox across the hillside. Over the gorse he sped, with Watt and Hawkins close behind him. But it was his country not theirs, and gradually the distance between them lengthened until he was only a remote figure sharply outlined on the hill crest, with what looked like a bundle of sticks clutched in his hand; a figure that stumbled and nearly fell, pitching the bundle sharply to the ground at his feet.

John Watt saw it go, and automatically shielded his face with his arm; Hawkins was caught by the searing flash that blinded him for a moment and made his heart start a sudden thumping. When he'd blinked his vision back again, he saw that on the hill crest nothing stirred. Next to him, John Watt shuffled his feet and coughed. There was no need of going to look for a body; with that much of an explosion there'd only be bits left. The night air was cold and there was a bitter taste in it; of exploded gelignite and drifting dust; of an investigation successfully carried out and a file closed; of a mother's heart broken and a young man's life thrown away.

MAIGRET

(BBC TV, 1960–1963)
Starring: Rupert Davies, Ewen Solon &
Helen Shingler
Directed by Andrew Osborn
Story 'Inspector Maigret Hesitates' by
Georges Simenon

Another television crime series also became essential viewing on Monday nights in the Sixties, *Maigret*, based on the best-selling novels by Georges Simenon. The methodical, pipe-smoking Parisian Commissioner of Police who had first appeared in the novel, *The Strange Case of Peter the Lett* in 1931, came to the small screen in October 1960 having already been broadcast on the radio in France and been adapted for several European and American films starring Albert Prejean, Harry Baur, Jean Gabin and Charles Laughton. But it was undoubtedly the performance by Rupert Davies, a stolid, heavy-set English character actor who also enjoyed smoking a pipe, that established the French detective as a top favourite with television audiences. Even Georges Simenon who had not been very impressed with any of the earlier impersonations of Maigret, congratulated Davies and gave his blessing to several years of adaptations. Sadly for the star, however, Rupert Davies became so typecast by *Maigret* that he found it virtually impossible to get any further acting roles after the end of the programme on Christmas Eve, 1963. The popularity of the character has remained undiminished, none the less: many of the Maigret novels are still in print, and in 1992 he was brought back to British television screens in a new series featuring the distinguished Shakespearean actor, Michael Gambon, which ran for two seasons until the star, probably fearing a repeat of what had happened to his predecessor, refused to make any more.

Georges Simenon (1903–1989) is one of the phenomenons of twentieth century literature. Born in Belgium, he began his working life as a police court reporter in Liege, but in 1932 moved to Paris where he launched what was to prove an amazingly prolific writing career producing crime stories under a variety of pen-names for various magazines. It was with the creation of Maigret in 1931, however, that Simenon found fame – and within a year his first three novels about the unique detective had been translated into a dozen languages and the detective was well on his way to challenging the worldwide popularity of those other two icons of the genre, Sherlock Holmes and Hercule Poirot. (Holmes has, of course, also been the subject of a hugely successful Granada TV series which ran from 1984 to 1994 starring Jeremy Brett, and Poirot has been equally well portrayed by David Suchet for LWT between 1989 and 1996.) Today, the majority of the Maigret novels have been adapted for TV in either the Rupert Davies or Michael Gambon eras, although a number of short stories still await adaptation for British audiences. One such is 'Inspector Maigret Hesitates', written in 1944, which was used in a German TV series, *Maigret* starring Heinz Ruhmann (1965–1968). Described as 'a case so puzzling that Maigret could not make up his mind to

take action' it is surely ideal for when – not *if* – the next series of this classic crime-fighter reaches the small screen . . .

Inspector Maigret stood still for a moment in front of the black-iron railings separating him from the garden. The enamel plate bore the number 47B.

It was five o'clock in the evening, and totally dark. Behind him a branch of the Seine flowed sullenly round the long unfrequented island of Puteaux, with its waste ground, coppices, and tall poplars.

In front of him, by way of contrast, on the other side of the railings was a small modern property of Neuilly, the Bois de Boulogne district, all comfort and elegance, and, just now, carpeted with autumn leaves.

Number 47B stood at the corner of the Boulevard de la Seine and the Rue Maxime-Baes. Lights were on in the second-floor rooms, and Maigret, standing with hunched shoulders under the rain, decided to press the electric bell set in the garden gate.

It is always embarrassing to disturb a quiet house, particularly on a winter's evening, when it is snugly self-contained and full of intimate warmth, and especially when the intruder has come from Police Headquarters with his pockets full of unpleasant documents.

A light appeared on the ground floor, the front door opened, and a manservant peered out, trying to see the visitor before crossing the garden in the rain.

"What is it?" he asked through the railings.

"Dr Barion, please?"

Maigret could see that the hall of the house was elegant, so he automatically stuffed his pipe into his pocket.

"Who shall I say?"

"You must be Martin Vignolet, the chauffeur?" asked the Inspector, to the great surprise of his questioner.

At the same time Maigret slipped his visiting card into an envelope, which he sealed.

Vignolet was a rawboned, thick-haired fellow of between forty-five and fifty, quite clearly a countryman.

He went up to the first floor and came back a few minutes later.

Maigret followed him up, past a child's stroller.

"Come in, won't you?" said Dr Armand Barion, opening the door of his consulting room.

He had the pale face and dark-ringed eyes of a man who has not slept for several nights.

As Maigret was about to speak he caught the sound of children's voices at play, coming from the ground floor . . .

Even before he went into the house the Inspector had already known what the household consisted of.

Dr Barion, a specialist in tuberculosis, and a former student of Laennec Hospital, had been living at Neuilly only three years, and, while taking private patients, he still carried on his laboratory research.

He was married, with three children – a boy of seven, a girl of five, and a baby of a few months, whose stroller Maigret had noticed.

The domestic staff consisted of Martin Vignolet, who was both chauffeur and manservant, his wife Eugenie the cook, and finally – until three weeks ago – an eighteen-year-old Breton girl, Olga Boulanger . . .

"I suppose you know what I have come about, Doctor? As a result of the post-mortem, Miss Boulanger's parents, on their lawyer's advice, have decided to bring an action, and it is my duty . . ."

His whole attitude seemed to express apology and, in

fact, Maigret felt a certain reluctance at tackling this case.

Three weeks before, Olga Boulanger had died in a rather mysterious way, but the doctor who was called in had, nevertheless, signed the death certificate.

The girl's parents had come up from Brittany for the funeral, a pair of typical hard, wary countryfolk, and they had discovered, heaven knows how, that their daughter was four months pregnant.

Somehow they had got in touch with Barthet, one of the most ruthless of lawyers. And on his advice, a week later, they had demanded the exhumation and an autopsy of the body.

"I've got the report with me," Maigret sighed, with a gesture toward his pocket.

"You needn't bother! I know all about it, particularly as I got permission to assist the police surgeon."

The doctor was calm, although he looked weary and even feverish. Dressed in his lab coat, he stood with his face under the light, looking Maigret in the eyes without trying to avert his own.

"Of course I was expecting you, Inspector."

A photograph of his wife stood on his desk in a silver frame, a pretty young woman of barely thirty, with a delicate appearance.

"Since you've got Dr Paul's report with you, you must be aware that we found the poor girl's intestine riddled with minute perforations which must have induced rapid blood poisoning. You know, too, that after intensive research we succeeded in determining the cause of these perforations, which had puzzled my learned colleague and myself.

"It had puzzled us so much that we felt bound to appeal for help to a colonial doctor to whom we owe the answer to the riddle."

Maigret was nodding restlessly and Barion seemed to guess what he wanted, for he broke off to say, "Please smoke, by all means. I don't smoke myself, for my patients are mostly children. A cigar? No? Then I'll go on.

"The method used to kill my maid – for there's no question that she was killed – is current, so it seems, in Malaya and the New Hebrides. The victim is induced to swallow a certain quantity of those fine bristles, as sharp as needles, that are found on some ears of grain, such as rye.

"These bristles remain in the intestine, the walls of which they gradually pierce, which inevitably causes—"

"Excuse me." Maigret sighed. "The post-mortem also confirmed that Olga Boulanger was four months pregnant. Is she known to have associated with anyone?"

"No. She seldom if ever went out. She was a rather awkward little thing with a freckled face . . ."

And the doctor hurriedly went back to his story.

"I must confess, Inspector, that since that post-mortem ten days ago I've been entirely taken up by this business. I've no ill-feeling toward the girl's parents, who are simple people and who obviously consider me responsible.

"But it would be an absolute tragedy for me if I did not succeed in finding out the truth. Fortunately, I've already done so to some extent."

Maigret found it hard to conceal his surprise. He had come to investigate a problem, only to find himself confronted, so to speak, with a ready-made investigation and faced by a calm, clear-headed man making a full statement.

"What day is it today?" said the doctor. "Thursday? Well, since last Monday, Inspector, I've had material proof that poor Olga was not the intended victim.

"How did I find out? In the simplest possible way. I had to discover in what article of food she could have swallowed the rye bristles. As she would never have thought of killing herself, particularly in such an unusual and extremely painful way, clearly some outside cause was indicated."

"Do you think perhaps your chauffeur Martin was involved with her?"

"He was. I know it for a fact," agreed Dr Barion. "I questioned him on the subject and he eventually admitted it."

"Has he ever lived in the colonies?"

"Only in Algeria. But I can assure you right away that you're on the wrong track.

"Patiently, with the help of my wife and the cook, I drew up a list of all the foodstuffs we have had in the house lately and I even analyzed some of them.

"On Monday, when I had almost given up hope of getting any results, as I was sitting here in the consulting room my attention was caught by the sound of footsteps on the gravel and I saw an old man making his way toward the kitchen, as if he were a familiar visitor.

"It was old Mr Monday, as we call him, whom I'd quite forgotten about."

"Mr Monday?" echoed Maigret with a smile of amusement.

"It's the children's name for him because he comes every Monday. He's a beggar of the old-fashioned sort, clean and respectable, who goes on a different round every day.

"Here, it's on Monday. And it has gradually become a tradition with us to keep a whole meal ready for him, and it's always the same meal, for on Mondays we have chicken with rice, and he sits quietly in the kitchen eating his share.

"He amuses the children who go and chat to him.

"I had already noticed some time ago that he used to give each of them one of those cream cakes they call eclairs, and I rather objected . . ."

Maigret, who had been sitting still for too long, got up,

and the doctor went on, "You know the way tradesmen have of giving presents out of their stock to the poor rather than money. I suspected that these eclairs came from a local pastry cook's and were probably stale. I said nothing to the old man for fear of hurting his feelings, but I told my boy and girl not to touch the eclairs."

"And the maid ate them instead?"

"Most probably."

"And it was in these eclairs . . . ?"

The doctor said, "This week Mr Monday came as usual with his two eclairs wrapped up in white paper. After he had gone I examined the cakes, which I shall show you presently, and I found there enough rye bristles to have caused the damage that brought about Olga's death.

"Do you understand now? The intended victim was not that poor girl, but my children."

The children's voices could still be heard on the floor below. It was quiet and warm in the room; from time to time the swish of motor tires sounded on the asphalt of the embankment.

"I've not spoken to anyone yet. I was waiting for you."

"Do you suspect that old beggar?"

"Mr Monday? Certainly not! In any case I've not told you the whole story and the rest of it will certainly clear the poor old fellow.

"Yesterday I went to the hospital and then I visited some of my colleagues. I wanted to know whether they had recently had to certify any cases similar to that of Olga Boulanger."

His voice was unemotional, but he passed his hand across his forehead.

"Now I have found out conclusively that at least two people have died in the same way – one nearly two months ago, the other only three weeks ago."

"Had they eaten any eclairs?"

"I couldn't find that out, for the doctors had unfortunately mistaken the cause of death and hadn't thought it necessary to demand an inquest.

"Well, there you are, Inspector. I know nothing more, but I've learned enough, as you see, to be terrified. Somewhere in Neuilly there's a lunatic who, I cannot think how, manages to put death into pastries . . ."

"You said just now that you thought your children were the intended victims?"

"Yes – I'm convinced of it. I know what your question implies. How can the murderer have contrived things so that it's only Mr Monday's eclairs that—"

"Particularly as there have been at least two other cases!"

"I know. I can't understand it . . ."

The doctor seemed sincere and yet Maigret could not help watching him surreptitiously.

"May I ask you a personal question?"

"By all means."

"Forgive me if it offends you. The Boulangers accuse you of having had an affair with their daughter."

The doctor hung his head and muttered, "I knew that would come out! I don't want to lie to you, Inspector. It's true, stupidly true. It all happened one Sunday when I was alone here with the girl . . .

"I'd give everything in the world for my wife not to know, for it would distress her too much. On the other hand I can give you my word as a doctor that Olga had already become my chauffeur's mistress . . ."

"So that the child—"

"Was not mine, I assure you. Anyhow, Olga was a good girl who'd never have dreamed of blackmailing me. You see—"

Maigret was anxious not to allow him time to collect himself.

"And you know nobody who . . . Wait a minute. You spoke just now of some lunatic—"

"Of course! Only it's impossible – physically impossible! Mr Monday never goes to *her* place before coming here! When he goes there afterward, she leaves him standing in the street and throws him a few coppers out of the window."

"Who are you talking about?"

"Miss Wilfur. You'll see that there's a certain justice in things! I adore my wife and yet there are two things I keep secret from her.

"You know the first already. The other is even more absurd. If it were still daylight you could see through this window a house where an Englishwoman of thirty-eight, Laura Wilfur, lives with her invalid mother.

"They are the daughter and widow of the late Colonel Wilfur of the colonial army.

"Over a year ago, when the two women came back from a long stay in the South of France, I was sent for one evening by the young woman, who was complaining of some pain or another.

"I was rather surprised, for one thing because I'm not in general practice, and for another, because I could find nothing wrong with the young woman. I was even more astonished to learn, in conversation with her, that she knew all about my movements, even my most trivial habits, and I only understood when I got back here and saw her window.

"To cut the story short, Inspector . . . Absurd as it may seem, Miss Wilfur is in love with me – hysterically in love as only a woman of her age is liable to be when she lives alone with an old invalid in a huge gloomy house.

"On two further occasions I let myself in for it. I went to

see her and while I was examining her she suddenly seized my head and pressed her lips against mine.

"Next day I got a letter beginning: *My darling* . . . And the worst of it is that Miss Wilfur seems convinced that we are lovers!

"I can assure you of the contrary. Since then I've avoided her. I have had to turn her out of this consulting room, where she came to badger me, and if I've never mentioned it to my wife it's been out of professional discretion and also to avoid arousing unfounded jealousy.

"I know nothing more. I've told you everything, as I had made up my mind to. I'm not accusing anyone! But I'd give ten years of my life to prevent my wife . . ."

By now Maigret understood that the doctor's previous self-possession had been deliberate, prepared in advance, achieved by a great effort of will, and that the man was now almost on the verge of tears.

"Carry on with your inquiry, Inspector. I don't want to influence you."

As Maigret crossed the hall a door opened and two children, a small boy and an even smaller girl, ran past him laughing.

Martin the chauffeur followed behind Maigret and closed the garden gate.

That week, Maigret got to know the district until he was sick of it. With laborious obstinacy he spent hours at a time walking up and down the embankment in spite of the persistently rainy weather and in spite of the astonishment of some servants who had wondered if this suspicious-looking stranger wasn't up to some mischief.

Seen from the outside, Dr Barion's house seemed an oasis of peace, professional activity, and quiet.

Several times Maigret caught sight of Mme. Barion pushing her youngest child in the stroller along the embankment.

And during an interval between showers one morning he watched the two older children at play in the garden, where a swing had been put up.

As for Miss Wilfur, he saw her only once. She was tall and solidly built, quite devoid of grace, with large feet and a mannish walk.

Maigret followed her on the off-chance, but she merely went to change her books at the lending library in a nearby English bookshop.

Then Maigret gradually widened the circle of his wanderings and went as far as the Avenue de Neuilly, where he noticed two pastry shops. The first, narrow and gloomy, with its facade painted an ugly yellow, would have fitted in quite well with the sinister story of the lethal eclairs.

But the Inspector scanned the window display in vain and inquired within. They never made eclairs.

The other was the smart *patisserie* of the neighborhood, with two or three small marble tables at which tea was served: *Patisserie Bigoreau*. Here everything was bright and fragrant and delicious.

A rosy-cheeked girl tripped gaily to and fro, while a distinguished-looking lady presided over the cashier's desk.

Was it possible? . . . Maigret could not make up his mind to take action.

As time passed and his conversation with the doctor grew more remote, the doctor's accusations, re-examined as it were through a magnifying glass, became more and more insubstantial.

So much so that sometimes the Inspector really had the impression of some ridiculous nightmare, some story invented lock, stock, and barrel by a megalomaniac or a desperate man.

And yet the police doctor's report confirmed Barion's

statement: poor freckle-faced Olga had really died as a result of swallowing bristles of rye!

And the following Monday's eclairs, brought by that mysterious figure, Mr Monday, had also contained a considerable number of these bristles, inserted between the layers of pastry.

But couldn't they have been put in later?

To crown everything, although Olga's father had gone home to the village inn he kept in Finisterre, his wife, wearing deepest mourning, had stayed in Paris and hung about police headquarters for days, waiting in the anteroom to waylay Maigret and get news from him. Another believer in the almighty power of the police!

Once she got angry with him and he could almost hear her say with grim features and pinched lips, "When are you going to arrest him?"

Meaning the doctor obviously! Who knew if she wouldn't eventually accuse Maigret himself of some sinister complicity?

Maigret decided to wait until Monday, although he felt almost remorseful about this, particularly as he saw, every morning, a vast tray of eclairs covered with coffee icing in the window of the Bigoreau *patisserie*.

Could he be certain that these were not lethal, too, and that the girl who was carrying three of them away with such tender care, the boy devouring one on his way home from school, were not doomed to suffer Olga's fate?

By one o'clock on Monday he was at his post not far from the cake shop, but it was two o'clock before he caught sight of an old man whom he recognised without ever having seen him.

This was surely Mr Monday, shuffling along with a calm philosophical air, smiling at life, tasting its minutes, treasuring every crumb of them. With a gesture he was obviously used to making, he pushed open the door of the cake shop, and Maigret, from outside, could see Mme. Bigoreau and her daughter good-humoredly exchanging jokes with the old man.

They were pleased to see him, no doubt of that! His poverty was not of the depressing sort.

He was telling them something that made them laugh, till the plump girl at last remembered Monday's ritual. Leaning forward over the window display she chose two eclairs which with a professional gesture she wrapped in a twist of white paper.

Mr Monday, without hurrying, went into the shoe-repair shop next door where he got nothing but a small coin, and then into the corner tobacconist's where he was given a pinch of snuff.

There was nothing unpredictable about his days – that was quite obvious. Monday's people here, Tuesday's people in another district, and Wednesday's people somewhere else – they could all set their watches by his visits. He soon reached the Boulevard de la Seine and his step grew livelier as he drew near the doctor's house.

That was the house he liked, the house where they gave him a real meal – the same meal the family had eaten a little while before; the house where he'd sit down at a table in a clean warm kitchen.

He went in through the back door, like someone who was used to the place, and Maigret rang at the front.

"I should like to see the doctor at once." Maigret told Martin, the chauffeur-houseservant.

He was taken upstairs.

"Would you have the two eclairs brought up at once? The old man's down below."

Old Monday ate his meal without suspecting that in the

doctor's consulting room two men were examining the gift he had brought the children.

"Nothing!" Dr Barion concluded after a close scrutiny.

So there were some weeks when the eclairs were filled with death, and others when they were harmless.

"Thank you," Maigret murmured.

"Where are you going?"

He was too late: Maigret was already halfway downstairs . . .

"This way, monsieur."

Poor Mme. Bigoreau was panic-stricken at the thought that one of her customers might discover that a policeman was visiting her. She took Maigret into a little parlor with leaded-glass windows, adjoining the shop. Tarts were laid out to cool on every available piece of furniture, even on the arms of the chairs.

"I'd like to ask you, why you always give two eclairs rather than any other cakes, to the old man who comes on Monday."

"That's simple enough, monsieur. To begin with, we used to give him anything we had – damaged pastries or stale cakes. Once or twice it happened to be eclairs. Then we gave him something different and I remember how on that occasion he insisted on buying two eclairs as well.

"'They bring me luck,' he said. So as he's a good old fellow, we fell into the habit—"

"One other question. Have you a customer by the name of Miss Wilfur?"

"Yes. Why do you ask?"

"Oh, nothing. She's a nice person, isn't she?"

"Do you think so?"

And the tone of that "Do you think so?" encouraged Maigret to go on.

"Of course, she's a bit of an eccentric—"

"You're right there! An eccentric, as you said, who never knows what she wants! If there were many customers of her sort we'd need twice the staff!"

"Does she come here often?"

"Never! I don't believe I've ever seen her. But she telephones, half in French and half in English so that we're always making mistakes. Do sit down, monsieur. Forgive me for having left you standing."

"I've finished. And please forgive me, madame, for having troubled you."

Three little remarks – enough to explain everything – echoed in Maigret's head.

Hadn't the woman in the shop said about Miss Wilfur: "An eccentric who never knows what she wants."

And then: "If there were many customers of her sort we'd need twice the staff."

And a moment later she admitted that this woman whom she had never seen "telephones half in French and half in English."

Maigret had not wanted to make a point of it. It would be time enough for that when the official examination took place, elsewhere than in the rather sickly atmosphere of the pastry shop.

Apart from the fact that Mme. Bigoreau might quite likely recover her business woman's pride and refuse to speak, rather than admit that she allowed people to send pastries back . . .

For that must be it! The three little remarks she had made couldn't mean anything else!

Maigret walked to Dr Barion's house, his hands thrust deep in his pockets, and as he reached the gate he almost collided with Mr Monday coming out of it.

"Well, did you bring your two eclairs?" Maigret remarked gaily. And as the old man stood dumfounded: "I'm a friend of the Barions. I know that you bring the children some cakes every Monday. But I can't help wondering something: why are they always eclairs."

"Didn't you know? It's a very simple story! Once when I had been given some eclairs, I had them with me and the children saw them. They told me those were their favorite pastry. So, as they're the kindest people on earth who give me the same sort of meal they have themselves, with coffee and all, you understand . . ."

Next day, when Maigret presented himself with a warrant in his pocket to arrest Miss Laura Wilfur, she got on her high horse and threatened to appeal to her ambassador; then she defended herself inch by inch with remarkable coolness.

"Which is just another proof of her insanity!" said the psychiatrist who examined her.

As were her lies – for she insisted she had been the doctor's mistress for a long time. And when the house was closely inspected, a large number of beards of rye were discovered hidden in a desk.

And finally it was learned through her mother that Colonel Wilfur had died in the New Hebrides from multiple perforation of the intestine brought about by a native plot . . .

Maigret saw Martin, the chauffeur, again at the last examination.

"What would you have done about the child?" he asked.

"I'd have gone off with Olga and we'd have opened a country inn somewhere."

"And your wife?"

He merely shrugged . . .

Miss Laura Wilfur, who was so much in love with Dr Barion that she had wanted to kill his children out of spite, had spied on all his movements, had poisoned the eclairs in her ferocious determination to attain her end – she had inserted the lethal beards of rye before telephoning Mme. Bigoreau, pretending there had been a mistake in her pastry order, and asking that the eclairs be picked up . . . Miss Laura Wilfur, who had the inspired notion of using innocent Mr Monday as her unsuspecting instrument, was confined for life in a mental institution.

And there for the past few years she has been telling her companions that she's about to become the mother of a son!

THE PROFESSIONALS

(LWT, 1977–1983)
Starring: Martin Shaw, Lewis Collins &
Gordon Jackson
Directed by Tom Clegg
Story 'The Embassy Incident' by Brian Clemens

The Seventies saw the arrival of the violent crime series in which agents of the law fought criminals with their own weapons: fists, guns and the uncompromising language of the backstreets. The first of these, *The Sweeney* (1975–1978) about the Metropolitan Police's Flying Squad which derived its name in cockney rhyming slang from the notorious Fleet Street mass murderer, Sweeney Todd, featured the exploits of Detective Inspector Jack Regan (John Thaw) and Detective Sergeant George Carter (Dennis Waterman), who were almost as bloodthirsty and earned their fair share of condemnation from viewers and sections of the press. The BBC's answer to the undeniable success of the series was *Target* (1977–1978) with Patrick Mower as the unscrupulous Detective Superintendent Steve Hacket who used tough and often unpleasant methods to combat the smugglers, murderers and bombers who 'targeted' his patch. *The Professionals* took the formula a step further in 1977 with stories about CI5 (Criminal Intelligence 5), an elite undercover crime-fighting squad whose most visible officers were Ray Doyle (Martin

Shaw) and William Bodie (Lewis Collins) reporting to their ruthless taskmaster, George Cowley, played by Gordon Jackson. (Originally, the roles of Doyle and Bodie had been intended for Jon Finch and Anthony Andrews, but both opted out.) The all-action series was an immediate hit – although as a result of complaints about the level of violence LWT ordered that there should be a maximum of two explosions per episode – and made media celebrities of its stars; though neither remembers *The Professionals* today with much affection.

The creator of the series, Brian Clemens (1931–) had been a freelance writer of plays for the theatre and TV before coming to widespread public attention in 1960 by devising the influential comedy suspense series, *The Avengers*, which started its life as *Police Surgeon* with Ian Hendry, but became a cult show once Patrick Macnee had become the dandified central character partnered in his crime-busting exploits by, alternately, three beautiful girls: Honor Blackman, Diana Rigg and Linda Thorson. Brian followed this in 1971 with another success, *The Persuaders*, about two wealthy adventurers, Roger Moore and Tony Curtis, fighting corruption all over the world, before working on *The Professionals* with Albert Fennell who had been an associate on the Patrick Macnee series. Clemens and his production team took full advantage of real life events while making the series – but this rebounded on them on one notorious occasion. After the tragic shooting of policewoman Yvonne Fletcher during the seige of the Libyan Embassy in St James' Square, London in April 1984, demonstrators in Libya apparently believing CI5 to be a real organisation staged their own demonstration around the British Embassy in Tripoli with cries of, 'Down with CI5!' 'The Embassy Incident', written in

1982, is also interesting because of the similarity it bears to another famous incident in May 1980 when members of the SAS stormed the terrorist-occupied Iranian Embassy in Knightsbridge to rescue 19 hostages. This time, though, there was no suggestion that Doyle and Bodie might have been involved . . .

Cowley's car turned into Pickwick Street and slowed to a halt a discreet distance from the Embassy. He gestured vaguely with his right hand as his left opened the suitcase on the seat beside him and began searching for some documents.

"Take a good look," said Cowley over his shoulder, "I'll give you plans of the inside later."

Bodie and Doyle studied the tall building with the large green and red flag over the door. On the first floor balcony a huge poster of a man in a uniform covered with medals drooped in the afternoon rain. A banner hung from the balustrade proclaiming FAISAK: SAVIOUR OF THE PEOPLE in both English and Arabic.

"Seems a popular sort of fellow," observed Bodie.

"He has a simple method of staying that way."

"What's that?"

"He has anyone who disagrees with him killed."

"It's one way to run a country, I suppose," said Doyle.

"It's why so many of his people have fled the country. But even then, his critics aren't safe. Faisak's secret police are sent after them." Cowley brought a folder from his suitcase. "It seems our General is a sensitive wee chappie – critics seem to bring the worst out of him, even from long distances. Listen to this . . ." Cowley began reading aloud from the folder.

"New York, September: Two outspoken exiles shot dead

on a Bronx subway. Paris, November: Attempted poisoning of an exiled family. London, November: Former leader's son falls from penthouse window. Rome, December: Exiled couple disappear." Cowley put the folder down . . . "There's plenty more."

"They're either bumped off or taken back home to stand trial for treason. When they're found guilty, they get shot. Quite a card is Faisak," said Doyle.

"But why should this concern CI5?" asked Bodie.

Cowley opened another folder and handed them a photograph.

"This is Professor Haroud Rashid," he said. "A scientist. He fled to England five years ago after Faisak's men killed his wife and children. He was granted asylum and given protection. He began working for the Nuclear Fuels Advisory Commission, and did very well for himself. Had access to some extremely sensitive information."

"Like where to find the makings of a nuclear bomb?"

"Among other things. Faisak is openly hostile to our country. If he could find out the weak spots in our nuclear power stations he could cause us a lot of aggravation."

"But Rashid wouldn't tell him anything, would he?" asked Doyle.

"Not voluntarily. The trouble is . . . Haroud Rashid disappeared three days ago."

"You reckon they've snatched him?"

"Looks like it. He told a colleague that two of Faisak's men had been following him the day before he disappeared."

"We're too late then," said Bodie, "they'll have him back home by now."

"Or dead," said Doyle.

"We don't think so," said Cowley. "We think they've got him stashed away in the Embassy there."

"Then it's stalemate," said Bodie. "They can't get him out of the country with us watching and we can't get inside because of international law."

Bodie studied Cowley's humourless smile and realised the danger of the forthcoming assignment.

"The Embassy may be out of bounds to CI5," said Cowley, "but since when did two fanatical terrorists pay attention to international law?"

Cowley started up the car and began the drive back to his office. On the way, he explained his plans.

"You get inside the building," said the Scot, "take the entire staff hostage then issue your demands. When these are refused you negotiate. Then you release some prisoners in exchange for concessions."

"What are our demands?"

"It doesn't matter. Just make sure you release Rashid. As soon as you've done that, you can surrender."

"Too simple," said Bodie.

"It can work," argued Cowley as they pulled up in the car park. He led them to the sliding doors of the basement weapons room. "Keep the hostages away from the window and I'll get the press to leave it alone. No-one will be any the wiser."

Inside the weapons room, the noise was deafening. On the practice ranges other CI5 agents fired at moving shadow targets and Cowley had to shout to make himself heard over the staccato explosions of their weapons. They approached a bench where a technician was working on a row of grenades. Cowley indicated a large green shoulder bag.

"Twenty-eight sticks of dynamite, fuses, detonators and eight grenades," he explained.

"What's he doing with the grenades?" asked Doyle, nodding toward the technician.

"He's making them safe. Taking the detonators out. The dynamite's already safe – it's made out of plasticine."

"Safe for whom?" asked Bodie.

"Safe for everyone. The people in the Embassy will never know the explosives aren't real."

"Maybe we should tell them," said Doyle with a grim smile. "After all, we don't want an unfair advantage."

That night Bodie and Doyle set out. Their first inkling that something was wrong came when they found no guard on the Embassy door. He was inside the darkened hallway with a big red hole where his left eye should have been. Bodie bent over the body, and was about to speak when a blinding flash of pain exploded at the base of his skull and fireworks started going off all over his brain.

When he came to, Bodie was still in the hallway. The lights were on and he was staring down the barrel of a Kalashnikov. A hooded figure held the rifle in shaking hands. Against the opposite wall, Doyle stood with his hands held high above his head.

"You're not going to believe this, mate," said Doyle, ignoring the second hooded figure, who was prodding him in the ribs with another Kalashnikov, "but these jokers have beaten us to the punch. The Cow's got a real siege on his hands."

The second man gave Doyle another prod. His voice was on the verge of hysteria.

"Do not speak! Do not move! You are the prisoners of the People's Liberation Army. Understand that we wish you no harm personally, but if you no obey – we kill you!"

Bodie groaned as he climbed to his feet and he and Doyle were hustled up the stairs to a first floor room. The curtains were closed and a third gunman stood over a line of hostages seated against a wall. Bodie and Doyle were pushed to the ground.

"English?" asked the hostage next to Bodie after some minutes.

Bodie nodded.

"You must understand the position. We are all prisoners of these extremists. They hope to engineer the downfall of General Faisak and the destruction of our country."

"What are their demands?"

"The release of all prisoners and the resignation of the government. Of course, General Faisak will not accept these demands."

"And what happens when he refuses?"

"Then we shall be killed," said the man in the same matter of fact tone. "But it will be an honour to die for Faisak, saviour of our people."

"Listen," said Bodie in a low, fierce whisper, "I don't intend dying for anyone just yet; not for Faisak, not for you, not even for your fat uncle Freddie. So tell us how many terrorists there are and just how they intend to blow the place up."

The man looked sullen and averted his gaze. Bodie grasped the man's arm and twisted until he began to talk. "There are three terrorists here. They brought that suitcase you see on the table, the one with the key in it. Inside is a bomb big enough to destroy the building. All it needs to detonate it is for someone to turn the key."

Bodie fingered the fake grenade he had taped to the small of his back. The terrorists had missed it. "Maybe we could bluff them with our grenades," he whispered.

Doyle shook his head. "These guys are too desperate, they don't care if they die. And I wouldn't count on any help from any of our fellow hostages either. They're under the impression that getting blown to bits for the great and glorious Faisak will make them heroes and martyrs."

"Someone should tell them about dead heroes," muttered Bodie.

Suddenly and eerily the sound of Cowley's voice, amplified and distorted by a loudhailer, drifted up to the curtained window from somewhere in the street below. He was asking the terrorists to negotiate.

One of the two hooded men crossed to the window, peered round the curtains and smashed one of the windowpanes with the Kalashnikov's barrel. "Our demands are already known. None of them are negotiable."

"Then release some of your hostages. Give us some assurance that you do not intend people to die needlessly."

"No hostages can be released until our demands are met."

"Then we shall talk again in an hour," said Cowley's voice.

Bodie turned worriedly to Doyle. "He doesn't know it's for real. He thinks that we're still calling the shots."

"I know. And these guys are working on a short fuse."

"We've got to make our move soon. There are only three of them and one is permanently downstairs in the hall. Now when Cowley calls from the street one of the remaining two is going to go over to the window to talk to him. That leaves just the one guarding us. We won't get a better opportunity. If we can get hold of one of those rifles then at least we stand a chance."

A tense hour passed in which the three gunmen argued fiercely with one another in Arabic and spat insults at their hostages. Then once more Cowley's voice came up from the street. "Can you hear me? Release some hostages and we can begin negotiations."

Once again one of the gunmen crossed to the window and replied. However this time it was with an angry, incomprehensible shout and a burst of fire. Bodie and

Doyle heard sudden, startled screaming from outside the window and knew it was time to act. Doyle dived head first at the man standing before them while Bodie endeavoured to knock the rifle barrel aside. He did so just as the guard fired, the bullets spattering into the plaster above the hostages' heads and leaving a scar across the wall and through a portrait of General Faisak. "The window, Bodie," yelled Doyle as his partner grabbed the Kalashnikov from the prostrate gunman. Bodie squeezed the trigger as he fell and the second gunman was spun round with the impact of the bullets, shattering what remained of the glass as he fell through the window onto the balcony. Bodie turned to see Doyle knocking the prone gunman unconscious with a rabbit punch. Behind him the third gunman appeared in the doorway. Bodie fired once more and the man crumpled up against the wall, the unfired Kalashnikov cradled in his lap. Doyle was already dragging the hostages to their feet. "All right. Down the stairs and out of the front door as quickly as you can," he yelled.

Outside Cowley had guessed that something was wrong after the first burst of automatic fire. Consequently, as soon as the hostages emerged into the daylight he was prepared and he and his men rushed them across the street to the safety of a protective cordon of cars. Bodie and Doyle were the last to leave the building, both grinning with obvious relief at how lucky they had been. "Are you all right?" Cowley called from across the street.

"Sure," called back Bodie. "There are three gunmen in there. Two of them are dead and the other's unconscious." But even as he spoke there was a tremendous explosion and the two men were lifted bodily into the air and then flung to the ground in a blizzard of flying glass and bricks. Behind them, in a roaring chaos of smoke and flame, melting metal and fragmenting stone, the Embassy had ceased to exist.

When Bodie awoke he was in a hospital bed. At its foot stood Doyle and Cowley. His head ached and reaching up he found it wrapped in bandages.

"What happened?" he asked.

"Just concussion. You should be out in a couple of days."

"But they blew up the Embassy?"

"Either the guy I hit wasn't unconscious or the other guy wasn't quite dead. One of them got to the suitcase and turned the key. Then Boom. Up goes the Embassy."

"Rashid?"

Doyle looked at Cowley and Cowley looked at his feet.

"Rashid's dead," said Doyle.

"He was still in the Embassy when it went up?" asked Bodie.

"He was dead before that," said Cowley. "You shot him."

Bodie's head began to ache. He rubbed his brow with his fingertips as Cowley explained.

"Intelligence got it wrong. Rashid had disappeared to set up a raid on the Embassy. He'd been in touch with other exiles and they'd asked him to do something to draw the world's attention to Faisak's regime."

"So he set up a siege," said Doyle. "Not very original for a professor."

"But I thought—" began Bodie.

"Don't worry," Cowley cut in, "it's not your fault these people chose London to settle their differences."

But the pain in Bodie's head wouldn't go away.

"We're sent to rescue someone and I killed him," he said quietly. "Faisak couldn't have planned it better himself."

"Rashid got what he wanted," said Cowley, "the story's

all over the papers. You saved innocent people from getting killed. As for Faisak . . ." Cowley's cheeks twitched as he gazed out of the hospital window. ". . . We'll just have to wait . . ."

JEMIMA SHORE INVESTIGATES

(Thames TV, 1983–)
Starring: Patricia Hodge, Yasmin Pettigrew
& Don Henderson
Directed by Tim Aspinall
Story: 'Your Appointment is Cancelled' by
Antonia Fraser

If the Seventies were the era of the violent cop series, then the Eighties can claim to have seen the arrival of the female crime fighter. In April 1980, LWT launched *The Gentle Touch* (1980–1984) which introduced Detective Inspector Maggie Forbes, played by Jill Gascoine, who is now acknowledged to have been Britain's first starring female detective. The hour-long episodes featured Maggie at work on her Seven Dials patch in the heart of London battling with the Soho criminal fraternity and the male chauvinism of some of her colleagues. Less than five months later, in August 1980, she had a rival on BBC in *Juliet Bravo* (1980–1985), with Inspector Jean Darblay (Stephanie Turner), combining the roles of a senior police officer and housewife in a small Lancashire town called Hartley. After three seasons of the series, Inspector Darblay was 'promoted' and Anna Carteret replaced her as Inspector Kate Longton and carried out the same duties without any decline in the show's popularity. While both these ladies were still on the small screen, Agatha Christie's classic amateur detective, Jane Marple, made her debut played by Joan Hickson in *Miss*

Marple for the BBC in which she gave a wonderfully authentic portrayal which continued in adaptations of the novels until the Nineties when age finally precluded her from playing the role any longer. Into this bevy of female crime fighters came perhaps the most unusual of all, Jemima Shore, an investigating TV reporter for Megalith Television who was forever stumbling into mysteries of one kind or another and solving them with a mixture of intuition and painstaking research. Based on the novels and short stories by Antonia Fraser, *Jemima Shore Investigates*, starred the beautiful and versatile Patricia Hodge who took on her first case, 'A Splash of Red' in August 1983 in which the authoress herself also made a brief cameo appearance.

Antonia Fraser (1932–) is, of course, no stranger to the world of television having appeared regularly on arts programmes where she is acknowledged as one of the foremost contemporary biographers. Apart from her critically acclaimed books such as *Mary Queen of Scots* (1969) which won the James Tait Black Memorial Prize for biography, Antonio has a strong affection for crime and mystery stories and created Jemima Shore as an outlet for this interest. A sophisticated, intelligent and music-loving woman, Jemima has a passion for driving fast cars and lying in hot baths where, she says, she does her best thinking when trying to solve mysteries. Two of the great supports in her life are Mrs Bancroft, her possessive landlady, and the resourceful Detective Inspector J.H. Portsmouth – nicknamed 'Pompey of the Yard' – who has more than once come to her aid in a tight corner. 'Your Appointment is Cancelled' is a typical Jemima Shore story which begins innocently enough with the cancellation of a hair appointment, but soon leads her into a case of mystery and brutal murder . . .

"This is Arcangelo's Salon, Epiphany speaking. I am very sorry to inform you that your appointment is cancelled . . ." In sheer surprise, Jemima Shore looked at the receiver in her hand. But still the charming voice went on. After a brief click, the message started all over again. "This is Arcangelo's Salon, Epiphany speaking. I am very sorry to inform you that your appointment is cancelled . . ."

In spite of the recording, Jemima imagined Epiphany herself at the other end of the telephone – the elegant black receptionist with her long neck and high cheekbones. Was she perhaps Ethiopian, Somali, or from somewhere else in Africa, which produced such beauties? Wherever she came from, Epiphany looked, and probably was, a princess. She was also, on the evidence of her voice and manner, highly educated; there was some rumour at the salon that Epiphany had been to university.

As the message continued on its level way, Jemima thought urgently: What about my hair? She touched the thick reddish-gold mass whose colour and various styles had been made famous by television. Jemima thought it was professional to take as much trouble about her hair as she did about the rest of the details concerning her celebrated programme looking into the social issues of the day, Jemima Shore Investigates. She had just returned from filming in Morocco (working title: New Women of the Kasbah) and her hair was in great need of the attentions of Mr Leo, the Italian proprietor of Arcangelo's – or, failing that, those of his handsome English son-in-law, Mr Clark.

But her appointment was cancelled and Jemima wondered what had happened at Arcangelo's.

A few hours later, the *London Evening Post* ran a brief front-page bulletin: a male hair-stylist at a certain fashionable salon had been found when the salon opened that morning with his head battered in by some form of blunt instrument. The police, led by Jemima's old friend, Detective Chief Inspector J.H. Portsmouth – more familiarly known as Pompey of the Yard – were investigating.

As Jemima was mulling this over, she received a phone call from Mr Leo who told her in a flood of Italianate English that the dead stylist was none other than his son-in-law, and that it was he, Leo, who had discovered the body when he unlocked the salon this morning. Epiphany, who normally did the unlocking, having been delayed on the Underground.

"Miss Shore," he ended brokenly, "they are thinking it is I, Leo, who am doing this dreadful thing, I who am killing Clark. Because of her, *mia cara, mia figlia, Domenica mia*. And yes, it is true, he was not a good husband, in spite of all I did for him, all she has been doing for him. In spite of the *bambino!*"

He paused and went on as though reluctantly. "A good stylist yes, it is I who have taught him. Yes, he is good. Not as good as me, no, who would say that? But good. But he was a terrible husband. *Un marito abominabile.* I knew, of course. How could I not know? Everyone, even the juniors knew, working in the salon all day together. *My* salon! The salon *I* have created, I, Leo Vecchetti. They thought they were so clever. Clever! Bah!

"But for that I would not have killed him. She still loved him, my daughter, my only child. For her I built up everything, I did it all. My child, Domenica, and the little one, Leonella, who will come after her. Now he is dead and the police think I did it. Because I'm Italian and he's English. You Sicilians, they say. But I'm not Sicilian. I'm from the North, *sono Veneziano*—" Mr Leo gave an angry cry and the flood poured on:

"What about *her* then?" he almost shouted. "Maybe *she* killed him because he would not leave Domenica and marry her!" He now sounded bitter as well as enraged. "No, Clark would not leave my fine business – the business he would one day inherit. Not for one of those *savages*, not he. Maybe *she* kill him – kill him with a *spear* like in the *films*!"

From this, Jemima wondered if Leo was saying that Epiphany had been Mr Clark's mistress.

"Mr Leo," she said. "When the salon reopens, I want an immediate appointment."

A few days later, Jemima drew up at Arcangelo's in her white Mercedes sports car. The golden figure of an angel blowing a trumpet over the entrance made the salon impossible to miss. Jemima was put in a benign mood by being able to grab a meter directly outside the salon from under the nose of a rather flashy-looking Jaguar being propelled at a rather more dignified pace by its male driver. She glimpsed purple-faced anger, rewarded it with a ravishing smile, and was rewarded in turn by the driver's startled recognition of the famous television face.

Well, I've certainly lost a fan there, thought Jemima cheerfully. She looked through the huge plate-glass window and saw Epiphany, on the telephone, austerely beautiful in a high-necked black jersey. One of the other stylists – Mr Roderick, she thought his name was – was bending over her. Epiphany was indeed alluring enough to make a man lose his head.

Pompey of the Yard, being a good friend of Jemima's from several previous co-operations beneficial to both sides, had filled in a few more details of the murder for Jemima. The blunt instrument had turned out to be a heavy metal hair-dryer. Mr Clark's body had been found – a macabre touch – sitting under one of the grey-and-gold automatic dryers. The medical examiner estimated the time of death as between ten and eleven the previous evening, more likely later than earlier because of the body temperature. The salon closed officially at about six, but the staff sometimes lingered until six-thirty or thereabouts, tending to each other's hair – cutting, restyling, putting in highlights, unofficial activities they had no time for during the day.

The night of the murder, Mr Clark had offered to lock up the salon. (Being one of the senior stylists and, of course, Mr Leo's son-in-law, he possessed his own set of keys.) At five o'clock, he had telephoned Domenica at home and told her he had a last-minute appointment: he had to streak the hair of a very important client and he might be home very late because this client was then going to take him to some film gala in aid of charity, to which she needed an escort – he couldn't offend her by refusing. Domenica, brought up in the hairdressing business and used to such last-minute arrangements, had a late supper with Clark's sister Janice, who had come to admire the baby, and went to bed alone. When she woke up in the morning and found Mr Clark still absent, she simply assumed, said Pompey of the Yard with a discreet cough, that the party had gone on until morning.

"Some client!" said Jemima indignantly. "I suppose you've questioned her. The client, I mean."

"I'm doing so now," Pompey had told her, with another discreet cough. "You see, the name of the famous client whose offer Mr Clark simply could not refuse, according to his wife, was *yours*. It was you who was supposed to have come in at the last minute, needing streaks in a hurry before beginning the new series."

"Needing streaks *and* an escort, to say nothing of what else I was supposed to need," commented Jemima grimly. "Well, of all the cheek—"

"*We* think," Pompey had interposed gently into Jemima's wrath, "he had a date with the black girl there at the salon after everybody had gone. There is a beautician's room which is quite spacious and comfortable, couch and all. And very private after hours."

"All very nice and convenient," Jemima said, still smarting from the late Mr Clark's impudence. "So that's where they were in the habit of meeting."

"We think so. And we think Mr Leo knew that – and, being Sicilian and full of vengeance—"

"He's Venetian actually."

"Being *Venetian* and full of vengeance. There's plenty of vengeance in Venice, Jemima. Have you ever been to the place? Mrs Portsmouth and I went once and when you encounter those gondoliers—" He broke off and resumed a more official tone. "Whatever his genesis, we believe he decided to tackle his son-in-law. That is to say, we think he killed him with several blows with a hair-dryer.

"Mr Leo has no alibi after nine o'clock. After a quick supper at home, he went out – he says – to the local pub, returning after it closed. But nobody saw him in the pub and he is, as you know, a striking-looking man. He had plenty of time to get to the salon, kill his son-in-law, and get back home."

"What about Epiphany? Mr Leo blames her."

"She admits to having been the deceased's mistress – she could hardly deny it when everybody at the salon knew. She even admits to having an occasional liaison with him at the salon in the evening. But on this particular evening, she says very firmly that she went to the cinema – alone. She's given us the name of the film. *Gandhi*. All very pat. What's more, the commissionaire remembers her in the queue – she is, after all, a very beautiful woman – and so does the girl at the box office. The only thing is, she had plenty of time once the film was over to get back to the salon and kill her lover."

"She has no alibi for her activities after the movie?" put in Jemima.

"Not really. She lives with a girl friend off the Edgware Road. But the friend's away – a very convenient fact if there was anything sinister going on – so according to Epiphany she just went home after the cinema, had a bit of supper, got into her lonely bed, and slept. Saw no one. Talked to no one. Telephoned no one. As for being late the next morning, that, too, was a piece of luck – stoppage on the Underground. We've checked that, of course, and it's true enough. But she could have come by a slower route, or even just left home later than usual so as to avoid opening up the shop and seeing the grisly consequences of her deed. As it was, we were there before she arrived."

With this information in her head, Jemima now entered the salon. Epiphany gave her usual calm welcome, asking the nearest junior – Jason, who had a remarkable coxcomb of multi-coloured hair – to take Miss Shore's coat and lead her to the basin. But Jemima didn't think it was her imagination that made her suppose Epiphany was frightened under her placid exterior. Of course, she could well be mourning her lover (presuming she had not killed him, and possibly even if she had) but Jemima's instinct told her there was something beyond that – something that was agitating, even terrifying Epiphany.

In the cloakroom, Pearl, another junior with a multi-coloured mop, took Jemima's fleecy white fur.

"Ooh, Miss Shore, how do you keep it so clean? It's white fox, is it?"

"I dump it in the bath," replied Jemima with perfect truth. "Not white fox – white nylon."

At the basin, Jason washed her hair with his usual scatty energy and later Mr Leo set it. Mr Leo was not scatty in any sense of the word. He did the set, as ever, perfectly, handling the thick rollers handed to him by Jason so fast and yet so deftly that Jemima, with much experience in having her hair done all over the world, doubted whether anyone could beat Mr Leo for speed or expertise.

Nevertheless, she sensed beneath his politeness, as in Epiphany, all the tension of the situation. The natural self-discipline of the professional hairdresser able to make gentle, interested conversation with the client whatever his own personal problems: in this case, a son-in-law brutally murdered, a daughter and grandchild bereft, himself the chief suspect, to say nothing of the need to keep the salon going smoothly if the whole family business was not to collapse.

At which point Mr Leo suddenly confounded all Jemima's theories about this unassailable professionalism by thrusting a roller abruptly back into Jason's hand.

"You finish this," he commanded. And with a very brief, muttered excuse in Jemima's general direction, he darted off toward the reception desk. In the mirror before her, Jemima was transfixed to see Mr Leo grab a dark-haired young woman by the shoulder and shake her while Epiphany, like a carved goddess, stared enigmatically down at the appointments book on her desk as though the visitor and Mr Leo did not exist. But it was interesting to note that the ringing telephone, which she normally answered at once, clamoured for at least half a minute before it claimed her attention.

The young woman and Mr Leo were speaking intensely in rapid Italian. Jemima spoke some Italian but this was far too quick and idiomatic for her to understand even the gist of it.

Then Jemima recognized the distraught woman – Domenica, Mr Leo's daughter. And at the same moment she remembered that Domenica had worked as receptionist at the salon before Epiphany. Had she met Mr Clark there? Probably. And probably left the salon to look after the baby, Leonella. It was ironic that it was Epiphany who had turned up to fill the gap. But why had Domenica come to the salon today? To attack Epiphany? Was that why Mr Leo was hustling her away to the back of the salon with something that looked very much like force?

Jason had put in the last roller and fastened some small clips on the tendrils Jemima sometimes liked to wear at her neck. Now he fastened the special silky Arcangelo's net like a golden filigree over her red hair and led Jemima to the dryers with his usual energetic enthusiasm. Jason was a great chatterer and in the absence of Mr Leo he really let himself go.

"I love doing your hair, Miss Shore – it's such great hair. Great styles you wear it in on the box, too. I always look for your hair-style, no matter what you're talking about. I mean, even if it's abandoned wives or something heavy like that, I can still enjoy your hair-style, can't I?"

Jemima flashed him one of her famously sweet smiles and sank back under the hood of the dryer.

A while later, she watched, unable to hear with the noise of the dryer, as Mr Leo led Domenica back toward the entrance. As they passed the reception desk, Jemima saw Epiphany mouth something, possibly some words of condolence. In dumb show, Jemima saw Domenica break from her father's grip and shout in the direction of Epiphany.

"*Putana.*" In an Italian opera, that would have been the word, *putana* – prostitute – or something similarly insulting concerning Epiphany's moral character. Whatever the word was, Epiphany did not answer. She dropped her eyes and continued to concentrate on the appointments book in front of her as Mr Leo led his daughter toward the front door.

"I am very sorry to inform you that your appointment is

cancelled . . ." The memory of Epiphany's voice came back to Jemima. Could she really have recorded that message so levelly and impersonally after killing her lover?

Yet why had Mr Clark lingered in the salon if not to meet Epiphany? He had certainly taken the trouble to give a false alibi to Domenica, who was expecting her sister-in-law for a late supper. Someone had known he would still be there after hours. Someone had killed him between ten and eleven, when Mr Leo – unnoticed – was still allegedly at the pub and Epiphany was at home – alone.

Jemima closed her eyes. The dryer was getting too hot. Jason, through general enthusiasm no doubt, had a tendency to set the temperature too high. She fiddled with the dial – and in so doing, it occurred to her to wonder under which dryer Mr Clark's corpse had been found sitting. She began, in spite of herself, to imagine the scene. Having been struck – several times, the police said – from behind by the massive metal hair-dryer, Mr Clark had fallen onto the long grey plush seat. The murderer had then propped him up under the plastic hood of one of the dryers to be found when the shop opened in the morning. The killer had left no finger-prints, having – another macabre touch – worn a pair of rubber gloves throughout, no doubt a pair that was missing from the tinting room. The killer had then locked the salon, pre-sumably with Mr Clark's own keys since these too had now vanished.

"At the bottom of the Thames now, no doubt," Pompey had said dolefully, "and the gloves along with them."

Jemima shifted restlessly, sorting images and thoughts in her head. Epiphany's solitary visit to a particularly long-drawn-out film followed by a lonely supper and bed, Mr Leo's alibi. Domenica entertaining her sister-in-law in Clark's absence, Jason's dismissal of abandoned wives – it all began to flow together, to form and re-form in a teasing kaleidoscope.

Where was Jason? She really was getting very hot.

Suddenly Jemima sat upright, hitting her head, rollers and all, on the edge of the hood as she did so. To the surprise of the clients watching (for she still attracted a few curious stares even after several years at Arcangelo's), she lifted the hood, pulled herself to her feet, and strode across the salon to where Epiphany was sitting at the reception desk. Both telephones were for once silent.

"It was true," said Jemima. "You *did* go to the cinema and then straight home. Were you angry with him? Had you quarrelled? He waited here for you. But you never came."

"I told the police that, Miss Shore." It was anguish, not fear, she had sensed in Epiphany, Jemima realized. "I told them about the film. Not about the rendezvous. What was the point of telling them about that when I didn't keep it?"

"His appointment was cancelled," murmured Jemima.

"If only I *had* cancelled it," Epiphany said. "Instead, he waited. I pretended I was coming. I wanted him to wait. To suffer as I suffered, waiting for him when he was with her – with her and the baby." Epiphany's composure broke. "I could have had any job, but I stayed here like his *slave*, while she held him with her money, the business—"

"I believe you." Jemima spoke gently. "And I'm sure the police will, too."

A short while later, she was explaining it all to Pompey. The policeman, knowing the normally immaculate state of her hair and dress, was somewhat startled to be summoned to a private room at Arcangelo's by a Jemima Shore with her hair still in rollers and her elegant figure draped in a dove-grey Arcangelo's gown.

"I know, I know, Pompey," she said. "And for heaven's sake don't tell Mrs Portsmouth you've seen me like this. But the heat of the dryer I was under a few minutes ago gave me an idea. The time of Mr Clark's death was all-important, wasn't it? By heating the body under the dryer and setting the time switch for an hour, the murderer made the police think that he had been killed nearer ten or eleven than the actual seven or eight when he was struck down.

"As it happened, ten or eleven was very awkward for Mr Leo, ostensibly at the pub, but not noticed in the pub by anyone – I have a feeling that there may be an extra-marital relationship there, too. Mr Leo is still a very good-looking man. That's not our business, however, because Mr Leo didn't kill Mr Clark. Between eight and nine, he was in the Underground on the way home, and there we have many people to vouch for him. As for Epiphany, the girl at the box office verifies that she bought a ticket and the commissionaire that she was in the queue. The timing lets her out, lets them both out, but it lets in someone else – someone who kept the appointment she knew Mr Clark had made. The abandoned wife. Domenica.

"Domenica," Jemima went on sadly, "entertaining her sister-in-law from half-past nine onward. Sitting with her, chatting with her. Spending the rest of the long evening with her, pretending to wait for her husband. And all the time he was dead here in the salon. Domenica had worked at the salon – she helped her father build it up. She knew about the rubber gloves and the keys and the hand-dryers and the time switches on the stationary ones.

"Pompey," Jemima paraphrased Jason: "it's heavy being an abandoned wife. So in the end, Domenica decided to keep Epiphany's appointment. She even left her baby alone to do so – such was the passion of the woman. The woman scorned. It was she who cancelled all future appointments for Mr Clark, with a heavy blow of a hand-dryer."

THE RACING GAME

(Yorkshire TV, 1979–1980)
Starring: Mike Gwilym, Mick Ford &
Alison Skilbeck
Directed by Jacky Stoller
Story 'Odds Against' by Dick Francis

The horse racing novels of Dick Francis have been con-
sistently among the top selling crime and mystery books
of the past two decades. But, sadly, when Yorkshire Television attempted to bring one of Dick's most interesting
characters to the small screen in a series about the seamy
side of the turf, *The Racing Game* failed to live up to
expectations although it is remembered with affection
by a group of enthusiasts who have lobbied for a second
series. The show was built around the character of Sid
Halley, a champion steeplechase jockey crippled by injuries which forced him to give up the track and set himself
up as an on-course private investigator working in the
main for wealthy stables under threat from criminals
organising betting coups or stealing racehorses. Sid had
made his debut in one of Dick's earliest novels, *Odds
Against* (1965) and having subsequently appeared in
Whip Hand (1979) and *Come To Grief* (1995) is his only
series character to date. *The Racing Game* was filmed in
and around a number of Yorkshire racecourses and the
track sequences were all colourful and dramatic. Mike
Gwilym brought Halley to life from the printed page,

robustly supported by Mick Ford as his sidekick, Chico Barnes. Although Yorkshire TV has not yet renewed its option for another series, Dick Francis said recently in an interview that he is constantly getting requests from viewers and readers to bring the ubiquitous Sid Halley back to the small screen.

Dick Francis (1920–) was for years famous as the jockey whose horse, the Queen Mother's Devon Lodge, dramatically collapsed while he was riding in the 1965 Grand National and in sight of a certain win. Born in Wales, he served in the RAF during the Second World War, and afterwards became an amateur and then professional National Hunt jockey, winning many important races and honours as well as being the National Hunt Champion in 1953–1954. Later Dick turned to journalism to write about his sport and was the racing correspondent for the *Sunday Express* for ten years before becoming a best-selling novelist with his first racing mystery, *Dead Cert*, published in 1962. As a man who took many hard knocks during his career in the saddle, a hallmark of Dick's novels is the violence done both to and by his characters. Sid Halley, a moody, bitter and tormented man is at the forefront of these ranks, and in this following extract from *Odds Against*, Dick Francis fills in some of the details of his perilous career. His return to the box is long overdue . . .

I was never particularly keen on my job before the day I got shot and nearly lost it, along with my life. But the .38 slug of lead which made a pepper-shaker out of my intestines left me with fire in my belly in more ways than one. Otherwise I should never have met Zanna Martin, and would still be held fast in the spider-threads of departed joys, of no use to anyone, least of all myself.

It was the first step to liberation, that bullet, though I wouldn't have said so at the time. I stopped it because I was careless. Careless because bored.

I woke up gradually in hospital, in a private room for which I got a whacking great bill a few days later. Even before I opened my eyes I began to regret I had not left the world completely. Someone had lit a bonfire under my navel.

A fierce conversation was being conducted in unhushed voices over my head. With woolly wits, the anaesthetic still drifting inside my skull like puff-ball clouds in a summer sky, I tried unenthusiastically to make sense of what was being said.

"Can't you give him something to wake him more quickly?"

"No."

"We can't do much until we have his story, you must see that. It's nearly seven hours since you finished operating. Surely . . ."

"And he was all of four hours on the table before that. Do you want to finish off what the shooting started?"

"Doctor . . ."

"I am sorry, but you'll have to wait."

There's my pal, I thought. They'll have to wait. Who wants to hurry back into the dreary world? Why not go to sleep for a month and take things up again after they've put the bonfire out? I opened my eyes reluctantly.

It was night. A globe of electric light shone in the centre of the ceiling. That figured. It had been morning when Jones-boy found me still seeping gently on to the office linoleum and went to telephone, and it appeared that about twelve hours had passed since they stuck the first blessed needle into my arm. Would a twenty-four hour start, I wondered, be enough for a panic-stricken ineffectual little crook to get himself undetectably out of the country?

There were two policemen on my left, one in uniform, one not. They were both sweating, because the room was hot. The doctor stood on the right, fiddling with a tube which ran from a bottle into my elbow. Various other tubes sprouted disgustingly from my abdomen, partly covered by a light sheet. Drip and drainage, I thought sardonically. How absolutely charming.

Radnor was watching me from the foot of the bed, taking no part in the argument still in progress between medicine and the law. I wouldn't have thought I rated the boss himself attendant at the bedside, but then I suppose it wasn't every day that one of his employees got himself into such a spectacular mess.

He said, "He's conscious again, and his eyes aren't so hazy. We might get some sense out of him this time." He looked at his watch.

The doctor bent over me, felt my pulse, and nodded. "Five minutes, then. Not a second more."

The plain clothes policeman beat Radnor to it by a fraction of a second. "Can you tell us who shot you?"

I still found it surprisingly difficult to speak, but not as impossible as it had been when they asked me the same question that morning. Then, I had been too far gone. Now, I was apparently on the way back. Even so, the policeman had plenty of time to repeat his question, and to wait some more, before I managed an answer.

"Andrews."

It meant nothing to the policeman, but Radnor looked astonished and also disappointed.

"Thomas Andrews?" he asked.

"Yes."

Radnor explained to the police. "I told you that Halley here and another of my operatives set some sort of a trap intending to clear up an intimidation case we are investigating. I understand they were hoping for a big fish, but it seems now they caught a tiddler. Andrews is small stuff, a weak sort of youth used for running errands. I would never have thought he would carry a gun, much less that he would use it."

Me neither. He had dragged the revolver clumsily out of his jacket pocket, pointed it shakily in my direction, and used both hands to pull the trigger. If I hadn't seen that it was only Andrews who had come to nibble at the bait I wouldn't have ambled unwarily out of the darkness of the washroom to tax him with breaking into the Cromwell Road premises of Hunt Radnor Associates at one o'clock in the morning. It simply hadn't occurred to me that he would attack me in any way.

By the time I realized that he really meant to use the gun and was not waving it about for effect, it was far too late. I had barely begun to turn to flip off the light switch when the bullet hit, in and out diagonally through my body. The force of it spun me on to my knees and then forward on to the floor.

As I went down he ran for the door, stiff-legged, crying out, with circles of white showing wild round his eyes. He was almost as horrified as I was at what he had done.

"At what time did the shooting take place?" asked the policeman formally.

After another pause I said, "One o'clock, about."

The doctor drew in a breath. He didn't need to say it; I knew I was lucky to be alive. In a progressively feeble state I'd lain on the floor through a chilly September night looking disgustedly at a telephone on which I couldn't summon help. The office telephones all worked through a switchboard. This might have been on the moon as far as I was concerned, instead of along the passage, down the curving stairs, and through the door to the reception desk, with the girl who worked the switches fast asleep in bed.

The policeman wrote in his notebook. "Now sir, I can get a description of Thomas Andrews from someone else so as not to trouble you too much now, but I'd be glad if you can tell me what he was wearing."

"Black jeans, very tight. Olive green jersey. Loose black jacket." I paused. "Black fur collar, black and white checked lining. All shabby . . . dirty." I tried again. "He had gun in jacket pocket right side . . . took it with him . . . no gloves . . . can't have a record."

"Shoes?"

"Didn't see. Silent, though."

"Anything else?"

I thought. "He had some badges . . . place names, skull and crossbones, things like that . . . sewn on his jacket, left sleeve."

"I see. Right. We'll get on with it then." He snapped shut his notebook, smiled briefly, turned, and walked to the door, followed by his uniformed ally, and by Radnor, presumably for Andrews' description.

The doctor took my pulse again, and slowly checked all the tubes. His face showed satisfaction.

He said cheerfully, "You must have the constitution of a horse."

"No," said Radnor, coming in again and hearing him. "Horses are really quite delicate creatures. Halley has the constitution of a jockey. A steeplechase jockey. He used to be one. He's got a body like a shock absorber . . . had to have to deal with all the fractures and injuries he got racing."

"Is that what happened to his hand? A fall in a steeplechase?"

Radnor's glance flicked to my face and away again, uncomfortably. They never mentioned my hand to me in the office if they could help it. None of them, that is, except my fellow trapsetter Chico Barnes, who didn't care what he said to anyone.

"Yes," Radnor said tersely. "That's right." He changed the subject. "Well, Sid, come and see me when you are better. Take your time." He nodded uncertainly to me, and he and the doctor, with a joint backward glance, ushered each other out of the door.

So Radnor was in no hurry to have me back. I would have smiled if I'd had the energy. When he first offered me a job I guessed that somewhere in the background my father-in-law was pulling strings; but I had been in a why-not mood at the time. Nothing mattered very much.

"Why not?" I said to Radnor, and he put me on his payroll as an investigator, Racing Section, ignoring my complete lack of experience and explaining to the rest of the staff that I was there in an advisory capacity, owing to my intimate knowledge of the game. They had taken it very well, on the whole. Perhaps they realized, as I did, that my employment was an act of pity. Perhaps they thought I should be too proud to accept that sort of pity. I wasn't. I didn't care one way or the other.

Radnor's agency ran Missing Persons, Guard, and Divorce departments, and also a section called Bona Fides, which was nearly as big as the others put together. Most of the work was routine painstaking inquiry stuff, sometimes leading to civil or divorce action, but oftener merely to a discreet report sent to the client. Criminal cases, though accepted, were rare. The Andrews business was the first for three months.

The Racing Section was Radnor's special baby. It hadn't existed, I'd been told, when he bought the agency with an Army gratuity after the war and developed it from a dingy three-roomed affair into something like a national institution. Radnor printed 'Speed, Results, and Secrecy' across the top of his stationery; promised them, and delivered them. A life-long addiction to racing, allied to six youthful rides in point-to-points, had led him not so much to ply for hire from the Jockey Club and the National Hunt Committee as to indicate that his agency was at their disposal. The Jockey Club and the National Hunt Committee tentatively wet their feet, found the water beneficial, and plunged right in. The Racing Section blossomed. Eventually private business outstripped the official, especially when Radnor began supplying pre-race guards for fancied horses.

By the time I joined the firm 'Bona Fides: Racing', had proved so successful that it had spread from its own big office into the room next door. For a reasonable fee a trainer could check on the character and background of a prospective owner, a bookmaker on a client, a client on a bookmaker, anybody on anybody. The phrase 'OK'd by Radnor' had passed into racing slang. Genuine, it meant. Trustworthy. I had even heard it applied to a horse.

They had never given me a Bona Fides assignment. This work was done by a bunch of inconspicuous middle-aged retired policemen who took minimum time to get maximum results. I'd never been sent to sit all night outside the box of a hot favourite, though I would have done it willingly. I had never been put on a racecourse security patrol. If the Stewards asked for operators to keep tabs on undesirables at race meetings, I didn't go. If anyone had to watch for pick-pockets in Tattersalls, it wasn't me. Radnor's two unvarying excuses for giving me nothing to do were first that I was too well known to the whole racing world to be inconspicuous, and second, that even if I didn't seem to care, he was not going to be the one to give an ex-champion jockey tasks which meant a great loss of face.

As a result I spent most of my time kicking around the office reading other people's reports. When anyone asked me for the informed advice I was supposedly there to give, I gave it; if anyone asked what I would do in a certain set of circumstances, I told them. I got to know all the operators and gossiped with them when they came into the office. I always had the time. If I took a day off and went to the races, nobody complained. I sometimes wondered whether they even noticed.

At intervals I remarked to Radnor that he didn't have to keep me, as I so obviously did nothing to earn my salary. He replied each time that he was satisfied with the arrangement, if I was. I had the impression that he was waiting for something, but if it wasn't for me to leave, I didn't know what. On the day I walked into Andrews' bullet I had been with the agency in this fashion for exactly two years.

A nurse came in to check the tubes and take my blood pressure. She was starched and efficient. She smiled but didn't speak. I waited for her to say that my wife was outside asking about me anxiously. She didn't say it. My wife hadn't come. Wouldn't come. If I couldn't hold her when I was properly alive, why should my near-death bring her running? Jenny. My wife. Still my wife in spite of three years' separation. Regret, I think, held both of us back from the final step of divorce: we had been through passion, delight, dissension, anger, and explosion. Only regret was left, and it wouldn't be strong enough to bring her to the hospital. She'd seen me in too many hospitals before. There was no more drama, no more impact, in my form recumbent, even with tubes. She wouldn't come. Wouldn't telephone. Wouldn't write. It was stupid of me to want her to.

Time passed slowly and I didn't enjoy it, but eventually all the tubes except the one in my arm were removed and I began to heal. The police didn't find Andrews, Jenny didn't come, Radnor's typists sent me a get-well card, and the hospital sent the bill.

Chico slouched in one evening, his hands in his pockets and the usual derisive grin on his face. He looked me over without haste and the grin, if anything, widened.

"Rather you than me, mate," he said.

"Go to bloody hell."

He laughed. And well he might. I had been doing his job for him because he had a date with a girl, and Andrews' bullet should have been his bellyache, not mine.

"Andrews," he said musingly. "Who'd have thought it? Sodding little weasel. All the same, if you'd done what I said and stayed in the washroom, and taken his photo quiet like on the old infra-red, we'd have picked him up later nice and easy and you'd have been lolling on your arse around the office as usual instead of sweating away in here."

"You needn't rub it in," I said. "What would you have done?"

He grinned. "The same as you, I expect. I'd have reckoned it would only take the old one-two for that little worm to come across with who sent him."

"And now we don't know."

"No." He sighed. "And the old man ain't too sweet about the whole thing. He did know I was using the office as a trap, but he didn't think it would work, and now this has happened he doesn't like it. He's leaning over backwards, hushing the whole thing up. They might have sent a bomb, not a sneak thief, he said. And of course Andrews bust a window getting in, which I've probably got to pay for. Trust the little sod not to know how to pick a lock."

"I'll pay for the window," I said.

"Yeah," he grinned. "I reckoned you would if I told you."

216

He wandered round the room, looking at things. There wasn't much to see.

"What's in that bottle dripping into your arm?"

"Food of some sort, as far as I can gather. They never give me anything to eat."

"Afraid you might bust out again, I expect."

"I guess so," I agreed.

He wandered on. "Haven't you got a telly then? Cheer you up a bit wouldn't it, to see some other silly buggers getting shot?" He looked at the chart on the bottom of the bed. "Your temperature was 102 this morning, did they tell you? Do you reckon you're going to kick it?"

"No."

"Near thing, from what I've heard. Jones-boy said there was enough of your life's blood dirtying up the office floor to make a tidy few black puddings."

I didn't appreciate Jones-boy's sense of humour.

Chico said, "Are you coming back?"

"Perhaps."

He began tying knots in the cord of the window blind. I watched him, a thin figure imbued with so much energy that it was difficult for him to keep still. He had spent two fruitless nights watching in the washroom before I took his place, and I knew that if he hadn't been dedicated to his job he couldn't have borne such inactivity. He was the youngest of Radnor's team. About twenty-four, he believed, though as he had been abandoned as a child on the steps of a police station in a pushchair, no one knew for certain.

If the police hadn't been so kind to him, Chico sometimes said, he would have taken advantage of his later opportunities and turned delinquent. He never grew tall enough to be a copper. Radnor's was the best he could do. And he did very well by Radnor. He put two and two together quickly and no one on the staff had faster physical reactions. Judo and wrestling were his hobbies, and along with the regular throws and holds he had been taught some strikingly dirty tricks. His smallness bore no relation whatever to his effectiveness in his job.

"How are you getting on with the case?" I asked.

"What case? Oh . . . that. Well since you got shot the heat's off, it seems. Brinton's had no threatening calls or letters since the other night. Whoever was leaning on him must have got the wind up. Anyway, he's feeling a bit safer all of a sudden and he's carping a lot to the old man about fees. Another day or two, I give it, and there won't be no one holding his hand at night. Anyway, I've been pulled off it. I'm flying from Newmarket to Ireland tomorrow, sharing a stall with a hundred thousand pounds worth of stallion."

Escort duty was another little job I never did. Chico liked it, and went often. As he had once thrown a fifteen stone would-be nobbler over a seven foot wall, he was always much in demand.

"You ought to come back," he said suddenly.

"Why?" I was surprised.

"I don't know . . ." he grinned. "Silly, really, when you do sweet eff-all, but everybody seems to have got used to you being around. You're missed, kiddo, you'd be surprised."

"You're joking, of course."

"Yeah . . ." He undid the knots in the window cord, shrugged, and thrust his hands into his trouser pockets. "God, this place gives you the willies. It reeks of warm disinfectant. Creepy. How much longer are you going to lie here rotting?"

"Days," I said mildly. "Have a good trip."

"See you." He nodded, drifting in relief to the door. "Do you want anything? I mean, books or anything?"

"Nothing, thanks."

"Nothing . . . that's just your form, Sid, mate. You don't want nothing." He grinned and went.

I wanted nothing. My form. My trouble. I'd had what I wanted most in the world and lost it irrevocably. I'd found nothing else to want. I stared at the ceiling, waiting for time to pass. All I wanted was to get back on to my feet and stop feeling as though I had eaten a hundredweight of green apples.

Three weeks after the shooting I had a visit from my father-in-law. He came in the late afternoon, bringing with him a small parcel which he put without comment on the table beside the bed.

"Well, Sid, how are you?" He settled himself into an easy chair, crossed his legs, and lit a cigar.

"Cured, more or less. I'll be out of here soon."

"Good. Good. And your plans are . . . ?"

"I haven't any."

"You can't go back to the agency without some . . . er . . . convalescence," he remarked.

"I suppose not."

"You might prefer somewhere in the sun," he said, studying the cigar. "But I would like it if you could spend some time with me at Aynsford."

I didn't answer immediately.

"Will . . . ?" I began and stopped, wavering.

"No," he said. "She won't be there. She's gone out to Athens to stay with Jill and Tony. I saw her off yesterday. She sent you her regards."

"Thanks," I said dryly. As usual I did not know whether to be glad or sorry that I was not going to meet my wife. Nor was I sure that this trip to see her sister Jill was not as diplomatic as Tony's job in the Corps.

"You'll come, then? Mrs Cross will look after you splendidly."

Dick Francis

"Yes, Charles, thank you. I'd like to come for a little while."

He gripped the cigar in his teeth, squinted through the smoke, and took out his diary.

"Let's see, suppose you leave here in, say, another week . . . No point in hurrying out before you're fit to go . . . that brings us to the twenty-sixth . . . hm . . . now, suppose you come down a week on Sunday, I'll be at home all that day. Will that suit you?"

"Yes, fine, if the doctors agree."

"Right, then." He wrote in the diary, put it away, and took the cigar carefully out of his mouth, smiling at me with the usual inscrutable blankness in his eyes. He sat easily in his dark city suit, Rear-Admiral Charles Roland, RN, retired, a man carrying his sixty-six years lightly. War photographs showed him tall, straight, bony almost, with a high forehead and thick dark hair. Time had greyed the hair, which in receding left his forehead higher than ever, and had added weight where it did no harm. His manner was ordinarily extremely charming and occasionally patronizingly offensive. I had been on the receiving end of both.

He relaxed in the armchair, talking unhurriedly about steeplechasing.

"What do you think of that new race at Sandown? I don't know about you, but I think it's framed rather awkwardly. They're bound to get a tiny field with those conditions, and if Devil's Dyke doesn't run after all the whole thing will be a non-crowd puller *par excellence*."

His interest in the game only dated back a few years, but recently to his pleasure he had been invited by one or two courses to act as a Steward. Listening to his easy familiarity with racing problems and racing jargon, I was in a quiet inward way amused. It was impossible to forget his reaction

220

long ago to Jenny's engagement to a jockey, his unfriendly rejection of me as a future son-in-law, his absence from our wedding, the months afterwards of frigid disapproval, the way he had seldom spoken to or even looked at me.

I believed at the time that it was sheer snobbery, but it wasn't as simple as that. Certainly he didn't think me good enough, but not only, or even mainly, on a class distinction level; and probably we would never have understood each other, or come eventually to like each other, had it not been for a wet afternoon and a game of chess.

Jenny and I went to Aynsford for one of our rare, painful Sunday visits. We ate our roast beef in near silence, Jenny's father staring rudely out of the window and drumming his fingers on the table. I made up my mind that we wouldn't go again. I'd had enough. Jenny could visit him alone.

After lunch she said she wanted to sort out some of her books now that we had a new bookcase, and disappeared upstairs. Charles Roland and I looked at each other in dislike, the afternoon stretching drearily ahead and the downpour outside barring retreat into the garden and park beyond.

"Do you play chess?" he asked in a bored, expecting-the-answer-no voice.

"I know the moves," I said.

He shrugged (it was more like a squirm), but clearly thinking that it would be less trouble than making conversation, he brought a chess set out and gestured to me to sit opposite him. He was normally a good player, but that afternoon he was bored and irritated and inattentive, and I beat him quite early in the game. He couldn't believe it. He sat staring at the board, fingering the bishop with which I'd got him in a classic discovered check.

"Where did you learn?" he said eventually, still looking down.

"Out of a book."

"Have you played a great deal?"

"No, not much. Here and there." But I'd played with some good players.

"Hm." He paused. "Will you play again?"

"Yes, if you like."

We played. It was a long game and ended in a draw, with practically every piece off the board. A fortnight later he rang up and asked us, next time we came, to stay overnight. It was the first twig of the olive branch. We went more often and more willingly to Aynsford after that. Charles and I played chess occasionally and won a roughly equal number of games, and he began rather tentatively to go to the races. Ironically from then on our mutual respect grew strong enough to survive even the crash of Jenny's and my marriage, and Charles' interest in racing expanded and deepened with every passing year.

"I went to Ascot yesterday," he was saying, tapping ash off his cigar. "It wasn't a bad crowd, considering the weather. I had a drink with that handicapper fellow, John Pagan. Nice chap. He was very pleased with himself because he got six abreast over the last in the handicap hurdle. There was an objection after the three mile chase – flagrant bit of crossing on the run-in. Carter swore blind he was leaning and couldn't help it, but you can never believe a word he says. Anyway, the Stewards took it away from him. The only thing they could do. Wally Gibbons rode a brilliant finish in the handicap hurdle and then made an almighty hash of the novice chase."

"He's heavy-handed with novices," I agreed.

"Wonderful course, that."

"The tops." A wave of weakness flowed outwards from my stomach. My legs trembled under the bedclothes. It was always happening. Infuriating.

"Good job it belongs to the Queen and is safe from the land-grabbers." He smiled.

"Yes, I suppose so . . ."

"You're tired," he said abruptly. "I've stayed too long."

"No," I protested. "Really, I'm fine."

He put out the cigar, however, and stood up. "I know you too well, Sid. Your idea of fine is not the same as anyone else's. If you're not well enough to come to Aynsford a week on Sunday you'll let me know. Otherwise I'll see you then."

"Yes, OK."

He went away, leaving me to reflect that I did still tire infernally easily. Must be old age, I grinned to myself, old age at thirty-one. Old tired battered Sid Halley, poor old chap. I grimaced at the ceiling.

A nurse came in for the evening jobs.

"You've got a parcel," she said brightly, as if speaking to a retarded child. "Aren't you going to open it?"

I had forgotten about Charles' parcel.

"Would you like me to open it for you? I mean, you can't find things like opening parcels very easy with a hand like yours."

She was only being kind. "Yes," I said. "Thank you."

She snipped through the wrappings with scissors from her pocket and looked dubiously at the slim dark book she found inside.

"I suppose it is meant for you? I mean somehow it doesn't seem like things people usually give patients."

She put the book into my right hand and I read the title embossed in gold on the cover. *Outline of Company Law.*

"My father-in-law left it on purpose. He meant it for me."

"Oh well, I suppose it's difficult to think of things for people who can't eat grapes and such." She bustled around, efficient and slightly bullying, and finally left me alone again.

Outline of Company Law. I riffled through the pages. It was certainly a book about company law. Solidly legal. Not light entertainment for an invalid. I put the book on the table.

Charles Roland was a man of subtle mind, and subtlety gave him much pleasure. It hadn't been my parentage that he had objected to so much as what he took to be Jenny's rejection of his mental standards in choosing a jockey for a husband. He'd never met a jockey before, disliked the idea of racing, and took it for granted that everyone engaged in it was either a rogue or a moron. He'd wanted both his daughters to marry clever men, clever more than handsome or well-born or rich, so that he could enjoy their company. Jill had obliged him with Tony, Jenny disappointed him with me: that was how he saw it, until he found that at least I could play chess with him now and then.

Knowing his subtle habits, I took it for granted that he had not idly brought such a book and hadn't chosen it or left it by mistake. He meant me to read it for a purpose. Intended it to be useful to me – or to him – later on. Did he think he could manoeuvre me into business, now that I hadn't distinguished myself at the agency? A nudge, that book was. A nudge in some specific direction.

I thought back over what he had said, looking for a clue. He'd been insistent that I should go to Aynsford. He'd sent Jenny to Athens. He'd talked about racing, about the new race at Sandown, about Ascot, John Pagan, Carter, Wally Gibbons . . . nothing there that I could see had the remotest connection with company law.

I sighed, shutting my eyes. I didn't feel too well. I didn't have to read the book, or go wherever Charles pointed. And yet . . . why not? There was nothing I urgently wanted to do instead. I decided to do my stodgy homework. Tomorrow.

Perhaps.

MINDER

(ITV, 1980–)
Starring: George Cole, Dennis Waterman &
Gary Webster
Directed by Johnny Goodman
Story 'Saint Nick Alas' by Tony Hoare

Comedy crime series are a comparatively new phenomena on TV. Although earlier police and detective series had quite often been unintentionally funny, the first to deliberately set out to get laughs from crime was *Porridge* (BBC, 1974–1977) with comedian Ronnie Barker playing an old lag in prison, with Richard Beckinsale as his young cell mate and Fulton McKay as a constantly frustrated prison officer. The series with its insight into life in jail as seen through the day-to-day activities of a group of characters ranging from unregenerate villains to sentimental guards was for years one of the top sitcoms on the box, and its popularity has resulted in frequent reshowings. Recently, *Porridge* has been in the same schedules as another very popular comedy series, *The Detectives* (1992–) which co-stars stand-up comedian Jasper Carrott and actor Robert Powell as two inept and accident prone sleuths forever bungling cases and infuriating their boss, George Sewell. ITV's contribution to comic crime, *Minder*, enjoys similar cult status to both of these series. Created by Leon Griffiths in 1980, the stories about a shady second-hand car dealer, Arthur

Daley (George Cole) constantly embroiled in dodgy deals from which he needs extricating by the muscle or nous of his 'minder', Terry McCann (Dennis Waterman) – superseded by Arthur's nephew, Ray (Gary Webster) – the series not only became a huge hit in Britain, but has also been shown in 70 other countries. Described once as 'the Richard Nixon of the forecourt', Daley's name has become a catchword both as an insult and a compliment, while his malapropisms are legendary. Interestingly, in the first series the emphasis of the stories was on the minder (hence the title) while Denholm Elliott was originally intended to play the Arthur Daley role. Since Dennis Waterman left the series, there have been fewer episodes, but the possibility of the occasional two-hour special still remains, according to ITV.

Leon Griffiths (1928–) has stated that Arthur Daley is 'an amalgam of lots of people' and the reason for his success is probably because of the public affection for 'slightly dodgy, anti-authority characters'. Prior to creating *Minder*, Griffiths was best known for his critically acclaimed TV dramas such as *Dinner at the Sporting Club* (1978) which Kenneth Trodd produced with John Thaw as the gritty manager of a young boxer just turned professional. For his contributions to television crime and mystery series, he won the Writers' Guild Award in 1964 and a BAFTA award in 1984. Although Leon Griffiths has frequently written scripts for *Minder*, the writer who has actually contributed more than any other and been responsible for some of the most amusing episodes and hilarious lines is Tony Hoare (1952–) who wrote the following short story for *TV Times* in December 1991. It is a superb reminder of Arthur Daley, the man known to millions as Thatcherism's funniest by-product . . .

Said Arthur Daley: "The thing about Christmas, it's a time for giving."

"Or in your case, receiving," Terry said, dismally watching the windscreen wipers push the lightly falling snow aside they headed for Arthur's lock-up.

Arthur changed gear, deliberately ignoring this, wanting to keep Terry sweet, trying to ease into the proposition without making it sound like a nice little earner. "A time for goodwill to all men . . . especially kids," he offered, glancing at Terry, searching for agreement. A way in. Terry cast him a suspicious look, sensing a move. Arthur smiled with a face that he hoped radiated sincerity and continued: "Nothing quite like watching their beamin' faces as they open up all the pressies Santa's brought them, right?"

Terry responded with a wary: "I guess so."

"You don't sound too sure," said Arthur. "What are you tellin' me, you don't like kids? You've got something about not making children happy?"

Terry sighed. All the signs were there. Arthur slipping whatever it was in sideways. Never direct. Which didn't stop him answering: "I like kids to be happy, okay?"

Fatal. He knew by the way Arthur smiled. It was confirmed when Arthur said: "I knew you were the right man for the job."

The car skidded slightly to a halt in the settling snow outside the lock-up. Terry didn't want to ask what job? In fact, he was thoroughly dispirited by the thought he had allowed Arthur to corner him yet again.

Detective-Constable Jones, sitting at a desk in the squad room, also felt dispirited. Here it was, Christmas Eve and here he was on duty. A mood guaranteed not to be enhanced by the fact that his superior officer, Sgt Rycott, was also on duty at the sparsely-manned station. He tried to cheer himself up by thinking of the three valleys and the Welsh Orpheus Choir singing *We'll Keep a Welcome in the Hillside*. He gave up. It made him homesick. But homesickness degenerated into a moment of despair when Rycott, pretending to be busy at *his* desk, said: "Don't just sit there daydreaming, Jones, *do* something." Dc Jones realised in that moment that his father had given him bad advice when he told him *not* to follow his footsteps down the mines.

"I am doing something, guv," he said.

"Really? I'm amazed. I'm agog," in a voice that exuded sarcasm. "Blinking vacantly into space constitutes serious activity, does it?"

Dc Jones glanced at the pathetic Christmas trimmings some desperate optimist had seen fit to drape around the room, and thought maybe it was time to consider a change of career – funeral director, something like that.

Terry didn't like the idea but Arthur kept laying the guilt trip on him about how he would be letting the kids down. Toddlers is what Terry was calling them by now. He also felt a right wally standing there in the lock-up dressed in the Father Christmas costume. It didn't help that the beard had a grey tinge and smelt distinctly unsavoury.

"I'm supposed to be meeting Arnie and a few of the chaps down the Winchester for a drink-up," he tried again as Arthur thrust what appeared to be a school bell in his hand – his voice overlapping: "Cop this . . . give it some stick and a few 'Ho, ho, ho's. Merry Christmas, children'."

Terry rang the bell, heard himself saying: "Ho! Ho! Ho! Merry Christmas, children," and experiencing a sense of unreality. "Forget the bell," he said, handing it back to

Arthur, whose face dropped while his brain told him not to push it when Terry had that look in his eyes.

"You're right," Arthur said, setting the bell aside, "you're going to need both hands anyway." Then he quickly realised now was not the time to go into that particular detail and added, ". . . for the sack of pressies." Like it was all one sentence.

"Sack?"

The snow was falling more heavily now. It was dark and visibility was poor as they headed in the car towards Mr Jackson's house. Mr Jackson was the man with the kids. A dear friend of mine, Arthur had said. "If he's such a 'dear friend' how come I've never heard of him?" Terry asked. Arthur muttered something about keeping his social life separated from his business life. Terry didn't believe a word of it. "So how much is my wack for doin' this job?" he enquired.

"Payment? Please, Terry, do not insult me an' demean yourself. This is an act of goodwill, suffer little children to come unto me, and all that. D'you think the geezers who shlepped across the desert humping gold, frankincense an' myrrh to Bethlehem were lookin' to be on an earner?" And before Terry could protest, Arthur slammed on the brakes, skidding and smashing into the curb. Whiplash caused the Santa hat to drop over Terry's eyes. Arthur, "oh my gawding" it, stumbled from the car to examine the damage.

"What the hell happened?" asked Terry. A cat had run out into the road. "Was it a black one?" asked Terry, trying to remember if it meant good or back luck. "Can't be good," groaned Arthur, pointing at the nearside front wheel sticking out from the wing at an unnatural angle.

"So what do we do now?" Terry asked.

"We'll have to walk it . . . it's only round the corner. Get the sack of pressies from the boot."

Around the corner turned out to be about half a mile away.

And so there they were, eventually, outside Mr Jackson's huge Gothic house, snow-capped and looking like Christopher Lee's castle in Transylvania against the black sky. Terry's feet were wet and icy cold in the synthetic boots with the white nylon fur trim. So what was he supposed to do, just knock on the door, or what, he asked Arthur – snuggled up in his Crombie overcoat and hand-made brogues.

"Nothing so mundane, my son," said Arthur, heading up the driveway. "D'you think Prancer, Dancer, Vixen an' Rudolf tug Santa from the North Pole across the rooftops of the world just to knock on doors? No, it has to be done proper, in keeping with tradition. You nip down the chimney."

"*What?*"

"Don't worry. Mr Jackson's had it swept 'specially'. As if *that* made a difference! "The kids'll be gathered waiting at the bottom. Think how surprised an' delighted they'll be when you drop, uh, show up in the inglenooky."

"Forget it, no way am I climbing *inside* a chimney! Are you crazy?"

"If being sentimental and filled with the yuletide spirit is crazy, then I cop a plea, Terence," Arthur said in tones that suggested great sacrifice and even greater humility.

"Arthur, I'm *twelve* stone!" Terry protested. "I couldn't get down the chimney even if I wanted, which I most definitely *don't!*"

"Not a problem, my son," smiled Arthur with breathtaking confidence, giving Terry a reassuring pat and guiding him towards the back of the house. "This gaff was built in the days when they shovelled kids up the flue to give 'em a dusting."

"Right, *not* grown men in Santa suits humpin' sacks of toys!"

"Sack, Terence. Singular."

"What difference, I ain't doing it!"

So Arthur explained how he and Mr Jackson had discussed the practicalities, how Mr Jackson even had a builder check out the measurements and remove the chimney pots to make room for access. Of course it might be a little *confined*, but nothing someone with Terry's suppleness and physical prowess couldn't overcome.

The two of them were at the rear of the house now, with Arthur pointing at the ladder reaching up to the roof, saying: "See, you don't even have to climb a drainpipe. Anticipation an' preparation is the hallmark of my continuing success, as you should well know, Terence."

"Oh really. I thought it was telling porkies and conning people," was the best defence Terry could muster against Arthur's onslaught of perverse logic.

"Uncalled for, Terry, not to add un-Christian," said Arthur, pointing a digit heavenward. "Shall we try and have some respect for His birthday?" Then glancing at his watch he indicated the ladder again and handed Terry a torch. "Up you go then . . . we're running late as it is."

Dc Jones still felt confused about his future. He thought about therapy as a solution to his disenchantment with the job – then decided against it on the grounds it would undermine his career prospects. A promotion board, if they found out, would view it as some sort of mental instability – a condition of the mind that immediately brought Sgt Rycott to the forefront of his thoughts.

Now there was a *real* nutter. Why else would the scourge

of his professional life decide it would be a good idea for them to leave the relative warmth and comfort of the squad room and 'patrol the manor' in search of criminal activity. Real villains took a break at Christmas to be with their families and *spend* their ill-gotten gains.

Suddenly Rycott was shouting: "Pull over, pull over!" Jones did as bid as Rycott twisted in his seat to peer and point dramatically through the rear window. "D'you see it?"

All Dc Jones could see was a badly parked Jaguar. "See what, guv?"

"Arthur bloody Daley," is what Rycott said.

Fortunately, the immediate area around the base of the chimney stack was flat and Terry was able to stand with relative safety, carefully wedging the sack of presents between his numbed feet, while he flashed the pencil torch down into the blackness of the flue. It appeared clear of soot. There was even a series of small iron lugs sticking out at regular intervals where he could get a toehold. That at least was reassuring. The actual width of the flue wasn't. Maybe he could just about squeeze down it. He could hold the torch in his mouth and sort of balance the sack on his head. "It gets wider as you descend," Arthur had assured him. But then he would.

"It's Daley's car, all right," Rycott said. "And those are his footprints. I'd recognise them anywhere!" The sergeant's obsessive preoccupation with the activities of Arthur were legendary on the manor, but to claim he could recognise the man's *footprints* . . . in the snow? Jones was incredulous. They were stood by Arthur's damaged car observing the two sets of footprints leading off into the distance.

"Remarkable observation, guv," Dc Jones said dryly. "And it's my guess there's someone with him."

"McCann!" Rycott exclaimed – then realising. "Is that supposed to be some form of Celtic wit, Jones?"

It took them about five minutes in the police car to follow the footprints to the entrance of Mr Jackson's residence. And a feeling of euphoria swept over Rycott as he peered around the corner of the house and saw Arthur standing near the foot of a *ladder* . . . staring up at the roof! Got the slippery sod at last. Bang to rights! Capturing Arthur Daley for burglary and in all likelihood his colleague in crime, Terry McCann, was the best Christmas present he could ever wish for! And he leaped from the shadows, calling: "Get the cuffs on him, Jones!" Startled out of his wits, Arthur tripped and fell over.

Mr Jackson was somewhat bemused. He had opened the door to reveal Arthur handcuffed to one police officer while the other one said: "Do you know this man, sir?"

Having first got his wife to usher the children upstairs so they wouldn't be upset, Mr Jackson led the trio into the living room, where he proceeded to confirm he knew Arthur and had hired his services to supply one Santa Claus.

Rycott's disappointment and frustration was immeasurable. Dc Jones could've sworn he saw tears forming in his superior's eyes as he released Arthur from the handcuffs, and squirming as Arthur demanded an apology for the unwarranted assault on his person.

It was during this exchange that a brick fell into the inglenook fireplace, and the muffled, distressed voice of Terry was heard calling for help.

It took the firemen three hours to release him.

Long before this, Arthur had felt it prudent to use Mr Jackson's phone to call for a taxi. Terry could be very unreasonable about this sort of thing. Sitting at home now, snuggled into his favourite armchair, sipping a glass of port, puffing on a cigar and warming his feet at the open fireplace while 'er-in-doors prepared his dinner, he mused about the evening's events.

Mr Jackson had been very understanding, apologetic even. He insisted on paying Arthur the hundred sovs fee that had been agreed upon a week earlier. Naturally Arthur had accepted it, feeling it was only fair considering the ordeal *he'd* been through. And, as an afterthought, Terry, too. Perhaps he should bung the boy, say, 20 quid. Tell him it was out of his own pocket.

After all, it was Christmas.

NEW COLUMBO

(Universal TV, 1989–)
Starring: Peter Falk, Patrick Bauchau &
Fionnula Flanagan
Directed by Roland Kibbee
Story 'The End of an Era' by Richard Levinson &
William Link

The advent of satellite and cable television has given a new lease of life to many of the classic crime series which are now being reshown to enthusiastic audiences of younger viewers. Among the crime fighters who have been particularly successful the second time around are *The Saint* (1962–1969) in which Roger Moore brought the exploits of Leslie Charteris's famous man-about-town sleuth, Simon Templer, to the screen; the long running saga of the man on the run, *The Fugitive* (1963–1967) with David Janssen as Dr Richard Kimble forever on the track of the mysterious one-armed man in episodes which engrossed audiences on both sides of the Atlantic for five years; and *Jason King* (1971–1973) starring Peter Wyngarde as the flamboyant enemy of law-breakers who wore the most outlandish shirts and romanced every beautiful woman who crossed his path. Perhaps even more successful than these has been *Columbo* (1971–1979), the cases of the rather down-at-heel Los Angeles Homicide Department detective who uses his mind instead of his gun to solve crimes, and has made its star, Peter Falk, into an international celebrity. The signs for the series were, in fact, auspicious right from the beginning when the first episode was directed by a rising young director named Steven Spielberg. Such an icon did Columbo become even after the series ended, that in 1989 Universal TV decided to bring him back in *New Columbo* which is now being shown on ITV while the earlier series is on cable. In the interim, however, nothing has changed about Columbo: he has the same eye for detail, the same taste in cheap cigars and the same crumpled raincoat. Peter Falk has confessed that there is a lot of himself in the character, and once revealed that he actually found his trademark coat in a cut-price store while escaping from the rain while waiting for shooting to begin – and then insisted on wearing it when the cameras began to roll. In that moment, the image of one of the most famous policemen created especially for television was set.

Richard Levinson (1934–) and William Link (1937–) are two of the most respected writer-producers in American television, having created some of the most popular crime shows of recent years including *Mannix* which starred Mike Connors, *McCloud* with Dennis Weaver, the long-running *Ellery Queen Mysteries* and *Murder She Wrote*, the recent triumph for Angela Lansbury. The partners have drawn the inspiration for these series from many sources; perhaps the most surprising being *Columbo* which Richard Levinson says was inspired by Porfiry Petrovich, the clever but unprepossessing police inspector in the classic Russian novel, *Crime and Punishment* by Fyodor Dostoevsky published in 1866! Like Petrovich, one of Columbo's most abiding qualities is his loyalty to the police force and his dedication to duty in the face of all manner of obstructions put in

his way not only by suspects. 'The End of an Era' is a rare short story written by Levinson and Link for *Alfred Hitchcock's Mystery Magazine* in January 1962 and also features a devoted employee who gets caught up in crime. The title, I am sure, has *no* bearing on the future of the crime series on television!

It was an absolute nuisance, something to be endured like a session in the dentist's chair. Mr Grubb found himself wishing he could close his ears with invisible plugs. They were talking about him, paying false tribute to his fifteen years with the firm, and the one thing he didn't want to do was listen. But he was forced to smile and nod, trying to look shy and grateful at the same time. He squirmed in his seat, consoling himself with the knowledge that it couldn't last much longer. And within forty-eight hours – he was delighted by the irony – they'd all see this little gathering in a totally different light.

"Those mornings by the water cooler," Miss Lemmon was saying. "Why, I'd just peek over at Mr Grubb behind his desk and I'd say to myself: 'There's the man for me.' But he never even gave me a tumble. Did you, Miles?"

There was laughter. Why shouldn't they laugh, he reflected; he was old enough to be her grandfather. The little flirt knew he was married, too, but that didn't stop her. She had to make a conquest of every man in the office, young or old, and he was no exception.

While they all laughed, he made himself smile the idiot grin of the good sport. Then Miss Lemmon sat down and there was a hush in the room as Mr Dougherty got ponderously to his feet. Well, here come the platitudes, thought Mr Grubb. The fifteen years of unswerving service to the firm, the feeling of personal loss at this particular retirement. Mr Grubb permitted himself a small smile. There'd be loss, all right, and much more personal than Dougherty expected. He settled back as his employer began to speak, wondering if they'd have the staggering effrontery to give him a wristwatch.

"I'll be brief," Mr Dougherty was saying, gazing out over his staff like a benevolent shepherd. "The end of an era is not a time for chatter, it's a time for thought. And when Miles Grubb leaves this office today it *will* be the end of an era, a moment for all of us here at Cumberland, Inc. to take stock of ourselves and our company."

Having promised to be brief, he launched into a lengthy oration. Mr Grubb, bored, cast his eye around the office. His co-workers were listening with the proper look of reverence; they sat behind their desks, completely absorbed, their thoughts no doubt winging to the day of their own retirement. He grunted under his breath. They were all such fools; their white collars were choking them and they didn't even know it. Well, it wasn't for him. He had intelligence and ambition; he intended to spend the last years of his life in unfettered luxury. And Mr Dougherty, poor, bumbling Mr Dougherty, would provide the means.

The speech ran down of its own sheer weight and Mr Grubb was asked to stand. "Miles," said his employer, "there's very little we can do to show our appreciation on this, your last day here at Cumberland." He held up a wrapped package. "But we hope this small gift will stand as a token of our esteem."

There was applause. Mr Grubb crossed the office, past the two buckets of iced champagne near the filing cabinets, past the desk where he had labored for fifteen years, and with just the right show of bashfulness he took the package from Dougherty's pink hands. "I'd like to thank—" he began.

"Open it," shouted Rudy Schmidt, the billing clerk.

"Yes, Miles, let's see," said Miss Lemmon.

Dutifully, he peeled away the layers of paper and opened the box. Inside was a matching lighter and ashtray set. A small card read: 'To Miles From The Gang At The Office.' He winced. "This is – this is very nice," he said. "Thank you."

Then everyone was standing around clapping him on the back. With twin pops the champagne corks were pulled and someone brought glasses from Mr Dougherty's private office. A toast was proposed, then another. Mr Grubb was compelled to drink to Miss Lemmon, to Cumberland, Inc., to the free enterprise system. It struck him that it would never do to get drunk; there was much to accomplish before the day was over. Fortunately, the big wall clock was inching toward six and a few people were already going for their coats.

Finally it was over. Mr Dougherty drove off in his limousine and the warehouse men came from the back to punch out. Mr Grubb stuffed his few belongings in his overcoat pockets, tucked the gift under his arm, and headed for the door. He was stopped by Alvin Griggle, the assistant comptroller.

"Gotta take you out and buy you a drink," said Alvin.

"Thanks, but I have to get home for dinner. The wife's expecting me."

Alvin's face drooped, then he brightened. "Yeah, guess so," he said. "But I'll miss you, buddy. You don't know how lucky you are, leaving this place." He shook his head. "I've been here ten years myself. And what does it get me? A hundred twenty-five less deductions. It isn't worth it, Miles. Look at you. Fifteen years. And you wind up with a lighter and a glass of champagne."

Mr Grubb was touched. The man seemed on the verge of tears. "I'll get by, Alvin," he said. Then he smiled. "I'll get by very well."

He left the office and went into a hotel across the street to phone his wife, telling her he'd be late for dinner. Then he bought a paper and read the news until seven-thirty. When it was dark outside he left the hotel and crossed the windy pavements to a bus terminal. There, in one of the wall lockers, he found the suitcase he had left that morning. Everything was fine, he told himself. Just fine.

It was almost eight o'clock when he let himself into the Cumberland office. The place was dark but he didn't need a flashlight; after fifteen years he could have moved around the desks and partitions blindfolded. He crossed to Mr Dougherty's office, went inside, and set down his suitcase, orientating himself. The safe was concealed by paneling to the left of the door. Mr Grubb chuckled. Its location was an open secret to everyone in the office.

He touched a hidden device to slide the panel aside, remembering quite clearly the day the safe had been delivered. Mr Dougherty had beamed proudly, instructing the workmen in the mechanics of its installation. Mr Grubb had come into the office to discuss an accounting error and had noticed, completely by accident, a slip of paper on his employer's desk. It contained in neat, ball-point lettering, the combination of the safe. Mr Grubb remembered those numerals. They had stayed in a corner of his brain for the past two years, always available and ready for use.

Now, with his fingers turning the dial, he felt a quiet touch of triumph. First the money, then the plane ticket resting in a drawer at home, and finally the flight to Hawaii, to Brazil, to some lush spot beyond extradition where he could sit on a beach and watch a hundred tropical suns come in and out with the tide.

All thanks to Mr Dougherty and his habit of keeping large amounts of cash on hand. Carefully, quietly, Mr Grubb opened the safe and lit a match. Ranged on the shelves before his eyes were neat stacks of currency in bank wrappers. He wouldn't even have to count them; each packet had its total value stamped on the wrapper. Mr Grubb brought his suitcase to the mouth of the safe and began removing the money. It was, he reflected, the last transaction he would ever perform for Cumberland, Inc.

The first thing his wife said when he came into the house was, "How was your party, dear?"

He examined her critically and decided he wouldn't miss her at all. In the beginning, when he was formulating his plan, he had hesitated for weeks over whether or not to take her with him. But now, looking at the wrinkled face, the gray hair and the vacant eyes, he was positive he had made the right choice. She didn't even ask him why he was carrying his suitcase; he had an excuse ready and waiting, but apparently all she could think of was the party.

"Very pleasant," he said. "They gave me a gift, a lighter and matching ashtrays."

"Oh, how lovely. Where are they?"

He suddenly remembered he had put them in the suitcase. "I have them," he said. "I'll show them to you later. Now I think I'd better wash up."

"Of course, dear."

She bustled into the kitchen and he went upstairs. In their bedroom he opened the suitcase and set the office gift on the dresser. Then he looked at the money for a long moment, trying to picture what would happen on Monday morning. Dougherty would be livid. Probably wouldn't even believe it at first. Not Miles Grubb. Not old, trustworthy, loyal Miles Grubb. How could he do such a thing? And after fifteen years with the firm.

He began loading a few essentials into the suitcase. He'd buy the rest, clothes and everything, when he reached his destination. Then he took the plane ticket from his drawer, went to the hall extension phone, and dialed the airlines. Flight 106 would be leaving for Hawaii on schedule? Eleven o'clock? Thank you very much. He closed the suitcase and went down to dinner.

The meal was uneventful. His wife chattered aimlessly and he only half listened while he ate. She was telling him that they could now enjoy the benefits of leisure. "You'll have all this time on your hands," she said. "So I was thinking . . . Dear? Did you hear me?"

"Yes. You were thinking."

"And I thought it might be nice if we took a drive across the country. You've always wanted to travel and we could stop by Cleveland and see my sister." The idea seemed to excite her. "We don't have to push it or anything. Just a slow, pleasant drive. After all, we're getting older, and we might not have the chance unless we do it soon."

She might be getting older, thought Mr Grubb, but he felt ageless. For a moment he was sorry for her; she'd live out the remainder of her days in this house, never once tasting, touching, or seeing, and death would come as a favor. He wondered how she'd feel when she found out he had betrayed her. Would she be angry, would she cry, would she condemn or defend him? No, she'd probably accept the whole thing with her usual passivity. Well, that was her problem, not his. She'd vanish from his memory the moment he got on the plane.

After dinner she went into the kitchen to do the dishes. Mr Grubb silently climbed to the bedroom, slipped the ticket into his breast pocket, and lifted the suitcase. He glanced around for the last time and was pleased to find that no chords were struck; there wasn't even a slight twinge of nostalgia. Smiling, he went downstairs and left the suitcase by the door. Then he strolled into the kitchen.

"I'm going to take a drive," he said. "Get some fresh air."

"All right dear. Bring back the paper when you come, will you?"

"Of course."

He bent to kiss the back of her neck. Then he left her there, arms plunged in soapy water, gray hair wispy in the steam. No, he decided, he wouldn't miss her at all.

Everything went smoothly at the airport. He left his car in the parking area with the keys in the ignition. It was a small gesture of kindness – now they wouldn't have to tow it away. Inside the terminal building he dropped his suitcase on the scales at the check-in counter and it was comfortably underweight. Well, money wasn't heavy, he reflected, at least not in the physical sense. He bought a few magazines and a box of cough drops, then browsed until loudspeakers began announcing his flight.

Settled on the plane, his seat belt fastened and his magazines on his lap, Mr Grubb sighed a sigh of contentment. He was safe; there hadn't been a single hitch in plans. Within a few minutes the motors would roar, they would taxi down the runway, and then, lifting, lifting, he'd be carried toward Hawaii and gilt-edged anonymity. He waited, his mind pleasantly occupied with thoughts of the things he would buy, for the propellers to grind into life.

And then the stewardess' voice was speaking over the PA system. "Ladies and gentlemen, due to mechanical difficulties we'll be unable to take off on schedule. We'd appreciate it if you'd leave by the rear door and go to the main waiting room until further notice."

There was a discontented murmur from the other passengers. Mr Grubb frowned. Always some idiotic fly in the ointment. And he had just been congratulating himself on how smoothly things were going. Well, they'd get it straightened out, whatever it was. He unfastened his seat belt and joined the others inching down the aisle.

As soon as he reached the waiting room he crossed to the check-in counter, "How long will 106 be delayed?" he asked.

"We don't know, sir," said the young man smoothly. "An hour, maybe more."

"What's the problem?"

"Just a few mechanical difficulties, sir. Nothing serious."

Mr Grubb found a chair and tried to read his magazine, but his eye was constantly drawn to the check-in counter. It seemed to be the meeting spot of a group of officials; they were talking animatedly among themselves, then one would hurry off and someone else would join the circle. He got up and moved closer to them, trying to overhear, but their voices were pitched too low. Finally, deciding it had nothing to do with his flight, he started back to his seat.

And then he saw the police officers, four of them, come into the building and move toward the desk. There was a hurried conference and they headed through double doors to the landing field.

He resisted a momentary impulse to run. But they couldn't be here after him. It was impossible. He made himself relax by an effort of will. No one would enter the Cumberland office until Monday morning. Then and only then would the police be interested in his whereabouts.

Mr Grubb paged through his magazine as time stretched on. His flight had been delayed a half hour now and he was growing nervous. The cluster at the check-in counter had dispersed and a new man – he seemed to be younger than the other, possibly new on the job – was weighing in luggage. Mr Grubb watched him for a moment. These airline people never tell you anything, he thought, but this fellow had the look of inexperience about him. Perhaps he could be bullied into parting with some information. Mr Grubb stood up and approached the counter.

"Look," he said in an angry voice, "we've been waiting here for thirty-five minutes. What's happening with 106 to Hawaii?"

"Just some minor diff—"

"I don't believe it," he snapped. "There's something else. Now do you tell me what it is or do I go to your superior?"

"Really, sir—"

"Don't 'really, sir' me! There were four police officers here a while ago. Why? What's going on?"

He continued to raise his voice and the young man looked uncomfortable.

"Well – if I tell you, sir, will you promise you won't tell the other passengers?"

"I promise."

The young man hesitated for a moment, then he said, "We got a crank call. You know, it happens every once in a while. Something about a bomb on the plane."

"A bomb?"

"No truth to it, of course. But we have to check. As soon as they're finished you'll be taking off."

Mr Grubb felt immensely relieved. Just a silly anonymous phone call. Some crank who hated the world. It had nothing to do with him at all. "I appreciate your telling me," he said, "and I'll keep quiet about it. How much longer will it take them?"

"Another ten, fifteen minutes, I guess. They have to search the luggage."

Mr Grubb stared at him. "Search the luggage?"

"Yes, sir. Just a normal precaution."

Mr Grubb felt his heart pumping abnormally. He reeled

away from the desk, just in time to see a police officer come through the double doors and start toward him.

The man held his suitcase in his hand.

"He wants you to call your family lawyer and come down to police headquarters right away," said the voice on the phone.

"But – I don't understand," said Mrs Grubb.

"Neither do we, lady. All we know is that he had a fortune in cash in that suitcase of his."

Mrs Grubb had difficulty speaking.

"We're at the airport," said the policeman. "We're leaving now and we'll be at the station house in twenty minutes."

"Is he – under arrest?"

"Yes, ma'am."

"Tell him – tell him I'll call Bill Moore and we'll both be down there right away. Tell him everything will be all right."

The police officer hung up and Mrs Grubb stood looking at the telephone for a long time. Then she dialed the airline terminal. When someone answered the phone she said, "I called you before, about that bomb on flight 106 to Hawaii."

"Who is this?" said the voice sharply.

"Never mind. I just wanted to say there isn't any bomb. You can leave now, if you want to."

"If you'd give me your name—"

"Tell them down there it was all a joke. That's all that it was. Just a joke."

She hung up, smiled, and began to dial the family lawyer.